PLEASE WELCOME MR. ARTHUR BEAN

SIDNEY ANNE HARRISON

ISBN: 978-1-7326796-1-0 [print]

To my father who inspires me,
To my friends who support me,
And to you, the reader, who gives this story life.

* * *

As a kid, I had this dog that was scared shitless of thunderstorms. Which was pretty bad for him, considering that we lived in one of the most storm-prone cities in the country. This poor dog would piss himself and shudder and yelp at every crash of thunder and every bolt of lightning. Even after the storm was finished, he was a wreck. Tail between the legs, flinching at a hand meant to pet him, huddling under the blankets of my bed, he was the textbook picture of fright.

I tried really hard to calm him down. I swaddled him like a baby and tried to distract him with food. Once, I even went so far as to buy some ridiculously expensive T-bone imported from Australia because I thought maybe the higher-quality meat would make him freak out less. Turns out that dogs don't really care if their beef is corn-fed or grass-fed, free range or kept in a cage its entire life. Put a fancy international steak in front of their faces, and they'll still make a puddle on your bedsheets when lightning strikes.

That dog died young, which was no surprise really, given how much stress he had to endure, but at the time it really bothered me. It made me feel like a bad person. Apart from the thunderstorms, I had been a rather decent pet owner. I woke up every morning at five just to take him on walks. And I didn't just let him out. I took him on a *walk*, sometimes for more than an hour, and I fed him good food. But despite all my best efforts, he still died—scared out of his mind during a thunderstorm. I didn't even know dogs could have heart attacks. That was the first time I learned that anything with a heart could have it attacked.

I'm not much one for psychology, but if I were, I'd probably attribute that dog's death to a lot of my fucked-up decisions in life. Like, for example, my decision to break up with a high school sweetheart when her family got a dog. Or my refusal to drive

1

during thunderstorms. Or—and this one I definitely think is the dog's fault—the fact that I allowed my only daughter to be raised as my half sister by my father, who thought *he* was her father, and the woman who had married him. A mouthful, I know.

My mother, you see, died when I was 14 years, 238 days, 17 hours, and 24 minutes old. I had kept my eyes on the clock as she was passing away. It was just too hard to look at her as she stopped living, even though I knew her eyes were on me.

After that, it was my dad and me for a while. I had been working in his diner part-time since I was twelve. When my mom passed, I took on a few more responsibilities that had used to be my mom's, like working out payroll and scheduling for our seven other employees. My dad was strictly a cook and nothing else. He hardly talked to any of the customers or the staff, not even the two other cooks who worked in the kitchen. After my mom passed, he became even more silent.

That is until one of our waitresses, who'd been working with us for over thirty years, broke her leg slipping on spilled coffee and decided that was the perfect sign from "G O D" to retire. So we had to hire a new one or run the risk of overworking our other three considerably aged waitresses.

Having older waitresses in cute little diner outfits had become kind of our thing. It reminded people of that soda shop in *Grease* where the dry but kindly middle-aged waitress doled out advice to unruly teens in leather jackets and pencil skirts. But for some reason, my dad chose the youngest and least experienced of the applicants to take the job.

She was 21. She was Cuban. She was beautiful. She was shifty. Her name was Mari.

Mari had a way of making people fall in love with her. She spoke Spanish to the cooks, poking fun at them in a way that was two-parts flirtation, one-part genuine interest. She also got the other women at the diner to go out with her to dance clubs that played Latin music. Imagine, fifty- and sixty-year-old women with grandchildren Mari's age shaking their drooping breasts to Selena. But that's what Mari did. She got people to do what she wanted them to do.

Mari was a thunderstorm. And my father married her.

If their difference in age caused any one of our friends and coworkers concern, no one ever let it show. The wedding was huge and festive, with lots of colors and dancing and food that was too spicy for me to eat. That was probably the high point of the marriage.

They went to Mexico for their honeymoon. Mari had wanted to go to Cuba, but travel restrictions were still in place for that country, and my father thought it was too risky. They didn't fight about it, but I could tell by the look in her eyes that Mari was furious.

Two nights after they came back from their honeymoon, Mari snuck into my bedroom. I was 15, 364 days, 2 hours, and 12 minutes old. I kept my eyes on the clock the whole time, because at that point, I was too afraid to look at lightning.

If the first time was scary, the other times were downright terrifying. Mari was too wild, too eager, and sometimes she didn't listen. She was always in control, and I always felt guilty afterward. It wasn't that I felt violated, not really. I didn't feel like those victims that you see on crime procedural shows. She always asked if I wanted it, and I always nodded my head. I didn't enjoy it most of the time, but I didn't feel like I'd been assaulted either. I didn't really start thinking about how Mari having sex with me affected my life until I was out of that house.

But I definitely knew it was wrong. In the legal sense, and more importantly, in the moral sense. I felt as if I was betraying my father, but he didn't have a clue. He'd returned to his semi-mute state apparently sometime during the honeymoon and never recovered. He never forgot a birthday, an anniversary, a dinner, or a party. He was always on time and always rubbed Mari's feet after a long day at work. But he was slow, and Mari was fast.

We only stopped sleeping together after she got pregnant. I

knew it was mine even before she told me, and when she said she wanted my father to raise the kid as his own, I had no reason to protest. I was almost seventeen, almost about to go to college, almost about to leave our corner of Florida for something bigger. And even if maybe I felt differently once I saw her—once my father placed that little baby girl into my arms with a soft "Meet your sister"—everything had already been done, and there was no going back.

I didn't actually get to college until four years after I graduated high school. My dad needed me at the restaurant, and I needed to see Grace take her first steps, speak her first words, laugh her first laugh. It was silly, really, because for the most part, I was so distant from that little girl that she hardly even knew my name when she started calling people by name. It wasn't until the second kid came along, a year and a few months after Grace, that I felt safe enough to be alone with her. As if another kid would take the attention away from me and how I interacted with her.

His name was Luke, after my grandfather on my mother's side. My dad had been close to my mom's father. I guess he wanted to honor that relationship somehow. Mari didn't care. She was starting to ignore my father more and more. I couldn't even tell if Luke really was his kid or not. All I knew was that he definitely wasn't mine.

Luke glommed on to me from the start. The kid was quite literally stuck to my side most of the time, and when he wasn't, he would throw tantrums until I got to him again. He liked Grace too, seemed to look up to her somewhat, but that intense, obsessive kind of love he seemed to reserve only for me. My father was good to both of them, but Mari hardly paid attention to either of them. I don't know if I was playing surrogate mother or what, but I do know that the day I left for college was the first day Luke showed just how violent he could be.

Another kid came along after I had been gone for three years. Barry, Mari called him, a pretty ridiculous name she thought up right after he popped out. By that point Grace was in kindergarten, reading and writing, and she would write to me almost three times a week, sometimes more if Luke had something to say. And I always came home for their birthdays and Christmases and Easters. If I didn't come back for them, there would've been no celebrations.

My dad wasn't old, per se, but he was tired, and I could already tell that he was getting sick. And Mari wasn't around. She still worked at the diner. She still came home every night, although the time varied greatly, and she still dropped the kids off at their various activities, but mentally she wasn't there. And she disappeared a lot. Grace would tell me all of these things.

She told me a lot in her letters. She got moved up a grade in elementary school. She was taking dance classes. She had one friend, Millie Arnold, but she thought Millie Arnold was only her friend because Millie Arnold didn't have any friends either. She was learning how to cook and do ceramics. She didn't like her Spanish teacher because he had a "boogie nose." To me it seemed a good enough reason as any to not like someone.

And she told me about the other two. Luke was having trouble in school. He was too rough with the other kids. They would make fun of him and he didn't understand why. Barry hardly spoke. He seemed sad and really didn't like to be touched. Barry and Luke fought sometimes, but other times they were the best of friends. Grace took care of them.

Sometimes, I felt bad for not going back to them after college, especially after my dad died, and Mari was the only person left for them to count on. Sometimes I felt like I should have just told Grace—who had been steadily proving that she was too smart for any grade they put her in—the truth and have her move in with me. Sometimes I wanted to go back to the diner and save my dad's business from failing under the hands of Mari.

But then there'd be a thunderstorm. Even far away from the tropics, I wasn't safe from them. There'd be a thunderstorm, and I'd remember that dog's face when I woke up one morning, after having fallen asleep, leaving him alone in his terror. I'd remember the legs shot out straight as if he were trying to run, the jaw open with the tongue lolling out, dried up and gray, and those eyes, bulging and searching and lifeless.

I'd remember that, and then no one could've convinced me to go back.

* * *

"I can't believe you're going to stay here for grad school."

It was midnight. It was a full moon, one of those huge shimmering ones that you could see even in the heart of New York City with a million fluorescents and LEDs drowning out the sky. We were swinging back and forth in the playground next to our apartment buildings. Technically you weren't supposed to go in there without kids, but it was midnight and all the playground junkies were asleep.

"Why? Tons of people stay at the same college for grad school." I said, my voice flat and unconvincing.

"Yeah, tons of people do. But do you want to be a ton?"

"Are you calling me fat?"

Thia laughed at that. She always laughed so well at everything I said. It was one of the reasons I was so insanely in love with her. It was also one of the reasons I was an idiot. I thought I was just really funny. Later on, I realized that Thia just wanted me to feel good. I suppose that isn't worse, but it definitely isn't better.

"You're, like, the least fat person I know. All you eat is vegetables and whey . . . stuff."

"Protein?"

"Yeah that's it."

"Well when you grow up in a diner, all that grease and smell, it kind of turns you off the fries and burgers."

It was true. I hadn't been a huge meat eater since I was a teenager, and I rarely ate greasy foods unless I was very drunk or very high. I also did track in high school and played ultimate frisbee and basketball in college clubs. But I'd like to clarify that I did not drink whey protein, or any other kind of protein for that matter. I wasn't a muscle head. I just liked to move and the smell of cooking red meat occasionally made me want to vomit.

"It's kind of a wonder you weren't a chubby kid, growing up around all that food." Thia paused there, and I knew she was

7

going to say more. So I didn't say anything. "Arthur, why are you staying here? The Iowa program accepted you. You should go."

"Yeah, it's a great program. But it's also Iowa. Not sure if going from the greatest city on earth to the middle of potato country is the best idea for me right now."

"Idaho is potato country. I think Iowa is corn."

"Whatever." I let the toe of my sneaker scuff deep gashes into the ground beneath me as I lazily swung back and forth. She watched me do it for a while before speaking again.

"Besides, New York is not the greatest city in the world. London is. And that's why I'm going."

"Yeah, that and you got accepted into a majorly British, prestigious acting program thing." I couldn't keep the bitter tone out of my voice.

"And *you* got accepted into a majorly American, prestigious writing program thing. You want to be a writer. So go write some stuff," she said.

"Columbia's education program is more practical."

"Since when did you care about that stuff?"

"I don't know. Seems like the time that I should be caring about that stuff."

"It's never the time to care about that stuff." She was starting to sound more annoyed than I wanted her to. I couldn't really understand why this mattered to her so much.

"Do you just want me to go because you're going?" I asked.

We'd already decided that we were going to break up at the end of the summer. Thia was going to be in London. I was going to be here. We would talk and see each other when we saw each other, but neither of us really wanted the long-distance thing. Or at least that's what we said to each other. It probably wasn't true for me.

We'd been traveling for a while after undergrad. My dad had left me some money, and when Mari sold the diner, she gave me almost everything from that. At first, I was shocked that she'd done it. My dad's will had said that the money from the diner was to be split fifty-fifty between us. But Mari just kept saying she didn't need it or want it. She had a new man who could pay her way, but more than that, I think she felt a little guilty. Guilty about me or my father or both, I wasn't really sure, but giving me the money was her best way of apologizing. So I took it and tried not to think about what it could mean. I put a lot of it into an account for Grace, and some away for Luke and Barry if Mr. Moneybags didn't come through for them. And the rest . . . Thia and I blew it all.

But then we came back to the real world, the world where you couldn't subsist entirely on sangria and seawater and street food. The real world without ancient temples and exotic animals and oversized hiking backpacks. And the real world meant grad school and breakups.

Thia sighed. "I want you to go because I think that you want to go. Do the writing thing, and then if that doesn't work out, do something else. People live to be one hundred these days. What's the rush to be normal?"

"Writing isn't normal?"

She threw her hands up into the air. "You know what I mean, Arthur."

I hated when she said my first name. She only really did that when she was angry or serious, and those weren't Thia's best emotions.

"I still have a month to decide. Just let me think about it, okay?"

Thia had known me long enough to recognize when I couldn't be pushed anymore, so she stopped pushing. We just kept on swinging.

My undergraduate years had been characterized by a lot of books, a lot of bad writing, not so much sex, and Thia. We had found each other at one of those freshman club fairs. I was two years older than every other kid wandering around, and she was two times cooler than any of them. Thia was pretty secretive about her past, even with me, but I knew that, like me, she'd had to grow up quick and before her time.

We were friends, and then best friends, and then lovers, and then in a "committed relationship." And now we were on the verge of being exes. We hadn't had a lot of other friends in college. I was a little more than surprised when Thia wanted to go so far away from this city. From me. But then again, I knew Thia. I knew that she was never really meant to be in one place for too long.

I saw her off at the airport. I'd turned down the Iowa program, but I told her that I'd try again after I did the Columbia thing. It bothered her and made her flippant toward the end. But she tried not to show it.

Two months later, her letters and calls stopped, and my letters and calls went unanswered.

Three months later, I tried asking her family if they'd heard from her and they wouldn't tell me yes or no.

Four months later, I went to the police to file a report that never had a chance at being taken seriously.

Six months later, I went to London to look for her and found nothing.

One year later, Thia was eternally missing, and I quit Columbia and went to Iowa.

***

I had bought a suit partly as a joke and partly because after Iowa I was convinced that I wasn't going to be a writer, so I might as well try to be an accountant or something. It had never been worn, so when I pulled it out of the depths of my closet, I'm sure it was surprised. Maybe it was like those mole people, hissing when they see the sunlight. Either way, the big plastic dry cleaner's bag I'd kept it stashed in had it looking like new. So I thought it would do.

Grace was getting married. She sent me a letter warning me about the invitation, and then I'd gotten the invitation. In that warning letter, she'd said that there might be a surprise for me at the wedding, and I shouldn't freak out when I saw it. I probably should have asked what it was, but the fact that Grace was getting married freaked me out enough. She'd also asked me to be the one to give her away because her stepfather was a giant butt-face (her words), and I was as close to a father figure as she was ever going to get.

The irony almost made me want to laugh, but definitely made me need to cry.

She wasn't even twenty-five yet, but she'd been dating this guy since her freshman year of college. I'd honestly found that problematic at the time because she was sixteen when she was a freshman and he was nineteen, but she said it was fine, and I couldn't really argue with her that much. Actually, I could have, but I didn't.

Apparently it was very fine because Grace had proposed to him, and he'd said yes, so they were getting married. And I was going to give her away. And Luke would be there, if he could stay out of trouble for long enough. And Beatrice would be there.

The last time I'd seen Luke, he'd been in a juvenile detention center for assaulting a teacher who had called him stupid, and the last time I'd seen Beatrice, people had been calling her Barry. Mari didn't really care when Beatrice revealed who she really was. Grace and Luke had been nothing but supportive. When Grace called me about it, I had a surprising non-reaction, or at least it was surprising to her. Going to school in New York, you meet all kinds of people, and you sort of just stop being surprised. But their ass rag of a stepfather called her a freak and kicked her out of his house. Mari didn't care about that either.

Luckily, I still had the money put away for her and Luke. Grace was already away at college on full academic scholarship and a work-study gig at the library, and Luke was . . . wandering. So I set up Beatrice in a studio apartment close to her school so she could walk to and from. Fortunately, she had friends who'd look out for her. She didn't need much else from me besides money, it seemed. We hardly ever spoke.

There was a lot of mental preparation that went down after I received the invitation. So much so that I hadn't ever prepared for the fact that the wedding might not happen at all.

I was trying on the suit a week before the wedding when I got the call. It was off. Grace and her fiancé had called everything off. Grace didn't reveal the details to me, but I had a sneaking suspicion the guy wasn't too happy. At least that's the feeling I got when he called me ranting about how Grace and her "chinky" friend were manipulative bitches. I'd hung up on him when I'd finally figured out who was yelling at me, and then I wracked my brain trying to remember if I knew any of Grace's friends who were Chinese. Not that it mattered. I didn't know many of Grace's friends anyway. I thought about asking Grace why she'd gotten so close to marrying a guy who threw around words like "chinky," but decided that it wasn't my business, and I also didn't really want to know.

So there was no wedding. No seeing Luke or Beatrice for the first time in years. No giving Grace away as her father. No suit.

That suit never got worn. I put it back in the dry cleaner's bag and never needed it again. I hadn't become an accountant. I'd become a teacher who scribbled nonsense in a long succession of

Moleskines and devoured books like a worm. And as a teacher at a New York public school, I got to wear pretty much what I'd wear to go grocery shopping on a Sunday. No suit needed.

I tried contacting Grace after it all fell out with the wedding. First I tried calling her, and then I tried writing her. And then I tried calling Luke, but he was in jail again for some minor infraction that he kept getting caught for and couldn't really tell me anything. He wouldn't have been able to go to the wedding anyway. And I tried calling Beatrice, but she had changed her cell phone number.

For a while I considered going to the police. Two weeks after the wedding had been called off, I almost did, even though I wouldn't have been able to give them much to go by. Plus, my experience with Thia's disappearance didn't exactly make me trust the police's ability to care about my problems. But then I got the note. Plain and simple. Just a few words.

Dear Arthur,

I'm fine. I've quit dancing because of an injury. I'm living in Louisiana now. I'll write more soon.

Love,
Grace

* * *

All the years I'd had a license and a car, I'd carefully avoided driving in thunderstorms. And then one completely caught me by surprise.

Rain was pounding against my windshield so hard I thought it might burst wide open and bring the downpour straight onto my face. Lightning and thunder erupted with foreboding frequency, meaning that the storm was pretty much right overhead. Flashes of unearthly electricity illuminated my decades-old car stuffed full of all my personal belongings. My hands trembled on the steering wheel as I tried my best to keep going straight on this one-way road to nowhere. I internally and externally cursed the imbecilic meteorologists who fed lies into the weather app on my phone.

I had quit my job. Partially because I was about to be fired, and partially because I didn't really like it in the first place. Teaching preteens was harder on the nerves than going to a rave sober, and I truly enjoyed neither of those things. As for the firing, well, you throw a book at a brat once, and that's pretty much the end of you as a teacher. Especially if you're not tenured.

The letter from Grace just seemed to be a signal that it was the right time for me to get the hell out of Dodge. After all, what was really keeping me there? I rented my house in Jersey, and, well, it was in Jersey. What really keeps anyone in Jersey? And I had no job. No girlfriend. After Thia, I became a perpetual bachelor of sorts. I just didn't see the point of getting into anything unless that person captivated me as much as Thia had, and no one did.

I didn't like my job. I didn't like where I was. And Grace was giving me a way out. Sort of.

I hadn't heard from her since that sparse letter telling me that she was living in Louisiana, and then she sent me a long letter explaining very little, if anything at all. In it she asked me if I wanted to help her, although she didn't say with what.

I've since lost that letter, but it went something like, "Dear

Arthur, Sorry I haven't written in a while, but I've been busy. I've been promoted to manage a hotel in Louisiana, but it's old and needs renovation. Wondering if you could help me out? Shouldn't take more than a month or two of your time. Love, Grace." At least that was the basic gist.

Grace always wrote and spoke a little bit like she was in the wrong century, but that was probably from all those old books that she read. She wasn't much into modern literature, but she loved stuff from way back when.

So I took her up on the offer, sent off a quick text (since I sometimes also communicated with twenty-first century technology) that I was coming, and got in the car. And then, thunderstorms.

I kept thinking that I should pull over and wait it out, but I was quite literally in the middle of nowhere with no idea how I'd gotten there or where I was supposed to go next. The rain had disoriented me so much that I'd lost my sense of direction and had forgotten to look at Grace's carefully drawn-out directions.

To say I was superstitious would be a bit of a leap, but I had seen one too many horror movies with this exact same situation played out to disastrous ends. A lone driver caught in a storm in the middle of nowhere gets lost and pulls off for directions, or to rest, and ends up with a knife in the middle of their forehead or their skin around someone else's face. And I was not about to be that person. So I kept going.

I kept going until a dark thing dashed in front of my car, followed by a light thing, small and quick, but not so quick that I didn't feel the need to slam on the brakes, pull the wheel hard to the left, and close my eyes. All those reactions combined caused my wheels to float on the rain, my car to practically fly off the road into a tree, my head to slam hard against the steering wheel, and my arm to snap against the driver's side door.

And all of that, probably combined with the blood I saw when I finally opened my eyes, caused me to black out.

* * *

"Excuse me sir, but have you seen this girl?"

"Lost your girlfriend, eh?" The man had one of those massive Santa-Claus beards, but somehow had managed to keep it free of debris. It was almost sparkling white. If I hadn't been so exhausted with worry and walking, I might have been fascinated by it.

"Yeah, kinda."

"Well then, give it here. Let me have a proper look."

The man took the photograph from me and peered at it, holding it an arms-length away. He covered one of his eyes with his free hand, and then switched hands and covered the other eye. I couldn't tell if he was fucking with me or genuinely had poor vision that required such theatrics, but either way I couldn't bring myself to care. He was my last stop of the day before I could make it back to my twelve-person dorm in a hostel whose bathrooms could've been in a Chernobyl exhibit. I was tired and wanted to sleep, but I didn't necessarily want to go back there either.

"Yeah I think I seen her once or twice in here. Like most of us, she didn't mind a pint or two at the end of the day." He handed the photo back to me.

"When was the last time you saw her?"

He stroked his beard. Sometimes I wished I could grow a beard that size to stroke when I was pretending to think hard about something.

"Not for a while now. She weren't a regular before either, but she'd come in every once in a while with her mates. All from that acting school. You know. The famous one?"

"Yeah. I know it."

"Yeah well they'd come in. I seen them around here. Not her though."

"Can you remember the last time you saw her?"

"Not sure. Not since a month at least." Another man called his name from down the bar. "Yeah, in a minute, you old fool. Can't you see I'm talking to an American chap?"

"Do you happen to remember if she was with anyone?"

"Some bloke, I guess. Don't really remember that much, I'm afraid. I got a lot of people in here, especially on a Friday or Saturday night."

He gestured grandly to his pub, which at seven in the evening held two old drunks and a quiet couple in the back eating shepherd's pie.

"Yeah I bet. Sorry, last question. Do you remember anything about the guy she was with? Like what he looked like? Maybe you caught a name?"

"No name, but I mighta caught something else from him."

I blinked. "Excuse me?"

"Bloke was sick as I recall. Not really the coughing up a bogey kind of sick, really, but he sure looked like he was on death's doorstep. Had that sunken look to him, you know? Like he hadn't eaten anything for a while. Thought it might've been AIDs or something similar. He got a nosebleed sitting there and I was too afraid to wipe up the blood. It spreads through blood, you know? I ain't been feeling well since. But that's really all I got for you."

I wasn't sure how valid those last few pearls of knowledge were, but clearly this guy had had his say and was done talking to me about stuff he hardly remembered. "Yeah. Thanks."

I started to pull my jacket off the barstool and the man grabbed my arm.

"Listen to me, lad. Breakups are tough and no one likes 'em, but sometimes you just gotta let 'em go. If you can't find her, that probably means she doesn't want you to find her."

"Thanks for the advice. But I'll . . ."

. . . *find him.*

"What do you mean how did I find him?"

"I mean how'd you know he'd be out on that road when you ran across it?"

"I didn't know. I just ran after Zorro because his leash broke

17

and he's afraid of the thunderstorm. I didn't know there was going to be a car there. Do you really think I wanted this to happen?"

"I don't know! Maybe you did. You don't know him like we do. This is really fucking bad! Shit! Bea, this is really fucking bad!"

"I *know* it's fucking bad! And just because I don't know him doesn't mean I'd want to kill him. Jesus, Luke, use your head for once, will you?"

"Beatrice, be nice."

Luke? Beatrice?

"Luke? Beatrice?"

"Oh shit, he's awake! Grace, what do we do? He's awake!"

"Grace?" I wasn't sure which world I was living in. Everything was fuzzy. I didn't feel awake.

"He doesn't look awake." A finger pressed into my right cheek. I winced. It hurt.

"Luke, please. Don't touch him right now. Mrs. K. said he needs to be left alone."

"Mrs. K. was a military nurse in like . . . the thirties or whatever. I can't say I fully trust her judgment on this." So many voices. I couldn't keep up.

"Yeah . . . shouldn't we take him to a doctor or something?"

"Oh yeah, let's take him to that clinic where Luke punched the pretty white nurse. Sounds like a great idea. Maybe they'll call the cops on us again and we can get almost shot for a change."

"You know I don't like needles!"

"Luke, enough. Mrs. K. has seen to him, now let's let him rest for a while."

"Don't you think one of us should stay? Just in case he, like, wakes up, or dies?"

"Shut up Bea!" That was loud. That was a shout.

"It's okay, Luke. Why don't you stay with him? You'll protect him, won't you?" That soft, sweet voice.

"Yeah. We don't need *you* in here, Bea."

"Whatever."

There was a whooshing sound of fabric being sent up into the air and coming back down. Then footsteps, a soft murmuring, and a door closing. A stinging in my fingers. Someone was touching me. It . . .

. . . *hurts.*

"Does it hurt?" Thia held my finger up to her face, squeezing it a little. More blood gushed out.

"It does when you do that." I laughed, pulling it away from her. I'll just clean it and put a Band-Aid on it. It's no big deal, really."

"Are you sure it doesn't need stitches?"

"I'm positive. We'll put that liquid bandage stuff on it. It's as good as stitches for something small like this."

"It's not small. I can see your bone!"

I laughed again. She was being dramatic. She knew she was being dramatic. And she liked that, really. A lot of life was a game for her, which I guess was a good way to live.

"Bone or no bone, I'm not ruining our first Thanksgiving in this apartment with an drawn-out trip to the emergency room over one little cooking accident."

"Did you know that the most dangerous kitchen task is slicing bagels?"

I rummaged in the kitchen drawers for Band-Aids and antibacterial cream. For good reason, we kept that stuff in there rather than in the bathroom. We were both good cooks, but not very graceful as far as knife skills went. Each of us sported a myriad of cuts and burns accumulated through years of trial and error. The accidents only grew worse as our ambitions grew larger than our bite-sized kitchen could handle.

"You know, I think I read that somewhere. I wonder if it's as much of a problem in New York. Because, you know, we eat so many bagels. You figure someone around here would've discovered the proper bagel-cutting technique by now."

"Well humans are flawed creatures. We never really learn from our mistakes, do we?"

"I suppose not. I keep using that damned ceramic knife even though it's betrayed me so many times."

"All our other knives suck though."

"That is true. Help me with this?"

Thia took the things I had gathered and started to work on my wound. Even though the cutting board looked like Glen Lantz's bed post-Freddy Krueger, my finger really wasn't that bad. Sure, I'd have to toss out that one chunk of butternut squash, but I was optimistic that the rest of the dish could be saved.

I'd always been a fan of the big, traditional Thanksgiving dinner. Of course, as I got older I put my own spin on the recipes, making them slightly more bourgie with heirloom this and organic that. Still, I wanted to keep to the historically inaccurate dinner that I knew and loved.

Thia's mother and father were Korean immigrants, so she had celebrated Chuseok instead of Thanksgiving. They ate sweet little rice cakes (the pronunciation of which I always butchered) rather than turkey and stuffing. She had never had an American Thanksgiving, or at least not one that didn't come from Columbia's dining hall.

After she wrapped me up, I asked her to check on the cranberry sauce, which I'd made from scratch. Food shouldn't jiggle. I stick to that belief even now. The only time I ever willingly ate Jell-O was when it came in shot form.

"So," Thia said as she gently stirred the sauce with a wooden spoon that had followed me from my mother's kitchen. "If the Pilgrims and the Indians didn't really eat this . . . and if the pilgrims then slaughtered the Indians for their land and their horses, why do you all celebrate this holiday again?"

"Because Americans are selfish, short-sighted idiots who like to eat a lot of food and pretend we are the best people in the world despite our dark, not-so-hidden history of genocide and colonialization."

"Colonialism."

"See? We don't even know the proper names for the atrocities we've committed!" I threw my hands, one of which was holding a knife, into the air. Thia laughed.

"Careful now. You might poke someone's eye out with that."

I set the knife down and went over to kiss her cheek. She leaned into me. At that moment, it was the purest indication of true love I knew.

"Sordid past or no, this food is fucking delicious, and you're fucking beautiful. Those are the only two reasons I need to celebrate."

"Okay. *That* I get." She twisted her neck to kiss me on the mouth. "How's the cranberry sauce look?"

"Looks good." I kissed her on the cheek again. "And . . ."

. . . *smells good.*

"Fuck. That smells good. I'm so hungry."

My eyes had that crusted feeling they get after a really deep sleep induced by copious amounts of liquor. Opening them turned out to be more exhausting than I could've anticipated, and once they were open, I couldn't muster the energy to close them again.

Above me was a ceiling, which was no surprise, I guess, except that the last thing I remembered was being in my car. So, I guess I had expected to be in my car. But it was fine that I wasn't because that meant someone had found me, and I wasn't going to die out there in a thunderstorm in the middle of nowhere.

Or it could be bad. It could have meant that the evil family of backwoods torture-cannibals had found me, and I was just waiting to be roasted and served up with mashed potatoes and gravy.

As if to send my mind into an even more paranoid state of confusion, the sound of a rumbling stomach broke the silence. I whipped my head to the side, an action I immediately regretted. It sent a sharp line of pain up my neck to my head and then back down to my fingertips.

"Oh shit, you shouldn't have done that. Are you . . . okay?"

I blinked disbelievingly a few times. This face, the one I so associated with courtrooms and juvenile detention center visiting rooms, was now out here in the real world asking me if I was okay.

I'd asked him that same question probably a million times before only to earn a grunt in reply.

Luckily, I wasn't a vindictive person, so I answered in a full sentence.

"I'm fine, Luke. My head just hurts."

He nodded. "I guess that happens after a car accident and stuff."

"Oh. Right. Where is my car?"

A flash of undeniable guilt flitted over his face. "Well it's kinda stuck in the mud, and we couldn't really get it out. With the rain and all. So we are going to go back for it tomorrow."

"Cool. Cool. Is it okay if I sit up?"

He stood up immediately and reached a hand around my back to help me. It hurt a little, but mostly because I was stiff and sore, not because anything was particularly or unbearably painful. I did, however, notice the cast on my arm, which looked slightly cruder than I was comfortable with. And there was acute pain radiating from somewhere in the vicinity of my forehead.

Once I was fully upright against pillows that Luke had taken a long time to fluff up just right, I got a better look at my surroundings.

I was in a room that looked old and dusty, but also somewhat homey and sweet. The bed I was on was a four-poster, with wood that wasn't shiny or new, but had some pretty intricate floral carvings. I was on top of the covers, a quilt made of what looked like old T-shirts and off-white sheets with those scratchy little balls of fluff that the insides of sweatshirts get after you've washed away the coziness.

There was a rust-colored rug on the floor with tassels bursting out of the edges like unruly baby hairs. In the corner to my right was a lumpy reading chair with a pinstripe cover, and on the wall directly in front of me was a generic and yet slightly unsettling picture of a barn housing a lone cow stranded in the middle of a thunderstorm. I quickly wiped my mind of any possible metaphor to be found in that.

Every other open space was taken up by bookshelves. Tall and thin ones, squat and short ones, ones with only a few shelves, and ones with dozens of varying sizes and shapes. Even the two bedside tables, both of which were adorned with shadeless lamps and rusty, old-fashioned alarm clocks, had shelves underneath them that were crammed full of books.

There were two windows in the room, but both of them were covered with curtains that looked like the von Trapp children's playclothes. Overall, the room had a sense of disarray and haphazardness, but the number of books that I saw gave me some amount of comfort. In my musings on what my future might look like, I always imagined that I'd be the owner of a world-renowned personal library, one that many scholars wanted to peruse to their heart's content, but only a select few would be allowed in.

I made a mental note to examine every book in this room while I was here, and, if I could, devour them one by one. Then I realized that I had been silently staring at my surroundings while Luke had been not-so-subtly staring at me, his stomach rumble growing to an increasingly loud soundtrack to our awkward and unexpected family reunion.

"Luke, what's up?"

I probably could've been more precise in my quest for answers, but Luke had always made me feel somewhat uncomfortable. Unfortunately for me, I was the kind of person who, when uncomfortable, became slightly idiotic as far as words went. Usually I was quite eloquent and had a well-developed vocabulary. My father had made sure that, even if I wasn't educated, at least I sounded it. He said that it would keep the white people confused, which apparently was better than them assuming that I was just some kid straight out of the inner city. But despite my father's training, my tongue still becomes tied and dull when taken out of my comfort zone.

Luckily for me, and quite flabbergasting at the same time, Luke understood what I meant.

"It wasn't supposed to be like this, Arthur. I'm sorry."

"Be like what?"

"Um, well, for one thing, you weren't supposed to come to us all broken and stuff . . ."

I knew he was referring to my arm and possibly my head, but at the time it felt slightly more poignant than that. Perhaps that was one of the reasons why Luke disturbed me so much. Despite his inability to control his own actions, his rage, his inconsistencies, he always managed to pinpoint everyone else's with alarming accuracy.

"Yeah, um, how'd that happen again?"

"It was so fucking stupid!" He erupted, like he'd been waiting to freak out about this ever since I'd woken up. "Beatrice was on the mainland with some of the others doing this crazy haunted hike thing and Zorro got off his leash. She followed him when he ran out into the street and well . . . you avoided hitting them, which was really great on your part!"

A goofy grin followed that last statement. I couldn't tell if he had intentionally made a joke, if he was simply amused by the situation, or if he was just smiling because he didn't know what else to do.

"Yeah. Bully for me."

"Bully . . . Roosevelt right? Teddy bear not wheelchair?"

"Yeah I think he's the one. So . . . I'm here then? At the hotel Grace wrote me about?"

I decided to stamp down possible questions I could've conjured about the very inconvenient coincidences of my car accident. It would just complicate things that were already overcomplicated.

"Yeah this is it. I mean part of it anyway. Just one room."

"Yeah I got that."

His eyes grew harsh at this particular piece of sarcasm.

"I'm not stupid!"

"Oh . . . I know you're not, buddy."

I only called him "buddy" when I sensed one of his outbursts coming on. He knew that, but he seemed to like it anyway.

"We just didn't think something like this was going to happen!

You could have died, man! I don't know what to say to you now. Beatrice should be the one apologizing, but they left me here to make dinner and stuff."

The mention of dinner renewed his stomach's frantic complaining. He grimaced, clutching a hand to the fabric of his T-shirt.

"You should go eat something."

"Yeah, I was going to ask you about that. Are you like . . . good to walk? You can come with me and meet everyone else. But we could also bring you something if you're not feeling up to it."

I considered my options. On the one hand, my arm was killing me, my head was killing me, and the rest of my body seemed about ready to jump on board with the massacre. I could just choose to stay up here, grab one of these books off the shelf, and eat whatever food they gave me.

On the other hand, I hadn't seen Grace yet. I had really no idea where I was and what I was doing here beyond the fact that Grace had asked me to come. Then I had gotten into a car accident caused by my half sister and something called Zorro. I was disoriented and confused and I had a lot of questions that would keep me up for hours, if not days, unless they were answered promptly. I was an impatient guy. The thought of staying in this unfamiliar room with all these unfamiliar things taking up space in my comfort zone seemed like a very bad idea indeed.

And I was starving. So that solved that, really.

"I think I'm good to go to dinner. But I might need your help."

"I have strong shoulders. I can do it."

"I know you can."

* * *

When Grace had first started out as a human being, it seemed as if she were going to live up to her name in every way. As a kid she was long-limbed, delicately featured, and soft-spoken. Her shyness was more often described as demure, and her delicate curls reminded people of old Hollywood stars who had to work much harder and pay much more to attain such effortless beauty.

Grace had café-mocha skin combined with honey-gold eyes that captivated everyone she passed. When she entered her preteen years, she seemed to miraculously avoid all of the awkward hormonal changes that plagued her peers. Apart from the development of peach fuzz on her upper lip, everything else about Grace's figure remained lovely and unblemished.

It wasn't until her later teenage years that the oddities of her personality really came to light. Despite being a very accomplished dancer, mastering various complicated styles, outside of the studio, Grace was clumsy and spatially unaware. She'd bump into the edges of doorways and catch her toes on the corners of bed frames constantly. As if to match her proclivity for inadvertently causing minor harm to herself on the regular, Grace also developed quite a sailor's mouth. Every jammed finger and bumped head was accompanied by a string of curses that would make a Tarantino film seem PG by comparison.

She also became extremely challenged as far as fashion went. After Mari stopped dressing her in the sweet pleated skirts and peter-pan necklines, Grace moved on to ill-fitting jeans, men's T-shirts bought in bulk, and a startling amount of flannel. She also only owned three pairs of shoes at any given time: ballet flats, off-brand sneakers, and hiking boots which doubled as rain boots on stormy Florida days.

On top of all that, Grace had a sense of humor that was impossible to describe. She never laughed at the common things that made people laugh. Fart jokes, slapstick, and wordplay were all lost on her. She was too aloof to pop culture to understand those references, and often the jokes of late-night hosts had to be explained to her in great detail before she even cracked the slightest of smiles.

However, there were things that were always guaranteed to make her laugh. Horror movies, for instance, specifically slasher films with innovative character deaths, made her burst out into powerful guffaws. She also found it amusing whenever someone or something in a movie or TV show got hit by a car, but she never liked to watch home videos where people were harmed because it was somehow too real for her. Her least favorite show in the whole world was America's Funniest Home Videos.

And she loved old songs from the twenties, thirties, and forties. Not for their musical value, but because the style of singing and lyrics made her giggle. She could never explain why, but it seemed to have something to do with the absurdity of it all.

So to say that Grace confused people would be a ridiculous understatement. No one could seem to grasp Grace's character. Myself included.

Maybe that's why, when I saw her standing at the head of a long, antique dining table in the middle of a ridiculously ornate dining room (cherubs painted onto the ceiling included), I felt something like a mixture of self-doubt and anger. It was like I didn't even know who I was looking at, and that frustrated me.

Luke had half-carried me down a long, wide hallway, turning a corner to reveal an open entryway surrounded on all sides with a banister that was failing in some areas. He had fully carried me down the unnecessarily steep staircase despite my protestations, and then let me walk the rest of the way to the dining room under his strict direction. I hadn't gotten a chance to fully absorb my surroundings, but I knew for sure that this place was big, old, and dying.

It'd been years since I'd seen Grace in person, and even longer since I'd seen a picture of her. The invitation to her wedding had not included a joyous photograph of Grace and her groom-to-be. It had been simple gold font on white cardstock. Nothing more or less.

She didn't look any older or younger than I had expected. In fact, she looked exactly as I had thought she would except that her signature long locks. They usually reached her buttocks when wet but had been shorn short at her jawline. Now her usually soft baby curls stuck out at odd ends from her scalp, and some even brushed the tops of her eyes.

Of course she was wearing flannel, this time a green color palette with the sleeves rolled up past her elbows. It was quite warm in the dining room, which made me think that the fire roaring in a medieval hearth behind Grace was probably unnecessary. But it added a nice atmospheric touch.

"Everyone. Please welcome Mr. Arthur Bean." Grace paused. "My brother."

"Half brother." Beatrice clarified.

"Close enough! Welcome, sir. Glad to see you're up and at 'em. You had us all quite frantic for a moment there." An elderly man sitting to Grace's left erupted out of his seat, only to lose his balance and plop right back where he'd been.

There were a lot more people at the table than I had expected to have to deal with at that moment. Across from the elderly man was a robust, elderly woman. Next to her was a giant of a man with a stony expression, and next to him was an angelic-looking little boy who couldn't have been more than ten years old. Across from them was a young woman with uncontrollable orange hair and similarly lawless freckles, and three men, two around my age and the other somewhere in his twenties. And there was a dog. A bloodhound sitting on the chair next to one of the men, drooling on the flatware.

"Um, thanks."

Luke guided me to an open chair on Grace's right. Once I was seated, he scuttled down to the end of the table, settling himself next to the boy. They pounded fists in way of greeting.

I felt all those eyes on me and immediately the ache in my head became sharper. I winced a little from the pain.

"Oh, you poor thing," said the older woman. Her voice was warbling and old-fashioned. "I hope my work was good enough for tonight at least. Perhaps you could make it to the clinic tomorrow morning to get a more thorough examination?"

"Yeah." I said, lifting my functional hand to rub at my temples. "I should do that. So, um, you're the one who set my arm?"

I realized that I should have probably been using that time to greet Grace and Beatrice, or perhaps introduce myself to all these new strangers. But like I said, I became remarkably unintelligent in uncomfortable situations. And this was probably the most uncomfortable I'd yet to experience. So needless to say, the niceties of social etiquette were lost to me at that moment.

"I am indeed, love. Although I must say I'm rather out of practice, and arthritic hands do not a great surgeon make."

Everyone laughed politely at this. Everyone, that is, except Grace, who, as always, did not get the joke.

"Oh, well, thanks. It doesn't feel too bad really. You all seem to be, um, taking this pretty well."

"Taking what well, sweetheart?" The older woman said.

"Well, I mean, finding me in a car accident. You don't seem too . . . bothered?"

"Oh we *were* very worried at first. Running around like chickens with our heads cut off. Luke couldn't stop crying." Luke shot her an unappreciative look but didn't say anything. "But you've been stable for a few hours now. You've just been asleep for a while. All that waiting tends to calm the nerves, you see."

"Arthur," Grace called my attention with a hand on my unbound forearm. "It's really good to see you again."

I smiled weakly at her. "Yeah, Grace, it's good to see you too. And you too, Bea."

"Yeah, sure." Beatrice had a way about her that made everything she said sound like sarcasm. And usually it was. "I put the

29

money for the last couple of month's rent and tuition and stuff back into your account. I wasn't using it."

"Oh, it's okay. That money's yours, so . . ."

"I don't need it."

"Okay."

"Well," Grace clapped loudly, which caused me to jump in my seat. Across the table from me, one of the men smirked slightly. "Mrs. K., shall we have dinner now? Introductions can be had after our stomachs are full."

"Yes, sweetie. Right away. I might need some strong arms to help me with the dishes though." She winked at the men on the other side of the table as she rose from her seat, her stomach knocking into the edge of the table as she did so.

Before they could even stand, the elderly man rose suddenly, this time able to keep his balance as he raised a fist into the air and pounded it hard against his chest. If you listened closely enough, you could hear his ribs rattling underneath his skin.

"Fear not madam! I will assist you in your plight."

"Oh you old geezer, your spaghetti noodles are no help to anyone. Now sit down and let the young ones help out a lady in need."

The elderly man sat down, slightly defeated, and proceeded to examine the squishy biceps on his "spaghetti noodles." Luke and two of the other men proceeded to follow Mrs. K. through a swinging door next to the fireplace. There was silence after that, everyone looking expectantly after them.

"I hope you didn't wait to eat because of me." A quick glance at Grace's watch showed that it was almost 9:30 p.m.

"We did." Grace said. "Usually we eat around six-thirty or seven, but with all the hustle and bustle of your arrival, dinner was completely forgotten until about an hour ago. Luckily Mrs. K. can whip up a feast in half that time."

Before I could respond to that, the swinging door slammed hard on the wall as Luke kicked it open. His hands were covered by oven mitts, and he carried a large tureen filled with something that smelled like nutmeg and lemon. The two men followed, one holding a salad bowl in one hand and a basket of bread in the other, and the other holding another covered dish that smelled just as exotic and delectable as Luke's.

Finally followed Mrs. K., who carried a bowl filled with something steaming and set it down in the middle of the table, revealing a rice pilaf of some kind dotted with specks of green herbs.

The scents assaulted my nose all at once. For a moment it was hard to breath. Spices, herbs, and juices all mingled in the air in front of us. I could see that the dog was no longer the only one at the table with a steady outflow of drool.

Luke and one of the men removed the tops from their serving dishes and revealed their contents. Inside Luke's dish looked to be some kind of stew, filled with carrots, greens, and lentils. It had a reddish-brown color that reminded me of newly laid brick. The other dish held cuts of a white fish, surrounded by caramelized onions and cloves of roasted garlic. Each filet was topped with a grilled slice of lemon. I remembered a show that I used to watch with Thia about fancy restaurants, their fancy chefs, and all the fancy food they served to fancy people. It felt odd to feel so fancy with a makeshift cast on my arm and an enclave of strangers surrounding me. Didn't spoil my appetite though.

"I'll get the butter!" Beatrice said, scurrying away from the table on nimble feet.

"Bon appétit!" Mrs. K. said before sitting down and spreading her arms wide to display the feast she'd prepared.

Despite the obviously ravenous hunger displayed on every diner's face, the serving was quite civilized. Everyone waited their turn and only took as much as they needed, at least for the first round. And everyone waited until everyone else had filled their plates and was ready to eat.

Then Grace said, "We are grateful for the food, Mrs. K.," and everyone started to eat.

That meal was undeniably a piece of art. Everything perfectly seasoned, balanced, and cooked. The skin of the fish was crispy and sweet, the flesh soft and savory, the rice warm and inviting, the lentils complex and hearty. Even the rolls I had assumed—erroneously, it seemed—were store-bought were as perfectly delicious as bread had ever been. And the salad, simple greens with no complicated sauce, made me feel as if I were eating at the best restaurant in New York City.

It wasn't until we had all finished our first helping, mostly in silence, and were moving on to seconds, of which everyone partook, that the introductions started.

"Well Arthur," Grace started, wiping her mouth with a cloth napkin, "I'm sure you have a lot of questions for us. But why don't we start with everyone's names?"

"Uh yeah," I said, holding back a belch I could feel bubbling up in my esophagus, "Sounds good."

"Excellent, well you already know Luke, Beatrice, and me. Or have you forgotten your siblings?"

"Nope. No, I know you guys."

"Always so literal." Grace rolled her eyes good-naturedly. Thia used to say that too.

"I'll start," said the elderly man. "My name is Thadeus Greenwood. But you can call me Thad. I am eighty-seven years young and as spry as any of you youngsters, so don't be fooled."

"Nice to meet you."

Heads turned to the woman next to Thadeus.

"Clancy. I don't think you need to know my last name, do you?"

"Not if you don't want to tell me."

"Good, then just Clancy. From Colorado."

"Cool. Nice to meet you."

They continued down the line. The man sitting next to Clancy was Caleb. He leaned into the table when he introduced himself, cupping his jaw in his hands and giving an unnervingly warm smile. It seemed like the kind of smile reserved for close friends and loved ones. When he finished introducing himself, Caleb leaned back in his chair and blew a kiss at me. I just blinked in return.

Rolling his eyes at his predecessor's antics was Diego, who spoke with an incredibly thick and incredibly false Spanish accent. He also introduced his dog, Zorro, a "Spanish bloodhound." Zorro's grunt was probably unrelated to the introductions being made.

Next to Diego was Sam. He introduced himself with that one word and nothing else. Sam was one of those classically good-looking men by the Aryan definition, but he had two long scars cutting down his right cheek. He never made eye contact with me.

Moving across the table was Mrs. K., who needed no introduction at this point but gave one anyway.

"The food was really fucking delicious, ma'am. Seriously. The best I've had in a while."

"Well thank you, my dear, but do watch your language. There are children present."

"Oh, right. Sorry."

The man next to Mrs. K. was named Francis and was apparently the guardian and tutor of the boy sitting next to him, whose name was Kiki. I assumed that was short for something but never asked. Kiki, it was explained, was the illegitimate son of a wealthy heiress who had died tragically last year. Kiki's grandfather had sent him away from the family homestead but continued to provide a monthly stipend for his living and his studies. Kiki did not seem bothered by Francis's explanation and simply waved his greeting at me with a wide smile.

"Well that's everyone. Now, Mrs. K., unless there is dessert, should we go into the library to continue the Q and A?"

"No dessert this time around, dear, but there is some ice cream. You can all grab a bowl yourself if you're so inclined."

Everyone stood, some immediately helping to gather plates and cutlery, some wandering through the swinging door in search of ice cream, and some wandering out the way Luke and I had come.

Luke arrived at my side, forcing my arm over his shoulders. With Grace and Beatrice behind us, we made our way out of the dining room. As we passed through the entryway, I noticed for the first time the chandelier hanging above us. Many of its lights were blown out. Many of the crystals that were supposed to be adorning it were missing. It swayed ominously back and forth, threatening to come crashing down at any moment.

* * *

Everyone seemed to have their place in the library. They settled into their respective chairs and spots on the floor with ease. The dog, Zorro, cuddled up to a fire that was already burning there, once again making the room unnecessarily hot. Luke helped me into a vacant spot on the love seat where Beatrice was already lounging. Grudgingly, she tucked her previously sprawled legs underneath her to make room for me.

The other guests, as I soon learned they preferred to be called, all had books or decks of cards or newspapers on their laps, but they were all looking expectantly at Grace and me. Clearly there was more to be discussed than simple introductions.

Grace had entered the room before me and was rummaging through one of the bookshelves. Eventually she turned around, a thin volume in her hand. She tripped over a corner of the rug, cursing under her breath, before placing the book on my lap.

"You might enjoy this one, Arthur. You prefer nonfiction, yes?"

"I'm a fan of both really. But yeah, this is great."

It was a book of letters from Confederate soldiers to their loved ones in the North. Grace remembered that I was somewhat of a Civil War nut in my youth, just like I remembered the time when she was positively obsessed with the mythology and history of ancient Egypt. It's strange the things the mind holds on to.

Once Grace had settled down in the spot that had been left open for her on a faded couch with red floral upholstery and clawed feet, her gaze settled on me. When I didn't say anything, she spoke.

"I'm sure you have a lot of questions for us, Arthur."

The situation suddenly struck me as extremely hilarious, and I struggled to hold back a chuckle. Luckily only a snort came out, which I passed off quite convincingly as a cough. At least I thought it was convincing, but the look on Beatrice's face showed that she was not so easily fooled.

It was just ridiculous. The way that everyone was arranged in an almost-semicircle around me, their eyes trained on Grace as if waiting for some signal. The elaborate dinner followed by quiet time in a library that belonged in the eighteenth century. It was as if I'd been transported into a mobster movie where Grace played the head of the family set in Civil War–era plantation country. It was a wonder to me that no one had donned a double-breasted suit and fedora or an antebellum gown complete with bustle.

And now that Grace had asked, I couldn't think of a single question I wanted to ask. All those musings about why Luke and Beatrice had happened to be here as well and who the hell all these other people were completely left my mind. I was left with a sense that this was Grace's world and I had stumbled unwittingly into it. These people belonged to her. I had to tread lightly somehow and earn my place here.

"Perhaps I should just update you on some things and then maybe you could ask me questions as we go along?"

"Yeah. Yeah that sounds good."

So Grace began. She started out with an introduction to the Hotel itself. I'm not just capitalizing Hotel to be funny. That's actually what the name of it was, at least until they finished repairs. It was all very *Breakfast at Tiffany's*: a hotel named Hotel.

The Hotel, as it turned out, was actually an abandoned plantation from the antebellum South, so at least I'd nailed that particular detail. Unlike most of those homes, which had remained within the family or been reclaimed by wealthy Northerners looking for a bit of southern charm, this one had not drawn the usual crowd of home hunters. This was for a variety of reasons, not the least of which being that it was falling apart. The location also left little to be desired. Many of these plantation homes found themselves far away from towns and neighbors due to the sheer mass of their land, but the Hotel didn't just have the usual solitude. It was also on an island.

The man who had first built this house had thought it charming to have a small stream of bayou water running through his front yard. At the time, the rest of the land was completely solid and viable for the production of various crops that he used for the household and keeping of a dozen or so cabins that housed his enslaved workers. He also owned land and a home in another part of Louisiana where he produced most of his cotton and spent most of his time. The Hotel was meant to be more of a temporary residence for him and a permanent residence for his daughters. He wished to expose them as little as possible to the horrors that cotton production in the era of slavery could produce.

Fortunately for the man, he did not live long enough to see the swampy marshland overwhelm his front yard, his gardens, and more than half of those cabins. And fortunately for Grace, it seemed, the fact that the Hotel was built on such an undesirable and difficult-to-reach piece of quasi-land made the purchase of such an enormous place remarkably affordable.

Unfortunately for everyone involved, the home itself was in such a state of decay that Grace wasn't sure if they'd ever be truly able to open for business. The grand columns at the front of the house were rotting and sinking into the earth. Most of the furniture was left from fifty or so odd years ago when a family had tried, for three months, to live there. Needless to say, it smelled of mold and mothballs. Grace had had just enough money, although she didn't say exactly where she received it, to renovate the kitchen entirely. But after that, they weren't sure how to proceed.

The roof needed fixing and so did the stairs. Furniture and rugs and curtains needed replacing or mending. The wallpaper was old and rotting and many of the rooms with painted walls were plagued with stains and scuff marks. The floorboards were creaky and inflated in places, probably caused by the plumbing, which was shoddy at best. Furthermore, the books had to be sorted through because Grace was certain that some of their bindings and pages had seen the last of their days long ago.

And if all that was fixed, then they could get to work on the remaining cabins on the property, which Grace hoped to use as honeymoon suites.

All in all, the Hotel was gargantuan and in great need of some TLC. Or a bulldozer.

There were four decent-sized bedrooms on the first floor which Thadeus pointed out might've been used for enslaved house workers, menservants, maids, and the like. On the top floor were six rooms that were clearly meant to be bedrooms, and another two that might've been designed as sitting rooms or office space but could be converted. And then there were six cabins in various spots on the land, of which Grace believed at least four could be salvaged.

At the time, Mrs. K., Thadeus, and Sam occupied three of the four rooms on the bottom floor. Diego, Caleb, and Luke all had their own rooms on the second floor. Grace and Beatrice shared a room, as did Francis and Kiki. I had been placed in the last vacant bedroom.

"Where do you stay, then?" I said, looking at Clancy.

"Behind the kitchen."

"Ah yes!" Thadeus said. "There is a very small room, hardly big enough for a bed really, behind the kitchen. Undoubtedly the former cook's quarters."

"Is that comfortable enough for you?" I was ready to trade the bedroom that had been assigned to me, but Clancy merely shrugged.

"It's fine for one."

Grace continued. Apart from the kitchen, the grand dining hall, and the library I had already seen, there was also a ballroom on the first floor as well as an attic, which could also be converted into a room. Unfortunately, at that time, the attic was filled with knick-knacks of owners past and infested by rats, which no one had yet summoned the willpower to battle.

Despite the dilapidated nature of the Hotel in its current state, Grace had very little doubt that it could be returned to its former glory given the proper expertise and a little bit of elbow grease. Then, they could start taking guests.

"So are all of you just here to help with the repairs?" I found it unlikely that Kiki, or Thadeus, or even Mrs. K., despite her clear expertise with kitchen knives, could possibly be handy with a hammer and nails.

"No, my dear boy," Mrs. K. said, "We are the guests."

Anticipating my confusion and surprise, Grace immediately jumped in. "At the moment, the Hotel is in no condition to receive formal guests. But these fantastic people found us and seem to enjoy it here. So they either pay a discounted price for their rooms, or they help the Hotel's functioning in some way. As you've already seen, Mrs. K. is our accomplished chef."

Sam handled a lot of the busywork around the Hotel: minor repairs, cleaning, and the like. But he had no training or skill with more complicated work. Diego was a landscape architect and former florist, so he was hard at work figuring how exactly to transform an island in the middle of the bayou into a lovely getaway for young couples and other travelers. Thadeus was a librarian in his day and was charged with the task of sorting through and organizing the Hotel's various books.

"But . . . how did you all find this place? Do you have ads out or something?"

Mrs. K. smiled. "One finds a way."

I opened my mouth to respond, then closed it again and shook my head a little. After another moment's worth of hesitation, I decided to let it pass. "Right, so when the Hotel is up and running, you'll all move on to other places?"

Everyone shifted uncomfortably in their seats, sharing sneaky glances with each other. I immediately knew I had caused some sort of disturbance, but at the time I couldn't really understand what it was. It only made sense that once the Hotel was ready to receive guests, the others that were paying their keep with work that was no longer needed would move on. After all, how could Grace expect to receive guests when only a few rooms were open to them?

"That's a thought for another time." Grace said soothingly. "For now, there's too much work to be thinking that far in the future. For now, we are all here and we are all needed."

That seemed to assuage everyone's nerves, although I still felt slightly uncomfortable with the obvious fact that Grace seemed to be the leader of some sort of haphazard gang of misfits. That thought brought my gaze to Luke, who sat next to Diego on the floor, and then to Beatrice. Both of them had remained silent throughout this entire history.

"How did you two get here? Luke, last time I checked you were still in prison."

"Got out on good behavior." He mumbled, but it was as obvious a lie as any.

"Luke is here to help with the repairs, just like you." Grace said.

"And you?" I turned to look at Beatrice. "Did you even graduate?"

"Yes. I graduated. Early. Then I needed a place to stay because I wasn't going to do college."

"And why not do college?"

"Because I didn't want to."

"Fair enough." There was really no argument against that. A pernicious thought suddenly entered my mind, and before I could even think to keep my mouth shut, the words slipped out. "Grace, did you invite me here because of my money?"

A sharp intake of breath from somewhere in the room, the sound of a book sliding from a lap and landing hard on the floor, a sudden chill that took advantage of the now dying fire. My mistake was evident, and yet it was out there, and, in my mind, it was valid. After all, Beatrice had returned the money to me that was meant to sustain her through college. Luke had never once touched my money, apart from the one time he needed bail and asked for it. And Grace had stopped accessing her account years ago. There was plenty of money in there. Money that could be invested in the Hotel's repairs. It made sense.

But it was deeply offensive to everyone sitting in that room. At the time, I still couldn't read the dynamic and understand that certain things were simply not tolerated. A lack of trust in a Hotel resident's good intentions, for one.

Grace, however, seemed to take the question in stride. She reminded me of Thia in that way. An expert at hiding true emotions when those emotions might cause more stress in a situation.

"While your money would be appreciated, Arthur, it is neither necessary nor the reason I invited you here. You are here, or at least I hope you are here, because a member of your family asked for help, and you graciously decided to extend that help. If you wish to use your inheritance to help our efforts, then it would be a sincerely generous offer on your part. But rest assured that we can achieve our goals without it."

Grace didn't do sarcasm. It wasn't in her tonal vocabulary. But her words, pleasant enough by definition, stung as if they were a diatribe against my character. I felt like a child being scolded for calling their parents a liar. A parent made to feel like a child by his own child. Maybe this was a common experience. If it was, then it was nothing that I was used to. Grace had always spoken to me with deference. It seemed she had hardened somewhat over the years. A part of me couldn't help but be proud, even though most of me simply felt deflated.

Before I could decide whether or not apologizing was the correct route for amelioration, Grace clapped her hands in that same jarring way that she had at the dinner table. It signaled the end of the conversation, the end of the questions, and the end of the evening. Everyone at once began to stand and gather their belongings. Confused, I whipped my head around like a bird on the lookout for some grub.

"You must be tired, Arthur, after your long day." Grace said by way of explanation. "And it is already late. Rest tonight, and we can talk more tomorrow."

I remained seated as they passed by me, and each of the guests touched me in some way. Kiki offered his fist for me to bump, which I did, because there is no more awkward a feeling than being left hanging. Francis, Diego, and Thadeus both clapped manly hands on my uninjured shoulder, and Caleb brushed my forearm with the tip of his index finger. Clancy booped my nose, which seemed an unlikely playful gesture for someone who, up until that point, had been so standoffish, and Mrs. K. planted a noisy, wet smooch on my cheek, an act which Zorro imitated on my hand. The only one who didn't touch me on leaving was Sam, who scurried by me so quickly that I didn't even have the chance to say good night.

Then it was just Grace, Beatrice, and Luke left.

"Do you need help up the stairs again?" Luke asked.

"No, thank you. I'm feeling much better now that I've eaten."

Luke took that as his cue to leave, and did so, offering his hand to Beatrice as he passed. She took it and hopped up from her spot beside me. They walked off hand in hand, Beatrice whispering something in Luke's ear.

I chuckled a little. "When did those two get so close?"

"You've missed so much, Arthur. Don't worry. We'll get you caught up in no time. Do you remember which room is yours?"

I nodded, standing from the couch and making my way toward the stairs. Grace followed me, eventually falling into step with me. When we arrived at the door to my room, Grace gestured down the hall.

"My room's just two doors down. Don't hesitate if you feel like you need something."

"Thanks, Grace. It's good to see you again."

"Good to see you too, Arthur."

* * *

I should've expected, with the Hotel being an old, creaky house, not being able to fall asleep that night. After all, old houses in the middle of nowhere were not only the favorite setting of many a horror movie, they were also prone to bumps and groans in the night. That along with the thunderstorm, which continued outside of my window, and the swirling cacophony of thoughts bouncing off the walls of my brain made sleep next to impossible.

It wasn't until the earliest hours of the morning that the storm finally passed, and it wasn't until the sun began its ascent, changing the sky from inky black to dusky gray, that I finally found a bit of sleep. It didn't last for long though. According to one of the rusty alarm clocks, which by some miracle still kept time, it was just after eight in the morning when Luke burst into my room claiming breakfast was ready. I remember thinking as I roused myself from my bed that for someone in his early twenties, Luke was bewilderingly a morning person. Maybe being in the system for so long did that to a person.

Luke had brought with him towels, a toothbrush, and toothpaste.

"Diego and Sam and me are going to go get your car today, so you should have all your stuff ready for you later."

"Oh really? Do you mind if I come with you guys? I'd like to go to the clinic that Mrs. K. mentioned last night."

Luke, who had been making my bed and was talking to me while I was in the bathroom, paused for long enough that I had to poke my head out just to check that he was still there. He was, but he had frozen over my bed, pillow in hand, eyes half-closed.

"Luke? Buddy?" Freezing on the spot was one of Luke's indicators. I really didn't have the energy for one of his outbursts at the moment.

Luke shook his head as if he were in some cartoon and then

43

looked at me, smiling. "Um yeah. We can drop you off there and then come back to get you later. If that's okay? Most of us avoid the clinic."

"Y'all not fans of doctors?"

"No. That's not it really."

"Oh. Okay. Well should I avoid it too?"

"No. No. They don't know you, so it should be fine." Luke threw down the pillow in his hands and turned to me with an unnatural grin on his face. "Breakfast is still going until nine, so you should come eat something. Then we'll go."

"Sure. Just let me finish brushing my teeth."

Luke nodded and then sauntered out of the bedroom as if I'd offended him. I shrugged it off and continued getting ready. I realized that the only clothes I had were the ones I'd fallen asleep in, the ones that I had woken up in after my accident, which were not the ones I had been wearing in the car. Those had conveniently disappeared and all I was left with were ratty grey sweatpants and an off-white undershirt. I felt slightly uncomfortable with the idea of entering civilization in these clothes, but there was nothing to be done about it.

The Hotel looked much bigger to me in the daylight. There were multiple large windows from which the curtains had been drawn to let in the sunshine. It seemed the storm had left behind lovely blue skies and soft, white clouds. Not a bad day to go to the clinic.

There was no food set out in the dining room, so I made my way back to the swinging doors. It was true what Grace had said about the kitchen. It was completely new in every way. Shiny stainless steel appliances, shiny backsplash in shades of blue, shiny tiles on the floor, and a shiny marble island with shiny stools lined up along one side. On two of those stools sat Caleb, who looked as if he had spent a significant amount of time that morning to look effortlessly attractive in his pajamas, and Sam, who sat close to Caleb and ate grapes from the other man's bowl.

Mrs. K. was at the sink cleaning dishes, but on the island in the same elaborate serving trays from last night, was a variety of foods that made my mouth water instantly. A huge pile of fluffy, scrambled eggs remained in one of the tureens, and next to it was a plate teeming with bacon and sausage, and right beside that was another plate piled high with pancakes and waffles. There were also many different kinds of breads, some of which had already been sliced up, and some of which had not. There were jams and preserves and honeys and syrups, and large bowls of fruits, grapes, apples, bananas, berries, and even lychees. A few pitchers held various juices, milks, and water. And there were also cereals ranging from the plain to the youthful. It appeared that Mrs. K. never made a meal that wasn't a feast.

As I was ogling the breakfast choices, Mrs. K. noticed my presence and halted her chore.

"Oh I was wondering if you'd show." She said, sending me a maternal smile and placing a rubber-gloved hand on her significant hip.

"Sorry. Had trouble getting started this morning. Is it still okay if I eat something?"

"Do you see food on the table?"

"Um, yeah."

"Then it's still okay."

I sat down one seat away from where Caleb and Sam were seated and began to fill a plate high with pretty much everything. I could tell I was being watched, a suspicion that was confirmed when I reached for the Cinnamon Toast Crunch instead of the slightly more adult option of Cheerios.

"So you eat kids cereal, I see." Caleb said.

"Yeah. I have a sweet tooth."

"Don't we all." Caleb said, popping a grape into his mouth. I held his gaze for a while before continuing to select food for my plate.

"I'll have you know," Mrs. K. said, "That breakfast and dinner are the only meals in which you'll find me in the kitchen. I take afternoon naps, you see, so you'll have to fend for yourself for lunch. Pretty much everything in the fridge and cabinets are up for grabs, unless specifically marked otherwise."

Caleb leaned over the empty seat toward me conspiratorially. "Don't let her fool you. She always makes something for lunch and just leaves it out for us. Yesterday it was roast beef sandwiches and tomato soup."

"Oh Caleb, hush."

"Jesus," I said, digging into my overfull plate, "I'm gonna get so fat."

"That's just fine." Caleb said. "None of us mind a man with a little something more."

I raised an eyebrow at him and noticed Sam blushing furiously before he pushed back his chair and took his plate to Mrs. K.

"Help?" He asked her simply.

"That's all right, sweetie. You're on dish duty tonight anyway. I'll make Mr. Flirtatious help me when he's done putting himself out there."

"Can't blame a guy for trying, isn't that right Arthur?"

I shrugged my shoulders and kept eating. Caleb was extremely handsome. He wouldn't be the first guy who flirted with me. If I had reciprocated, he wouldn't have been the first guy I had flirted back with. But at that moment, flirting with anyone was the furthest thing from my mind.

At my dismissal of his efforts, Caleb simply laughed and stood up. "All right, Mrs. K. Put me to work."

Both Caleb and Mrs. K. sang while they washed dishes. Caleb hummed some kind of soothing, lilting tune, and Mrs. K. occasionally burst out into an operatic aria. Weirdly enough, their dissonant melodies matched each other quite well.

I had just finished polishing off my plate when Luke burst through the door, followed by Diego and Sam.

"Are you ready?"

I coughed, startled by the slam of the swinging door on the

46

wall. Then I nodded and said, "I was wondering if there were some other clothes I could change into before we left. I'm not usually the one to wear sweatpants outside of the house."

"A man of fashion. Be still my beating heart." Caleb said from the sink.

"Control yourself." Diego said, and then turned to me. "You look like you're about my size. I bet I could find you something in my closet. Come on."

"We are going to be late!" Luke called after us as we left the kitchen.

"The car's not going anywhere, Luke. It can wait." Diego said.

Going through Diego's closet only caused a three-minute delay to Luke's schedule because, despite what Caleb assumed, I was not in fact a man of fashion. I borrowed a black T-shirt and black jeans from Diego and a pair of socks. Diego told me that there were galoshes near the front door that anyone was welcome to use.

"Where are my shoes from last night? When you all found me?" I asked, following him down the stairs.

"I think they had too much blood on them. So someone threw them away."

"Oh." I had loved those shoes. Fashionable or not, it was hard to find perfect shoes. Those had been perfect shoes.

Sam and Luke were waiting for us by the front door, Luke shifting impatiently from foot to foot. When he saw us coming down the stairs, he immediately shoved open one of the two large, heavy doors. Its hinges greatly protested at being disturbed, but it opened easily enough. In my mind, I was already making an inventory of repairs that needed to be done and how much those would cost. The renovation that had already been done on the kitchen alone must have cost an astronomical amount. If Grace had more money, she might have finished the whole thing herself and never asked me to come. But the fact that nothing else had been done made me think that she had exhausted all of her funds in one spot.

Walking out those doors was my first time getting a look at the exterior of the Hotel. If I had been pessimistic about restoring the place just by the state of its innards, then seeing the outside made me downright hopeless. It looked like the set of a Tim Burton movie. The columns were warped and bent, the foundation sunken into the earth on one side, which gave it a lopsided appearance, and the porch bloated and rotting. Next to the front doors was a lone wicker chair whose bottom had burst open long ago. Ominously, a crow crouched low on the porch railing, cawing at us as we made our way across the surprisingly solid front lawn. Truthfully, I had expected my feet to sink into the ground when I saw the building.

The Hotel really was on an island. Although the mainland was visible from the shore that ended the Hotel's front lawn, according to Luke, the water was not only surprisingly deep at this particular point in the bayou, there were also alligators.

"How do you keep the gators from coming up on land then?"

"Electric fence. Keeps Zorro out of the water as well."

There was a newly made dock jutting out slightly into the water. An airboat was tethered to its posts along with two kayaks that knocked into each other at rhythmic intervals.

Noticing my quizzical glance, Luke said, "Thought kayaking might be a fun activity for the guests."

"Might not be safe if there are alligators."

Luke just shrugged and clambered into the boat after Sam. I settled myself on the back bench where Diego sat, and Luke started up the engine.

It took less than five minutes to get to the opposite shore, and as we disembarked at another dock that looked just as new as the one we left, I noticed two large concrete structures that also had a new look to them. As we walked around to their fronts, I realized that they were garages, each with four parking bays. Luke grabbed a clicker from his pocket and opened the last door to one of the garages, revealing an old Ford truck with a questionable paint job.

Sam went to sit in the front seat with Luke, but Luke jumped in front of him.

"What are you doing?" Luke's arms were outstretched as if he were protecting the truck from a possible attack.

"Sam always sits in the front, Luke. He gets carsick. You know that." Diego said. Sam simply nodded, looking slightly lost. He wrung his hands together, causing his fingertips to turn red.

"But my brother has a broken arm."

Sam looked down at the rebuff. His eyes glanced at me furtively, but immediately returned to the garage floor when he noticed I was looking at him. Slowly, Sam made his way toward the bed of the truck.

I reached out to touch his arm so he'd stop. "It's okay, Luke. I'll sit in the—" My fingertips just barely grazed Sam's arms before I felt myself being shoved backward.

I stumbled, reaching out to grab at something to stabilize myself. I ended up grabbing a rake, which came crashing down with me as I landed hard on my ass. I remember thinking that I'd have to get checked out for a broken tailbone as well as a broken arm. The shouting began immediately.

Rising to my feet, ignoring the pain in my ass, my arm, and my head, I stumbled forward to the writhing mass that was Diego and Luke. Luke must have lunged at Sam after he pushed me, and now had him pinned to the floor. Sam was frozen underneath Luke, eyes squeezed shut. He made an odd whimpering sound that reminded me of a baby that was uncertain of whether it was going to cry or not.

Diego was attached to Luke's back, struggling to get him off of a petrified Sam. But Luke had gone wild. He was a strong kid to begin with, but when he lost control, it was like the adrenaline gave him superpowers. He was an immovable object that no amount of force could shake.

Sam started to whisper over and over again. "Sorry. Sorry. Sorry."

Diego was shouting. "Hey! Hey! You know how Sam is. It's not his fault."

But Luke remained hunched over Sam, his hands gripping

Sam's wrists so fiercely that I was afraid they might break. I knelt down next to Sam's head, leaning down as far as I could to make sure that Luke would look into my eyes.

"Buddy. Buddy, there's no need for that. I'm fine. See? Just fine. Why don't you let him go now?"

I'd only had to bring Luke back from the edge four or five times before this point. I wasn't nearly as practiced at it as Grace or maybe even Beatrice. But there was a script to dealing with him depending on what had set him off. In this case, he thought someone was trying to hurt his family. That was a big trigger for Luke, who was fiercely loyal and had a strong sense of blood being thicker than water. So I went with the script, and Luke responded.

His panting slowed to normal breathing, his hands loosened on a still paralyzed Sam, and slowly, with Diego still attached to his back, he began to stand. I made to help Sam up, who had finally opened his eyes, but Diego immediately held out a hand to stop me.

"Don't! Don't touch him. He doesn't like to be touched." There was a tone in his voice that suggested I was to blame for disrupting the tentative equilibrium Luke and Sam seemed to have achieved within themselves and each other.

I felt moronic, standing there with a broken arm, a massive headache, and a sore bottom, staring at a catatonic grown man on the floor of a garage in the middle of the bayou. It didn't seem right just to leave him there. But eventually Sam did come to and quietly got into the bed of the truck as if nothing had happened. Diego followed him, and I went to Luke.

He was standing hunched over. Luke didn't find it easy to cope with his own actions. In the moment, it was like he had no control. He could hardly even see what he was doing. But after he came down from his fury, he had a hard time dealing with the guilt that always seemed to follow him.

I placed a hand on his shoulder. As I had expected, because Luke was predictable even if he was uncontrollable, he took a big step into my arms and placed his forehead onto my shoulder. Patiently, I patted the back of his head until he straightened and made his way silently to the front seat of the car.

* * *

The town where Luke dropped me off was one of those small ones that one could happen upon during any road trip across America. The whole country was littered with tiny, next-to-nothing populations all conglomerated around a church, or a gas station, or a grocery store. This one was no different.

We'd driven past a few lone houses on the way to the main street. Like so many other towns, it seemed that this one had only one main thoroughfare, where almost all the restaurants, shops, and public spaces were situated. The clinic, because this town wasn't big enough for a real hospital, shared space with the funeral parlor and the vet. It was across the street from a three-screen movie theater that also acted as a museum of town history, according to the marquee.

I had to say that it was more than troublesome to have to be within sight of a casket showroom while waiting for my checkup. Also, the smell of dog, cat, and hamster was so strong that I felt as though I might as well have just gone to the zoo for a new cast.

But the doctor was quick and efficient. She had a few questions about how I'd received my injuries and who had put on the rudimentary cast and why I hadn't immediately come to the clinic. I fabricated some story about my cousin being a nurse practitioner and the accident having happened late at night and so on and so forth. She seemed to take what I said at face value, and I felt my anxiety ease a little. But then, when I winced as she moved my arm into the cast, she chuckled and said, "I'm surprised you even felt that. Your lot usually handle pain better than most."

I turned my head slowly to look at her and blinked disbelievingly. "Excuse me?"

"Oh, you know. Black people handle pain better. Every medical professional knows that." She said it so matter-of-factly that I was completely at a loss for words.

I opened my mouth and closed it again. Staring at the door, I

52

tried to switch off my brain until she was finally done and I could get the hell out of there.

I realized as I left the clinic that my cell phone was in the busted car that Luke, Sam and Diego were now retrieving. The whole visit to the clinic had taken only slightly over an hour, and I had no idea how long it would take them to finish their task. I didn't know where my car had hit the tree, how far away that was from the town or the Hotel, and whether the sedan was at all drivable. If it were a complete wreck, they'd need to tow it somehow, which could take hours. I got the feeling, based off of their unwillingness to come to the clinic in the first place and their general secretiveness about the Hotel itself, that they would not hire a service to do the towing.

So I was left with two options. I could sit on the curb in front of the clinic, which would undoubtedly arouse suspicion. Small town residents were extremely observant, which in turn made them extremely nosy. They were used to a certain kind of routine and a certain cast of characters. A guy like me, a stranger lingering outside the local doctor's office, would definitely make people curious, perhaps even a little angry. Especially given the fact that I looked nothing like any of the people I saw.

The second option was to find someplace nearby where I could anonymously linger while also keeping an eye on the clinic's storefront to see when the truck, an easily recognizable vehicle, came. But there was a problem with that option as well. Not only did I not know the layout of the town or any of the shops, I also did not have any money. My wallet was in my car along with my cell phone.

I felt a surge of anger at Luke for not having given me more precise instructions. He could've recommended a coffee shop where I could wait, given me an estimate on how long their task would take, or even just loaned me twenty dollars so I could've bought lunch.

Realizing that as I was standing there considering my options, passing locals were already starting to throw me quizzical looks, I crossed the street to the museum. Luckily enough, entry to it was free.

The only exhibit this museum hosted was set up just to the right of the concessions stand for the movie theater. A bespectacled teenager reading a science fiction paperback nodded at me without looking from in front of the popcorn machines. She was absent-mindedly twirling one fine blond lock of hair of the few that had escaped from underneath her baseball cap. As far as I could see, she was the only person inside the movie theater.

I wandered over to the exhibit. There were a few glass cases holding some memorabilia, including an aging baseball, a charter signed by the town's founders, and the large head of an alligator who had apparently terrorized the town for almost ten years before its capture and consequent execution.

There was also a plethora of pictures, paintings, and drawings. Some of them were obviously old, from the town's history, and others were pieces done by local artists. There were even a few ceramics and one sculpture made of wire and twinkle lights. From far away it sort of looked like an angel, but the closer you got, the more it just looked like a jumbled mess.

I continuously glanced out of the window to see if Luke had reappeared, but so far there was nothing. On one wall of the exhibit was a small bookshelf and next to it a large reading chair. The bookshelf held a few old magazines with articles about the town, some old copies of a discontinued town newspaper, and two novels written by an author whose name I vaguely recognized. I picked up one of the newspapers and began to flip through it.

The date on the paper was December 12, 1953. The main head-line read "Soviet Union Strikes Again!" Underneath it the author clarified, "Town official revealed to be head of secret Communist organization." The town official was the local treasurer, who was also the vice principal of the local K-12 school. Apparently, he had been revealed by a group of students he had tried to recruit. Being the good Christian boys that they were, they had immediately reported him to the proper authorities.

Other notable headlines were mostly just accounts of local goings-on, including a rather lengthy obituaries section, all of them black people with only the vaguest and somewhat triumphant descriptions of how they'd died. I ignored the uncomfortable shiver that sent up my spine and kept reading. I was just about to delve into a reader-submitted recipe for ambrosia salad when a shadow passed over me.

"Anything interesting in the paper, son?"

An older white man with a significant salt and pepper beard and no other hair to speak of stood in front of me with an amused grin on his face. Clearly he had found his joke to be quite funny. I, however, felt slightly uncomfortable. As a rule, being alone in the presence of an older white man who I didn't know tended to make me slightly uncomfortable. I guess you could have called it a learned defense mechanism.

"There's a recipe in here for ambrosia salad." I said, trying to keep my voice light. "Thinking about trying it out for dinner tonight."

The man apparently thought this was extremely funny and let out a loud belly laugh. I glanced out the window behind him, but there was still no sign of Luke.

"Say, son," the man said once his laughter had subsided, "I don't think I've ever seen you around here. And yours is a face that I'd remember."

I had to stop myself from cringing at the implication. It was already clear to me from the waiting room at the clinic and the passersby on the street that this was a monochromatic town. I stood out like a spot of blood on crisp white sheets.

"Where is it that you come from?"

"Florida. Jacksonville." I could've said New York, but decided to go the more southern route.

"Never been there. But I bet it's nice."

I nodded.

"So what brings you to our little museum then? Just passing through town or looking to stay?"

"Passing through."

"Uh-huh. Dr. Maeve mentioned that you'd been in to see her. Had an accident nearby?"

So much for doctor-patient confidentiality. "Yes, sir."

The sir seemed to please him. He uncrossed his arms and shoved his hands into his pockets instead.

"Where's your car now, then? At the local mechanic's, I'd assume."

"Actually, I have cousins nearby who are taking care of it for me. I just saw the museum and thought I might stop in for a bit." Out of the corner of my eye, I noticed a man lingering near the entrance to the museum, a sheriff's badge pinned to his chest and his hand resting on his gun. I gulped. "But I should be going now."

I made to stand up, and by some miracle, the Ford truck pulled up in front of the clinic. For a brief moment, I thought the man might try and stop me, but he let me slip by easily enough. I walked slowly toward the sheriff, trying to keep my hands where he could see them and my face passive. As I passed him, he said to the old man, "This guy bothering you, sir? Got a call about a suspicious character in the museum."

"No, no." The old man said. "He's just *passing through*."

"It was a pleasure meeting you, sir." I said as I ducked past the sheriff.

"Sure. You too, son." He said. "Say hello to your cousins for me." It was impossible to ignore the slightly sinister note in his voice.

I quickly crossed the street without looking and slid into front seat next to Luke. Diego and Sam were no longer in the back. Luke looked filthy from sweat and mud, but he grinned at me.

"All fixed up?"

"Yeah, all better. Now let's get out of here. This place is creeping me out."

Luke didn't ask me what I meant. He just pulled out and headed home.

* * *

Sam and Diego were waiting for us outside of the garage when we pulled up. They both looked as muddy and filthy as Luke did.

"My car?" I said as I stepped down from the cab.

"It is in the garage. We were able to drive it here after digging it out and changing a tire, but we think it will need a lot more repairs before it is safe to take over long distances."

"How far away was it?"

"Only a few miles." Luke said coming up behind me. "We got lucky."

I failed to see how my car being trashed was lucky, but I decided not to fight him on it.

The car was pretty badly beat up. The entire front looked like it was frowning, metal crumpled up into a morose grimace. I could see a bit of the engine sticking out from under the hood. There was a long, jagged crack traveling the length of the windshield and both headlights were completely smashed. Diego said they had changed a tire, and it was obvious which one because all the others were either completely deflated or on their way there. I could empathize with the poor thing. We'd both had a rough couple of days.

Sighing, I opened the front door to gather my phone, wallet, and briefcase. The phone had probably flown into the dash during the accident because its screen was cracked. Otherwise it was functioning, which I was slightly more relieved about than I had been expecting. It's not like anyone was going to be calling me, but at least I had some kind of link to the outside world. At the time I didn't know that service in the hotel was nonexistent at best.

Luke and Diego gathered my two bags from the trunk and started to lug them over to the airboat. Sam waited for me at the door to the garage while I searched the rest of the car for anything

57

I might've forgotten. When I came out, he took out a clicker and brought the doors down.

"Sorry you guys had to get all dirty for me."

"It's nothing." Diego and Luke both said. Sam just nodded.

When we got off at the dock in front of the Hotel, I offered to take my bags up to my room myself, but Luke immediately brushed me off, gesturing to my broken arm as if it were obvious.

"Besides," Diego said, "It looks like someone is waiting for you."

I looked up at the Hotel. Grace stood on one of the balconies that overhung the patio. I immediately wanted to yell at her to get down from there because I was doubtful of the decaying columns' ability to hold even her meager weight. She waved at me and made a gesture that she would be coming down.

She met us in the entryway, insisting that we take off our shoes. Sam, Diego, and Luke disappeared up the stairs with my things. There were noises coming from the dining room and music drifting in from the library, but Grace and I were alone together for the first time in years.

"How did it go at the clinic?"

"Fine. They put a new cast on me and checked me out for a concussion. They said I'd need to come back in a few weeks to get the cast off."

Grace nodded. "Perhaps your car will be fixed by that time and you can drive yourself."

"You all don't like to go into town much, do you?"

Grace smiled wryly. "We've had some issues in the past. Nothing major, but now we usually only send a select few of our residents for errands and chores."

"What kind of issues?"

Grace just shrugged. "Nothing major. Are you hungry? Mrs. K. set up a lovely lunch before she went for her nap."

"I thought she didn't cook for lunch."

"Usually she doesn't. But I think she might be showing off for you a bit."

Showing off was an understatement. I had been expecting leftovers from the incredible dinner last night, or even some of those roast beef sandwiches that Caleb had mentioned that morning. But the assortment of sandwiches, salads, and soups laid out on the table could've given Golden Corral a run for its money. There was even a whole roasted chicken that still had tendrils of steam floating off its golden skin. And at the end of this long procession of savory delicacies were two cakes, one covered with the most decadent-looking chocolate frosting I'd ever seen, and the other dotted with strawberries and fresh cream.

I must have been staring with my mouth hanging open because I felt a gentle finger tap at my chin.

"Ah, here comes the man of the hour now!"

Thadeus, Caleb, Clancy, Kiki, and Francis were all seated at the dining table, their plates and mouths full. Thadeus stood upon noticing Grace and me.

"Lad," he said, holding up a drumstick as if it were a sword, "We owe all of this to you. Let me tell you, Mrs. K. does not usually roll out such a feast in the afternoon."

"Sometimes she does," Kiki said through a mouthful of food. "When it's leftovers day."

Francis tutted at Kiki's poor table manners. The kid only grinned bashfully before resuming his attempt to see exactly how much food he could stuff in his mouth.

"But it is not leftovers day, my dear boy. I imagine that leftovers day this week will be something of a bonanza due to this spread. We could not possibly eat all this food."

"I'll give it my best shot." I said, grabbing a plate.

My effort to fit as much food as I could onto one nine-inch plate was valiant, but after much debate over a platter of sandwiches, I decided I'd simply have to have seconds to fulfill my duty. In truth, I was not hungry at all. Not only was that morning's meal larger than my usual banana and coffee, but the trip to town and the doctor's office unsettled my stomach. The doctor's comments and then the old man in the museum taking an interest in me both gave me flashbacks to a far more uncomfortable time in my life. I couldn't stop thinking about them and how much they reminded me of a group of far less subtle bullies from my past. Still, it felt beyond rude to refuse something that apparently had been specially made for me. Just because I wasn't hungry didn't mean I couldn't eat.

I sat at the same seat I had last night. Grace seated herself next to me with a plate that had significantly less food on it. Being at the Hotel was a bit like traveling. When you first arrived somewhere, all the food seemed exotic and irresistible. But once you'd been there for a while, you stopped eating everything you saw and started eating like you could actually gain weight again.

"So how was the doctor?" Caleb asked. "Hope they didn't poke and prod you too much?"

"It was fine." I nodded.

"That's good. Wouldn't want you all battered and bruised for too long, now would we?"

"God, Caleb." Clancy said. "Must you jump on every man you see?"

"I'm not *jumping*. Just making polite conversation." Caleb rolled his eyes at me so hard that he looked like a possessed person. I tried not to laugh. I didn't want to get in the middle of something between him and Clancy, especially because Clancy hadn't exactly taken a shine to me yet. But something about Caleb made me want to laugh, made me feel like it was okay to laugh. I wasn't going to flirt back at him, if what he was doing really was flirting. The only person I'd ever initiated flirtation with was Thia, and my success rate for reciprocating flirtation was even sparser. "Besides," Caleb continued, "If I were jumping, there's no harm in seeing if someone will jump back."

"And what makes you think that Arthur's going to jump back, as it were?" Thadeus asked. Out of context, the question might've sounded accusatory at best, but Thadeus's tone was simply curious, as if he were fascinated by the study of homosexual intuition.

"It's called instinct. Same as a man and a woman. Sometimes you can just feel if a person is receptive."

"I don't know about that." Clancy said. "Your instinct is usually off. Like with Luke. And Sam."

"I wasn't wrong about Sam. I said he wasn't attracted to women and he isn't."

Clancy shook her head somewhat violently. "He's also not attracted to men."

"Well just because he isn't attracted to anyone doesn't make my original statement wrong."

"He isn't not attracted to anyone. He just isn't attracted to everyone." Clancy said indignantly. She seemed slightly more offended by the line of conversation than expected. Caleb noticed this and, blinking, put his hands up in a sign of defeat.

"That doesn't make sense, does it?" Kiki whispered to Francis. Francis, smiling, shook his head.

I rose from my seat to get a second helping of chicken. In my mind I was trying to envision what it was like when Caleb flirted with Luke. I imagined he not only would've been very confused, but also very angry. Not because Caleb was a man. But just because any kind of sexual stuff, like flirting or seeing an R-rated scene in a movie, was one of his triggers. I'm not sure if it was a maturity thing or an experience thing or maybe he just didn't like the idea of sex at all, but Luke did not like to be exposed to the intimacies of human relationships.

"So Arthur, why don't you break the mystery for us?"

"What mystery?" I said, purposefully being obtuse as I helped myself to another grilled cheese as well.

"Oh, Arthur has slept with men before." Grace said from the end of the table.

"Grace!" I wasn't surprised that she knew. When I was in Iowa, Grace had visited and one of the people I was having sex with at the time had answered my apartment door in his underwear. Iowa had been an uncharacteristically adventurous time in my sexual life. Grace was smart enough to put two and two together.

"I'm sorry. Is it some kind of secret?"

My eyes darted over to Caleb, who had a huge self-satisfied grin on his face, but this time he was looking at Clancy. "No, it's not a secret. But there's a kid here. Not sure if discussing my sex life is really appropriate."

"Oh don't worry." Kiki said. "Francis has been educating me on the complexities of sexual orientation since I was very young. He feels that it is best that I am exposed to as many kinds of people, beliefs, and lifestyles as soon as possible so I can become a fully rounded adult in the future."

Francis nodded sagely.

"Um, that's very smart. But I still don't feel comfortable discussing this in front of an audience."

"Oh don't be such a prude, lad." Thadeus was obviously thoroughly enjoying his lunchtime entertainment.

If I had to give the guests credit for one thing, it was their stubborn persistence. "Fine." I sat back down next to Grace. "Yes. I have been with both men and women and enjoyed both of those situations very much. But right now I am not interested in being with anyone, so that's that."

"Well said," Grace said.

Caleb looked as if he were going to say something more, but then Luke came careening through the dining room doors.

"Did I miss it?" Clearly, he was referring to the spread of food because when he saw it, his entire face lit up. He immediately lunged for a plate.

"Where's Beatrice?" I asked Grace.

"She usually skips lunch. After you finish we can go to your room to talk."

"Okay."

The guests began to finish their lunches one by one and drifted out of the dining room. Francis guided Kiki away for his afternoon lessons. Caleb agreed to Thadeus's offer of a game of chess, and Clancy asked Luke where Diego was. When Luke said he was taking a shower, Clancy whistled, summoning Zorro seemingly out of thin air. She informed everyone that she was going to take the dog for a walk and disappeared into the kitchen. Grace chatted amiably with Luke about how he'd managed to get my car unstuck from the side of the road until I finally cleared my plate.

Once I was done, she rose out of her seat and told me to forget the dishes. Usually everyone washed their own dishes at lunch time, but Grace was sure that Luke would gladly take care of ours for us. Luke nodded, too preoccupied with his chicken noodle soup to respond verbally.

"So," Grace said as we made our way up the stairs to the second floor. "You've seen a bit of our place now. What do you think?"

"You mean about the repairs?"

"That. And just in general."

"Well in general I think it's pretty . . . interesting. I mean, how did you even come to get this place, Grace?"

"I'll explain that somewhat in a minute. What do you mean by interesting?" She opened the door to her shared room with Beatrice and waited until I entered.

There was an obvious difference in style between the two sides of the room. The bed closer to the door was obviously Grace's—if the flannel bedspread was anything to go by. It was clean, simple, and organized. The desk was also obviously hers, but there were no bills scattered across the top, no pens displaced from their holder; no sign of any work having been done on it at all.

The other bed was unmade, revealing purple jersey sheets and a crumpled gray blanket. Next to the smashed pillows was an oversized teddy bear that had obviously been well loved. I recognized it immediately as the gift I had given Beatrice for her sixth birthday. It was missing its red bow tie, and it had lost some of its original shape, but it was the same bear nonetheless. Beatrice had surrounded her bed in a gauzy canopy that hung delicately from the ceiling.

Grace gestured to her bed for me to sit. She sat in the desk chair, which she spun around to face me.

"I'm really very glad you're here, Arthur. It's been too long."

"Yeah, tell me about it."

"So what did you mean by interesting?" She repeated.

"Oh, just that it wasn't what I was expecting, I guess, when you said that you were working at a hotel that needed repairs."

"What were you imagining?"

"Um, some kind of bed and breakfast that was a little run down or something like that. You know, charming and out of the way but still . . . on the way."

"Yes, the Hotel is pretty inconveniently located."

"Yeah and way more busted than I can fix."

"I was afraid you'd say that."

"I mean, come on Grace. The place is practically falling apart. It's a wonder it hasn't been condemned yet."

I could tell I was pushing it. For some reason, Grace and the others were fiercely protective of this old place. That was just how people got when it came to their homes, I supposed. It explained why, in the face of impending natural disasters, people chose to remain in their houses and wait it out instead of abandon ship and search for safer shelter.

Maybe I could've been kinder in my diagnosis of Grace's choice of establishment, but I had always been a strong believer in honesty being the best quality. Thia also reminded me on many occasions that while honesty was the best policy, it was also sometimes my worst quality.

If Grace was offended by my words, though, she did not let it show. "You're right. It is a challenge. But I think it can be done. I know it can be done."

"But, by who? I mean I can help with a lot of stuff. And I'm sure the other people here . . . they can help too. But there are some things that I am just not qualified to do. And honestly it seems like this place is going to need more than just a few nips and tucks."

"Well," Grace said, "We have considered hiring a crew to help us work on it."

"Is that what you did for the kitchen?"

"Oh well, we lucked out with that one really."

"What do you mean?"

"Just that we had help from a friend. She got her own crew in here and fixed it up."

"Why didn't she finish the job?"

Grace smiled a little and shrugged. "She had more important matters to deal with. She offered to have her crew stay, but they were missing their families. I assured her that we could do it all on our own."

"Missing their families?"

"Yes." Clearly, she wasn't going to elaborate.

"Okay so, um, we need to hire another crew. But with this amount of work the price won't be cheap."

"Money isn't an issue."

"What . . . what do you mean money is no issue? If it's no issue, then why haven't you started work already? And how is it that money isn't an issue? Did you suddenly become a whiz at the stock market or something?"

"Arthur," Grace said, sighing, "I understand that you're confused and maybe even a little upset, but I'd appreciate it if you kept the sarcastic tone to a minimum. I am trying to explain myself."

"Well do better." At that point, I was pretty exhausted by all the secrecy. It seemed like everyone in the Hotel was part of some secret society, and they were hazing me before I could join them. I hadn't joined a fraternity in college for a reason. I wasn't good at playing those kinds of games.

"You're right." Grace said, so understanding and sweet that it made me feel guilty for getting upset in the first place. "I have been kind of vague, haven't I?"

"Yes. Yes you have."

"Well let me try to do better. You see, after my wedding was called off, I felt slightly lost. I felt like my entire life plan had been put through the shredder, which I suppose is not an uncommon thing to feel after the dissolution of an engagement. And for months afterward that listless feeling followed me until I thought I was going to go crazy."

She paused to allow me to take in all of this information. It was the first time Grace talked candidly with me about her feelings, and she knew that. I had always wondered who exactly Grace talked about these kinds of things with, because as far as I knew, she never shared it with anyone in our family.

"Luckily, before that year was up, an old friend contacted me with an interesting proposition. This friend told me that they had recently purchased an unlikely property in the heart of the Louisiana bayou, and they needed a team of people to help prepare it to be a hotel. They knew that I had a way with people and a talent for managing financial and personal affairs, so they offered me the job of manager. Nothing was tying me to where I was, so I said yes."

I could tell the lack of gender pronouns was deliberate, but I didn't think it mattered. It was not the time to nitpick small details.

"So this friend of yours," I said, "They have a lot of money?"

"Oh, they were well-off to begin with, but the death of a family member and an unexpected employment situation left them with more money than they knew what to do with. That is why money is no issue. Because they are funding us through whatever we need. I, of course, would need to submit a carefully thought-out budget and have it approved. We can't just spend willy-nilly. We shall need to do our research."

"Yeah, of course. So then, how did everyone else get here? Were they hired by your friend too?"

"Not exactly. I had already known Beatrice had no interest in going to university, so I invited her to join me as my assistant. And Luke, well you might not know this, but he had voluntarily checked himself into a facility after his latest stint in jail. I told him what was happening in my life, and he checked himself out to join us too."

"And the doctors were okay with that?" If this afternoon's incident with Sam was anything to go by, Luke was far from in control.

"They were not entirely convinced. I did my best to assure them that the Hotel would be a safe and productive environment for Luke. And at the end of the day, Luke was there under a voluntary basis. They had no right to hold him."

"What about his parole officer?"

Grace just shook her head. "Such an overworked man. He didn't really need to be informed about any of this."

"But . . ." Last time I checked, leaving the state without permission was expressly against parole, but the lazier part of my mind was starting to see Grace's logic. What the parole officer didn't know wouldn't hurt him, or Luke. "Okay. And the others?"

At this Grace paused. She seemed to be considering her next words carefully. Her silence offered me a chance to gather my own thoughts. The mysterious benefactor I could easily come to terms with because it seemed to have nothing to do with me. I was more worried about Grace's judgment when it came to Beatrice and Luke.

Beatrice not attending college wasn't really my concern. College wasn't for everyone and plenty of people were successful without it. I often felt as if the money spent on my college education had been a waste. But Beatrice was a young girl. A young girl with, I assumed, some pretty specific medical needs. I wasn't fully persuaded that a place like the Hotel was the best for her.

And Luke. Grace knew as well as I that Luke was damaged. It wasn't his fault. None of us had ever treated him that way, but it was a blessing that he had sought treatment on his own. Perhaps she had been reluctant to reject him, but it seemed to me that allowing Luke to remove himself from the hospital and place him in this entirely unstable situation was doing him more harm than good. It was irresponsible, something that Grace had never been.

I was about to say as much when Grace continued. I'm glad that I hadn't voiced my thoughts, though. If I had, I doubt Grace wouldn't have said what she did next.

"Maybe you've noticed, Arthur, that our guests are not your usual sort."

"You mean they're weird."

She laughed. "Yes, they are odd. But it is slightly more than that. Take Caleb for example. He is obviously a gay man. A gay man from deep in Georgia. A gay man from a highly religious, Baptist family whose father chose to beat him into submission whenever he dared speak his mind and whose mother sent him to conversion therapy starting at twelve years old."

"God."

"Yes. And then there's Mrs. K. Her family and friends disowned her decades ago for marrying 'the wrong sort.' For fifty years it was just her and her husband, the love of her life. They traveled the world together, and then he was murdered just before he turned seventy-five. It was as if her life was torn away from her. Most of her friends had passed or were lost to her. She was alone."

"I . . . why are you telling me all of this?"

"These are not secrets. If you got to know either of them well enough, they would reveal these stories to you. Just like Diego would tell you that he was hitchhiking to California when Luke picked him up on the side of the road. Or just like how Thadeus came to us after seeing us in the grocery store in town because his kids were about to put him in a home so they could sell his house. Or just like how Kiki would tell you how he begged Francis to bring him here after stumbling upon our website."

"You have a website?"

Grace chuckled. "Yeah, but it's not very good."

"I didn't even know you had computers."

"Well this *is* a business, Arthur. But my point is that this place has a sort of attraction for people who feel like they have lost their place in the world, or who never had a place to begin with."

"It's secluded?"

"Yes. It's secluded and private and safe for the most part. But it is also open and warm and accepting. I do not mean the architecture itself. I mean the way it feels. The people who are here now have a sort of understanding. It is my hope that I can make this place suitable enough for guests so that we can offer this sort of comfort to more—you might say—outcasts."

"Is that what you feel like, Grace? An outcast?"

"I suppose I do. Don't you?"

Yes, I supposed I did.

* * *

To some, the word outcast has a rather romantic connotation. Those people usually re-watched John Hughes movies on Saturday nights and read books about serial killers. To others, the word outcast was one of those despicable nomenclatures used to describe people who were less than them. So, the word could be used in a positive or negative light. It all depended on your audience.

Thia thought of it as a good thing. In college, we'd gained a sort of reputation for being each other's only friend. She was double majoring in theater and psychology. I was majoring in English with a minor in creative writing. This normally would've meant that our paths would have never crossed. All of our classes were in buildings on opposite ends on campus, but we were brought together anyway. We stayed together like that for four whole years.

It wasn't that we were closed off to the idea of more friends. Well I was, but Thia was charming and sociable. She could make someone feel at ease after just a few short minutes. She liked to go to parties hosted by her various peers in the theater department. (Psychology majors' parties, however, she avoided like a rabid dog because they were, according to her, too "shrinky"). I didn't mind tagging along with her whenever she went somewhere. Sometimes I was even the one to come up with plans, mentioning that a group from one of my classes was going to go to the midnight showing of *Rocky Horror*, or that there was a student sit-in to protest the school's food provider.

We weren't holed up in our dorms, only talking to each other, breathing each other's air, and admiring each other's smiles. We were active in college life. There was just something about us, purposeful or not, that discouraged anyone else from attempting to foster a close relationship with either of us.

I remember one instance in particular when I realized that the

70

way that Thia and I were made it impossible for anyone else to integrate.

We were at a dinner party. Thia was starring in the coveted lead of the theater department's latest play. I can't remember what the play was, but I do remember the uproar around campus when people realized that a sophomore was going to take the spot that was usually offered to seniors looking to impress prospective agents. At the time, the star of the senior class was bound for Broadway, or at least that's what everyone thought. It was a major blow to her reputation and future possibilities to not have been given the main role in the last collegiate play she would be able to participate in.

So Thia was getting some campus-wide recognition, both positive and negative. With that recognition came a multitude of party invitations. We were discerning in choosing which ones to attend, but this particular dinner party invitation had been extended by her male counterpart in the play. Thia felt that we needed to go to "save face."

The guy wasn't really a good cook. He was floundering in the kitchen by the time the two of us arrived. So Thia and I offered to help. Most of the party guests were gathered in the kitchen even though it was way too small and dangerous to have more than three people in there when knives were used and fire was burning. Still, they all mingled, sipping cheap wine and talking about theater-y stuff. I wasn't really listening, but Thia would offer her two cents every once in a while.

The guy had clearly meant to make some kind of pasta dish, if the jar of marinara on the counter was anything to go by. Once Thia and I took over, the ambiguous Italian food turned into four-cheese lasagna with roasted zucchinis and eggplant on the side, along with a salad that we let the guy make just so he could feel somewhat involved in his own dinner party.

I quite enjoyed cooking. It was one of the things that I was undeniably good at. My father cooked diner food for a living, fast and simple, but he had the skill and creativity of a classically trained chef. Our most memorable moments of father-son bonding were had over a cookbook. He taught me everything I knew about cooking. It was the greatest inheritance he left me.

Thia was also very skilled. For a brief moment in her childhood, Thia's mother had harbored hopes for her daughter's future as a mother and wife. She taught her the necessary skills to please a man's stomach. It wasn't until after Thia had mastered the kitchen that her mother realized Thia's future was going in a far, far different direction.

Whenever we cooked together it became this sort of mindless dance. It was built into our muscle memories, how we moved in the kitchen, how we used knives and seasonings, where we liked to put our cutting boards and dish towels. If I hadn't been so absorbed in layering the noodles, I would've noticed that the gentle, semi-intellectual chatter that usually flavored these kinds of parties had ceased. I would've noticed the eyes that were fixed on me and on Thia.

I would've seen that when Thia passed me a knife, wordlessly, without prompting, without looking, and I took it, my hand cupping hers over the handle, eyebrows raised and a murmur passed through the other partygoers.

I would've seen the host of this party set down his salad-tossers and watch gobsmacked as Thia tossed me both the salt and pepper at the same time as I was seasoning the vegetables. I caught them without so much as a glance.

I would've seen how two girls whispered to each other when Thia skirted around me, a hand passing over my back as a way of warning, as I bent over to place the baking dish in the oven.

When everything was finally in the oven and set to be eaten in under thirty minutes, when I picked up my glass of wine, coming down from that focused, unrelenting headspace that cooking often put me in, I finally turned to the other guests. That was when I first realized it.

They were all staring at Thia and I, some with incredulous looks of amusement, others with an almost harsh jealousy. I realized how exactly Thia and I must have seemed to other people. Like two parts of an inseparable, impenetrable whole. It was as if people were realizing that their attempts to integrate us into a wider life were futile. We were always going to be a house of two. No entry. No exit.

Thia and I were mostly quiet and tipsy as we wandered back to our shared apartment from the dinner party. It had two bedrooms, but by that time we had already started sharing a bed, even though we had not started having sex yet.

As we closed in on our doorway, I turned to Thia and placed a hand on her arm so she would stop. She did, turning to me and smiling softly.

"Everything okay?" I hadn't given any indication that something was wrong, but that's just how well she knew me. A touch on the arm was all it took.

"Do you think people think we are . . . snobs?"

"Snobs?" She laughed a little.

"Well, not snobs exactly. I guess more . . . cliquey. That would be the word."

Thia pretended to consider this for a moment. She was humoring me, I could tell, but I was grateful for it. "Can it be a clique if there are only two people?"

"I don't know."

"Are you upset that we don't have more close friends?" Thia was always blunt when it came to things like this. Some people might find it offensive. I found it relieving.

"I'm really not, but sometimes I feel like I should be. Sometimes I feel like we are alienating people, even if we don't mean to, and that it's something that I'm supposed to try and change."

"I understand." And she did. I knew she did. "But I think that's a problem with other people. Not with us."

"What do you mean?"

Now Thia considered what she was going to say for real. "I mean that . . . um how should I put this? I mean that a lot of the time in life, and especially in college, relationships appear superficial. People interact with other people and pretend to be great friends because that's what they are supposed to do, but a lot of the time they don't feel any real connection with the people they've chosen to include in their lives. And so when they see something like what we have, a genuine, authentic attachment that isn't motivated by any kind of ulterior purpose, then they get threatened and angry and want to remove themselves from the thing that reminds them how artificial their lives are."

"Threatened and angry, huh?" We started to walk again. Thia slipped her keys into the front door. It always required a little bit of finagling with the pressure and twist. It usually took us two or three minutes just to get through the front door.

"Yep. They are just plebes."

I laughed out loud at that. I knew that Thia didn't mean it. She had no sense of superiority. In fact, at times she could be annoyingly humble. So I knew that she was doing it for my sake because, if anything, I had an inferiority complex that could make Napoleon blush.

We made it into the kitchen of our apartment. Thia poured two glasses of water, one lukewarm and the other over half ice. She knew that cold water when I had been drinking alcohol just made me throw up.

"So you think we are okay? Just the two of us like this?"

"I think that, for now, it works and it's right. If things change later on, then they change. But we live now, so that's enough for me. Is it for you?"

"Yeah. Yeah. Let's go to bed."

When Grace asked me if I felt like an outcast, and I said that I did, I was thinking of that specific conversation. That time with Thia in college was the only time I didn't feel somewhat removed from the world. She had made me feel at peace with myself. And when I had asked Thia if she thought we were okay with just the two of us, I think her answer was completely wrong.

The thing is, when you're an outcast and you find another outcast and you two become a part of something together, that means that when the other one goes away, you're back to being just one. But now you're just the one who had a brilliant glimpse at what life could've been, which is even sadder than having just been the odd one out, ignorant forever.

In a way, that made what Grace was doing so brilliant. Sure, they were dependent on each other, all of the guests, but at least they were a group. Not just two. Comfort in numbers.

* * *

G race and I decided not to do any serious thinking about fixing up the Hotel until my arm was healed. I had a feeling that she also wanted me to become better acquainted with the other guests before we started working together. So she and I settled to flipping through interior decorating catalogues and researching possible contractors on the Hotel's spotty internet connection while I set my mind to figuring out the people I was living with.

Some of them were easy to read. Now that I was somewhat aware of Caleb and Mrs. K.'s darker moments, it was easy to see them more clearly. After a few days, Caleb's initial flirtation toward me just disappeared. It seemed like I'd proved myself to him somehow. At first, I thought it was because he just wasn't interested in me anymore because I'd told him, and everyone else, that I wasn't interested in anyone. As I paid more attention, though, I began to see that the reason Caleb had come on so hard at first was because he was testing me. I was new and he knew nothing about me. He wanted to see if I was closeting any hostilities, and, if I was, to get them out in the open as soon as possible. But as soon as he saw that I would just let him do his thing, his personality did a total one-eighty. Little by little, the southern gentleman he'd been hiding started to peek through.

Caleb always stood when a lady entered the room. He pulled out chairs at the dining table. He carried a silk, monogrammed handkerchief that he offered to Mrs. K. to wipe her brow in the kitchen or to Clancy when she sneezed. And he was subtly protective of Sam in a way that I hadn't expected. Everyone at the Hotel seemed deeply connected in one way or another, but with Sam and Caleb it was like there was a tether drawn between them. Where Caleb went, Sam followed. Caleb was soft with him in a way he wasn't with the others. He usually had a cocky sense of humor and a playful, teasing way of showing affection, but with Sam he immediately became more subdued. After dinner, the two usually sat in the library reading a book together. Caleb would always finish the page first and watch Sam until he was done. Then he would softly turn the page and they'd continue.

If Caleb and Sam's relationship was surprising, then Mrs. K. and Thadeus's one was entirely predictable. Mrs. K. often went into moods. Apart from being a skilled chef, Mrs. K. was also a trained opera singer and had performed for many a captivated audience in her youth. So she was theatrical at best, melodramatic at worst. Thadeus seemed to appreciate that in a woman. In fact, he seemed to appreciate everything about Mrs. K.

Despite the fact that Mrs. K. consistently rebuffed him at every turn, Thadeus's bright, boy-in-love attitude never faltered. They both seemed perfectly pleased with the arrangement. I thought it reminded them of the time when they were young adults courting lovers and enjoying those little games that people play when they are handling attraction. Besides, Mrs. K. must've been somewhere in her late seventies or early eighties, and Thadeus perhaps ten or so years older than that. At that age, a little youthful flirtation could be more satisfying than an actual relationship.

Diego and Clancy were both intriguing to me. Although Zorro was Diego's dog, Clancy took charge of most of his care. Oftentimes, she was the one to feed him, take him on walks, and play with him. But at night, when we all gathered in the library for various after-dinner activities, Zorro's head always found its way onto Diego's lap.

Diego himself seemed perhaps the most down-to-earth of all the Hotel's guests. He wasn't over-the-top or painfully introverted. He seemed to me to just be a guy who was extremely invested in the upkeep of his home. He often sat in with Grace and I as we talked about possible repairs and prospective workers. He had a lot to say about the quality of products we were choosing and the timeline we had set out. I once asked Diego how he knew so much, and he said that long ago he had trained with a master carpenter in Madrid. It took a lot of effort to keep my skeptical eyebrow from rising.

That was the only real thing that made me suspicious of Diego: his fake Spanish background. It would've been clear to anyone that his accent was forced. Most of the time he wasn't even able to stamp down a Midwestern twang to his speech, but no one ever mentioned it. They all allowed him to live out his delusion. That was a common theme among the Hotel guests. Whatever was shared was shared, and whatever was secret was secret. No one ever asked me questions about my past life, so I learned really quick not to ask them any questions about theirs.

Clancy also seemed somewhat normal, at least what most people considered normal. She was dry and sarcastic, but also had somewhat of a playful side to her. She liked to perform minor pranks on the other guests. It wouldn't be odd to hear a loud of eruption of her name coming from one of the bedrooms when another guest discovered that she had cut holes into the backs of their T-shirts or that a tube of toothpaste had been mysteriously replaced by superglue.

Even though all the guests kept their secrets, Clancy was particularly reluctant to talk about herself. She avoided any mention of the past and would excuse herself on the rare occasion someone would bring up their own memories or histories. She also cringed whenever someone would compliment her in any meaningful way. I don't mean the kind of random, everyday compliments that one receives, like "you look nice," or "cool shoes." I mean the deep ones that showed how fully someone did or did not understand us.

Clancy was a painter. I once got a glimpse inside her room, which was more a studio with a mattress shoved into one corner. Her work was sporadic, colorful, and at times violent. She'd transfer from photorealistic character studies to warped, demented landscaped dripping in colors that one would never find in nature.

I found her work to be mystifying and controlling. It made me nervous in the way that waiting in line for concert tickets made you nervous.

But despite her brilliance and talent, she did not like to be recognized for it. I wondered if no one had ever told her how amazing she was growing up. Or, maybe they'd told her all the time but it had been lies. Either way, she preferred for her art to be viewed wordlessly if it was going to be viewed at all.

Sam and Francis were similar in that they both were mostly quiet, expressionless, and attentive. But with Francis it was intentional. I had a feeling that when Francis was not acting as tutor to Kiki, he was playing the part of combined father and bodyguard. He kept up this strong poker face whenever Kiki spoke to someone other than him, as he was if trying to intimidate the other party. But when he and Kiki interacted, he immediately melted into the kind of father figure that was both hard and soft, disciplined and lenient. He let Kiki test his boundaries, but only just so far before pulling him back.

Sam, on the other hand, did not seem to be at all in control of his outward personality. He was like a raw nerve constantly rubbing up against sandpaper. He couldn't control his facial expressions with the mastery that Francis did. Sometimes he reminded me of a squirrel trying to cross the highway. He would linger on the edges of conversations, eyes darting back and forth between people and things involved. Then, just as he began to make his first steps into participation, an unexpected phrase or topic would come careening down the road. At that point, caught in the middle, Sam could either scurry back to the safety of where he had come from or he could make a mad dash for the other side. And if he couldn't make his decision fast enough: roadkill.

Caleb calmed Sam in some mysterious way, kept him grounded, but Kiki brought him out of his shell. Admittedly, it was hard to deny that kid anything. Out of all of the Hotel guests, he was the most open and willing to share about himself. He was jovial, intelligent, and wise beyond his years. He enjoyed puzzles and working with his hands. He eagerly looked forward to the day when we started work on the Hotel so that he could learn a new skill. The kid's passion for education was something that you didn't often find in a ten-year-old. He devoured books like they were cookies and had a vivid imagination that he often put to use at the guests' expense.

Playing a pretend game with Kiki was like getting swept into Narnia. All you could do was accept that this was now your reality and follow the faun to his cottage. The scenarios that governed these games ranged from deep space expeditions to tea with the royal family of Yesteryear (a mythical world he had created himself). Kiki was the kind of kid that I wish I'd had in my class back when I was still a teacher.

In the month and a half it took for my arm to heal, I felt that I was finding my place among the Hotel's guests. I quickly discovered that Caleb was both entertaining and pleasant to be around. Thadeus enjoyed regaling me with stories about his time on the Western Front in World War II and his subsequent career as a tightrope walker in a traveling circus. Mrs. K. allowed me to help in the kitchen and taught me her little secrets for every recipe. Francis employed my help in teaching Kiki Shakespeare, even though most of the material was well below his level. Even Clancy sometimes allowed me to go on walks with her and Zorro, although those were mostly silent.

The only one who didn't seem to embrace, or at least accept, my presence in the Hotel was Beatrice. In fact, most of the time she was downright hostile, which annoyed Luke and exasperated Grace. I was completely at a loss on how to gain her trust, so for weeks I ended up just letting her be. Thia and I had always agreed that if a person proved without a doubt that they did not like you, then it was best just to accept that fact and move on. In Beatrice's case, however, it was probably just the cowardly lion rearing his ugly head in my mind. Out of the three of my family, I knew Beatrice the least. I hadn't really been there for her except financially, and I didn't know the kind of person she'd become. That made me nervous, and I had always been bad at overcoming nerves.

Granted, it was slightly harder to simply let Beatrice dislike me because not only did Grace and Luke both desperately want us to get along, but she also did not make it easy for me to "move on." Every time I spoke in a group setting, she would scoff or roll her eyes in the perfect picture of teenage angst. Apart from dinner, if I entered the room, she would leave it, making sure that I knew I was the reason for her departure. In every way she could, Beatrice seemed determined to make sure I felt uncomfortable.

Thadeus and Diego once asked me about it.

"I'm not really sure, honestly. Is she not that way with you guys?" It was a stupid question because anyone could see that she wasn't.

"Absolutely not." Thadeus said. "I always took Beatrice to be quite mature and sweet for a girl her age."

"I agree." Diego said. "You can usually expect a few tantrums from a teenager, but Beatrice was always pretty lovable. Until you got here."

"Are you sure there's nothing from your shared pasts that could be making her upset?"

I shrugged my shoulders. "Beatrice and I don't exactly have a shared past. I was out of the house by the time she was born, and I never really had that much contact with her since. Except for the occasional birthday or Christmas gift."

"And you paid for her education and livelihood for a bit, right?" Diego asked.

"Yeah. Up until she came here. I would've done the same for Grace and Luke, had they needed it, but she got into college on a scholarship and he never even finished traditional high school."

They both nodded sagely, as if having found the key to Beatrice's disdain in something I had said, but they didn't let me in on the secret.

I can't say that I was desperate to discover why Beatrice seemed to hate me so much. At the time, I was far more concerned about my relationship with Grace. I never once considered telling her the truth about her parentage, but that didn't mean that I didn't have the desire to treat her like a daughter. I only really began to think about my lack of a relationship with Beatrice when it started to affect the one I had with Grace.

* * *

"**W**hy don't you take Beatrice to town with you today, Arthur?"

My spoonful of Cheerios froze halfway to my mouth as I looked over at Grace to figure out whether she was being serious. Mrs. K. had her usual extravagant breakfast spread laid out on the kitchen island, but I had recently downsized the amount of food I allowed myself to eat at each meal. For the first two weeks at the Hotel, I ate like a ravenous dog. Then I realized that all my jeans were feeling slightly tighter than they had before, and I figured it was probably time to stop eating like I was on vacation. So my breakfast that morning consisted of a small bowl of Cheerios in skim milk, some mixed berries, and a mug of green tea.

"Um, okay? But would she even want to come with me?"

Grace's back was turned as she washed her own plate, so I couldn't read her expression. Sam was the only other person in the kitchen at the time. As per usual, his opinions on the matter were impossible to discern.

"Beatrice enjoys going into town. And we don't go enough. Maybe you two could see a movie?"

I found it hard to believe that Beatrice actually liked going to that small little town. It was clear that everyone else at the Hotel felt uncomfortable enough there to avoid it entirely. Like I had said before, it was monochromatic. Beatrice and I would stick out like sore thumbs. My plan had been to go there, get my cast off, and leave without any detours or stops. But I knew that if I refused to at least try to get Beatrice to come with me now, Grace would be upset.

"Sure. I'll ask her. Luke said it was okay that I borrowed the truck, right? My car still needs some work."

"Why don't you take Francis's car instead? It's a sedan. Easier to park than the truck, I'm sure. He won't mind."

"Yeah all right." I took my last bite of Cheerios and brought my dishes to the sink. "I'll go ask him for the keys now."

"And then you're going to ask Beatrice? They should both be in the library right now. If Beatrice isn't there, then try Clancy's room."

Before I could respond, Grace had dried her hands off on a fraying dishtowel and left the kitchen. Once she was gone, I thought I heard a low mumble over the sound of running water. I turned my head to look at Sam.

"Did you say something?"

Sam went bright red and ducked his head to continue eating. I shrugged. He had never talked directly to me. In fact, I'd hardly heard him talk at all. If he did, it was one or two words only. His muteness was just one of those little oddities that had become part of my daily life.

Diego and Grace were in the library, but Francis was nowhere to be seen. Diego was hunched over a piece of drafting paper. Now that my arm was about to be set free, he felt a sudden urgency to start making some concrete plans about the Hotel's renovations. He had been cranking out sketches like an industrial printing press for a week. The one he was currently working on looked like some kind of plan for updating the banisters on the second-floor landing and staircase. Zorro sat upright by Diego's chair, snuffling at his writing arm every once in a while. I patted his head as I walked by.

Beatrice sat contorted into a small, curled-up ball, her feet tucked under her, her chin resting on top of her knees. She held an oversized novel in front of her face. It looked too big for her arms to support, which is probably why her elbows were pressed firmly into the arms of her chair. Beatrice was slight, just a sliver of a thing really, even though she ate just as voraciously as I had when I first came to the Hotel. At first I thought maybe she had some kind of eating disorder that kept her so thin. I even asked Grace about it, but she laughed at the idea of Beatrice having any kind of mental instability. According to Grace, some of Beatrice's medications raised her metabolic rate. She just burned stuff off quicker than most of us. I found it as plausible an explanation as any.

"Hey bumble Bea." I said, utilizing the nickname in hopes of piquing her interest. I'd heard Luke and Grace call Beatrice that with great success multiple times.

"I'm reading."

"Yeah, I see that. Want me to let you finish your page?"

Beatrice heaved a great, angsty sigh. Teenagers seemed to inherit the mastery of that particular skill as soon as they turned thirteen. She shut her book, keeping one index finger between the pages to keep her place, and begrudgingly looked up at me.

"Just tell me what you want so you can leave me alone."

"Um, okay. Well I'm going into town today to get my cast off. I was wondering if maybe you wanted to come with? Grace mentioned that you never really get to go into town. We could grab lunch and see a movie . . . or something."

As I was talking, I became more and more convinced that Beatrice was just going to deny my offer. Her face had definitely become harder as soon as I mentioned Grace. She was a smart girl. She knew that this little jaunt into town together was not my idea, and that offended her. Everything I did seemed to offend her.

"You want to hang out with me?"

"Sure."

"And you would've wanted to hang out with me even if Grace hadn't told you to?"

I was fighting a losing battle, both with Beatrice and with my own tongue, which couldn't seem to form an answer to that question. Luckily, a sweet little voice came to my rescue.

"Do you mind if I join you both, Arthur?" Kiki and Francis had just entered the living room. Kiki immediately crossed the room to greet Zorro, cooing about how he was a good dog.

"Don't you have studying to do, Kiki?"

Kiki was a good kid. Under normal circumstances I would have been more than glad to watch him for a day, take him out to lunch and a movie and maybe even something more exciting, like the park or an arcade. But Kiki was a beautiful, blond-haired, blue-eyed boy. He looked like those kids in fifties milk ads or Nazi propaganda posters. In short, he would fit in perfectly in that town.

But not if he were accompanied by me.

I was more than certain that the sight of me with him would raise a certain amount of suspicion. They would wonder why I was with him, maybe even be afraid of what I might do to him, and, misguidedly, they would act as Good Samaritans. They would ask Kiki where his mommy and daddy were, if he was lost, if the big scary man took him away—it was all in all something that I desperately wished to not deal with.

"It's Veterans Day today. Francis observes all national holidays, just like they do at real schools. When Francis and I were in town earlier shopping for books, I noticed a flier advertising a parade in honor of our troops. I really want to see it."

"A parade?" After effectively getting me to shut up, Beatrice had returned to her reading rather pointedly. She perked up at Kiki's last statement.

"Yes. There will be a parade and also a fair I believe. With games and hot dogs and things like that. I think it would be very fun. I was going to ask Francis to chaperone, but he also deserves a day of rest. Don't you think, Arthur?"

This whole situation was just getting worse and worse. A big festival meant that I wouldn't just have to avoid the probing eyes of a few hostile passersby. I'd have to avoid the leering gaze of a large crowd. But Kiki was a kid. A kid who lived in a decrepit quasi-hotel on an island in the middle of the bayou. He deserved those precious childhood memories just like everyone else.

"You're okay with this, Francis?" It was my last-ditch effort at avoiding this whole ordeal.

"Sure. As long as you're home before dinnertime."

"But Francis," Kiki said, halting his generous petting of Zorro, "I really want to see the fireworks. Can I please stay out until nine? The flier said that fireworks were set to go off at seven p.m. That would give us plenty of time to view the show and then head back. Please Francis."

My heart clenched. Until nine at night was a long time to spend in that town. More than the few hours I had been willing to sacrifice for Beatrice.

Francis gave a hearty laugh at Kiki's bargaining and reached down to pat him on the head. "All right, you little crook. Did you hear that, Arthur? Nine sharp."

"You have my word." I was glad to hear that my voice didn't come out sounding quite as stressed as I felt. Remembering my initial mission, I turned to Beatrice. "What do you say? Up for some fireworks?"

Beatrice regarded me carefully and then nodded once.

I couldn't help the big grin that swept across my face. It kind of caught me off guard, how happy I was to have Beatrice agree to spend some time with me. It definitely surprised her, if the shock on her face was anything to go by.

"Excellent," Kiki said. "We must leave soon then. Or else we will miss the start of the festivities!"

"When does it start?" Beatrice asked.

"The parade is supposed to start at noon, and the fair is going to go all day until the fireworks. Oh, it will be such a marvelous time! Francis, come on, let's pack my day bag. I'll be back in a minute!"

"Oh, um Francis?" I said as they began to leave.

"Yes?"

"Can I borrow your car? Mine's still busted."

Francis nodded. Kiki ran out of the room and Francis followed, laughing and rubbing the back of his neck.

"I'd like to change before we go." Beatrice said. I realized somewhat belatedly that she was talking to me.

"Oh yeah, sure. Go ahead. Let's meet down here in fifteen minutes?"

She nodded and left. I stood in the middle of the room, somewhat unsure what to do with my body. My mind was racing with dozens of different scenarios as to how this day could be a complete and utter disaster. I could lose Kiki, or he could get taken away by child services, or someone might try to harm Beatrice, or I could get . . .

"Don't worry so much." Diego said. He had been quiet this whole time, working on his sketch, but now he was looking at me intently.

"Why do you all avoid the town?" It was maybe the first direct question I'd asked any of them. I'd learned that direct questions like that didn't go over well with the other guests. But Diego always seemed more open to a bit of bluntness.

"For all the reasons that you'd expect. But really, we've never gotten anything more than thinly veiled bigotry. And Kiki's been to town quite a few times with Francis. They won't do anything too extreme while that kid's around. He has a way of making people believe what he wants them to believe."

That much I knew. Diego's words didn't exactly make me feel any better, but they didn't make me feel any worse. At least that was something.

K iki practically vibrated with excitement as we sat in the clinic's waiting room. Out the window we could see the various floats going through last-minute checks for the parade. Groups of teenagers lingered on the edges, donned in cheerleader and band uniforms, stretching and testing their instruments. A group of army vets, some young, some old, some in uniform, some not, were milling through the lineup and finding their places for the parade. American flags hung off of every light post. Red, white, and blue tinsel wrapped around the trunks of trees like highly patriotic boa constrictors.

Kiki had changed into a blue-and-white striped T-shirt with red pants and a black blazer. He carried around a backpack filled with snacks, bottles of water ("Because, Arthur, water at these events is so overpriced."), and a pretty expensive-looking DSLR camera. Kiki, apparently, was doing photography as his creative art this year. He hoped to get a fascinating glimpse into small-town rituals of celebration.

I had been a little shocked by Beatrice's choice of outfit for the event. Usually she wore pretty punk-leaning clothing. Lots of leather and denim and black. However, today she had gone for a slightly more girlie-girl look. She wore a navy-blue dress with a floral print that went down to her mid-calf and a cozy knit cardigan. High white socks disappeared under the hem of her dress and red Mary Janes added a sweet touch rather disparate with her personality. Her hair, which usually tumbled around her face in wild, unkempt curls, was swept up into a sweet little ponytail which bounced back and forth as she walked. She'd even put on a bit of makeup.

I wanted to play the part of the older brother and tease her about her outfit, but I thought that maybe she wouldn't find it as harmless as I would mean it to be.

"I wish the doctor would hurry." Kiki said impatiently, his

head craned to look out the window. "It looks like things are about to get going."

As if answering his prayers, the doctor who had set my arm came out to the waiting room to gather me. Last time, someone had just called my name and I had followed them back. I tried not to look too much into that particular personal touch.

"All right, Mr. Bean. I'm ready for you." But she didn't move when I stood up. Instead she gave Kiki and Beatrice a rather bemused look and said, "And who are your friends?"

"This is my sister, Beatrice." Beatrice looked momentarily surprised that I had introduced her as my sister. So did the doctor, it appeared.

"Oh your *sister* is it?" Her voice was sickly sweet, but it didn't hide the note of sarcasm in her voice.

"Yes. My sister. And this is Kiki. A friend of the family. I'm taking them out to the parade once we are done here."

"Well young man," the doctor said, leaning down to be at eye level with Kiki, "Perhaps you'd like a piece of candy or two to munch on while you wait?"

"Thank you, doctor. That sounds lovely. Maybe I could get some candy for my friend, as well?" Kiki slipped his hand into Beatrice's.

The doctor ill-hid her look of mortification at seeing Kiki's small, pale fingers intertwined with Beatrice's long, brown ones. My stomach turned. For a moment I just wanted to abandon the whole thing, go back to the safety of the Hotel, and have Mrs. K. remove my cast. If my arm got completely messed up, well to hell with it all. Living in New York and mostly keeping to myself had given me the joy of somewhat forgetting the ignorance of people and how to deal with that. There was no such escape in the doctor's office.

After composing herself, the doctor made a harsh gesture to the woman at the desk who wandered over with a warm smile and a bowl full of red, white, and blue candies. The doctor began to lead me back, but I heard the girl say, "Don't you two look so nice today. Did you dress up for the fair? Go ahead and take all the candies you want."

The doctor, who had been positively chatty the last time I came in, said next to nothing as she went about removing my cast. I was almost sad to see it go. Over the past few weeks, the cast had become the home of the signatures of every guest at the Hotel, even Sam's, whose signature was more a child's scrawl than actual cursive. Clancy had also taken to using it as a canvas. Every night after dinner she'd taken my arm and set it on a table and began to draw with a pungent permanent marker. Doodles, sketches, and calligraphy done by her hand weaved in and out of the guest's names.

"Could I keep that?" I asked the doctor when my arm was finally freed.

She didn't respond. For a second I thought she might not give it to me. Her cool air was easily linked to Beatrice's presence. Whether the doctor realized that Beatrice was trans or not, Dr. Maeve definitely sensed something she didn't approve of about my sister. Eventually, though, she just placed it on the bed next to me and asked me to test out my new and improved limb. Warning me that I would have to make sure to exercise it slightly more than my other arm for a few weeks, she led me back to the waiting room. Right before we got to the desk, though, she stopped me and gave me a look that was at the same time sweet and sickening.

"I do hope you'll be more careful from now on, Mr. Bean. I'm not sure if we'll have room in our schedule for any more accidents."

It would've been a fool who didn't take this as a threat. Panicked, I looked back to where Beatrice and Kiki were sitting. Relief washed over me when I saw the two of them sitting there, laps full of candy wrappers, chatting amiably with the receptionist who had taken a seat next to Beatrice. From what I could hear, they were talking about the different floats that were going to be on the display at the parade, and all of the delicious food that the fair had to offer.

Feeling slightly settled, I turned back to the doctor, mimicking her facial expression. "Oh, I'm sure you won't have to worry about seeing me in here again, doctor. I'll be careful." I began to walk away, only to turn once more and say, "Maybe we'll see you around town."

It was petty of me and probably unwise, but every so often I was swept away in moments of bravery or foolishness. It was worth it to see the infuriated look of terror that passed over her face. I'm sure she was running through a list of town officials to whom she'd have to complain. Pretty much everyone in my life had trained me to not stir up trouble where these things were concerned, but at the moment, I was not at all sorry to have made her feel just as uncomfortable as she had made me feel.

"Hey, kids." I said, walking up to Beatrice, Kiki, and the receptionist, who stood upon seeing me and the doctor.

"I'm not a kid." Beatrice said.

"I am." Kiki said.

"Oh, well beg your pardon. Hello grown-up woman and kid. You two ready to get out of here?"

The receptionist and Kiki laughed at this. Even Beatrice cracked a smile.

"Yes! Ms. May here was just telling us all we should expect out of the day's festivities. I told her that she should come find us when her work is finished today. Which will be at what time again?"

"Just a little bit after one, sweetheart. My husband and I will be sure to find you."

I surprisingly did not feel quite so stressed about Kiki having invited her to join us, but that was probably because Ms. May had already proven to be a somewhat normal person. At least normal in the way that she didn't seem to care what we looked like, or even who we were. In fact, Ms. May helped me calm down a bit.

We made our way outside and immediately Kiki began to drag Beatrice and me along the road until he found a slight gap in the crowd. He sidled forward, forging a path for Beatrice and me. The crowd gladly gave way for him, chuckling at the sight of this intrepid boy so eager to support his veterans. Their amused smiles fell into confusion or irritation as they saw Beatrice and I follow. I sighed loudly. Beatrice glanced my way. As we settled behind Kiki, Beatrice put her hand on my shoulder.

I jumped. She had never touched me before. She hardly acknowledged my presence.

"Everything okay?" I asked.

Beatrice nodded. "It would be a lot easier if you just stopped caring so much."

"What . . ."

"We can't change them. At least not right now. So let's have fun. Okay?"

I noticed that she was speaking quietly. It might've been because she didn't want the crowd to hear, or she didn't want Kiki to hear. Either way, her words had disarmed me, and I had no intelligent response to give. I didn't even have an unintelligent one. I just nodded, and then the parade started with a blast of horns from the marching band and an uproarious cheer from the crowd.

Kiki was delighted by every float that passed, clapping his hands and waving a little plastic American flag that had been handed out to the crowd by some of the boy cheerleaders. At one point, an oversized teenager had shifted in front of Kiki, blocking his view. I hoisted him up to my shoulders, which earned me an approving look from Beatrice and a giggle from him. He grabbed my hair with one hand as he continued to furiously wave his flag with the other.

I had to admit that the parade itself was pretty impressive. I'd been to the Macy's Thanksgiving Day and Halloween parades in New York. My own Floridian hometown had a fair few parades for high school pride and the Fourth of July. But given the size of the town, I hadn't expected anything quite so grandiose. Not only did it look like the entire population was either viewing or participating in the parade, but the floats looked like they'd been made by experts. A pretty hilarious MC talked us through the whole parade, introducing each new spectacle with jokes and flare. The cheerleaders flipped and spun through the floats and the band played their instruments with a controlled frenzy; there was even a color guard made up of veterans and students spinning flags and rifles like they were born to it.

The parade lasted for almost two hours. That entire time Kiki cheered and waved and laughed. I finally let him down from my shoulders as the last float rolled by. The crowd had already started to disperse. Per Beatrice's advice, I ignored all of the pointed looks that we got as people passed by.

"Well that was really something, wasn't it?" Kiki said.

"The floats were pretty." Beatrice said. "Clancy would've liked that one that the art club did. Of the famous paintings."

"That was great!" Kiki said. "But I liked the one from the library better. With all the famous characters and places from books. I mean that was really, really cool. What did you think, Arthur?"

Kiki's enthusiasm was infectious. "It was a blast. That color guard team was out of this world."

Kiki grinned. "They were. So talented! Should we make our way over to the fair now?"

"Does that start immediately after the parade?" I asked as we started to walk down Main Street.

"Well Ms. May said that there would be a brief intermission since a lot of the people who were in the parade are also running the games and booths at the fair. So we might have a little time."

"Did you have something else in mind?" Beatrice asked.

"Nothing really. It's just that I was thinking we could grab some food somewhere and have a bit of a picnic before we check out the fair."

"But there will be food there." Beatrice said skeptically.

"Yeah. Well I think Mrs. K. and Francis would kill me if I allowed you guys to subsist entirely off cotton candy and popcorn for the day. Besides, the real food, the burgers and dogs and all that, they won't happen until around dinnertime, right?"

"You're absolutely right, Arthur," Kiki said. "And Ms. May did say that a lot of people have a picnic between the parade and the fair. Apparently it's a tradition. If we hurry, we still may find a good spot. There's a diner over there."

We crossed over to a place that looked like the epitome of a small-town diner. It had a little bell that rung cheerfully as we stepped through the swinging doors, black-and-white tile floors, and booths with red plastic seats. I noticed a sign above the cash register letting people know that the diner would be closing early to observe Veterans Day. We had just twenty minutes left before closing time, but the people behind the counter didn't seem to mind.

"Hello there. Didn't pack a picnic I guess?" said the woman behind the counter, who was wearing one of those classic diner outfits with the pin-striped dress and bright red apron. She immediately reminded me of so many of the women who used to work at my dad's place. Warm and maternal, with a take-no-prisoners kind of humor and a way of knowing what you were going to say before you even said it, she a blew a bubble with her gum and let it pop without flinching.

"We did not. The kitchen still open? We don't want to ruin your closing routine."

"Don't worry about it, darling. You're the first customer we've had all day, except for old Mr. and Mrs. Carter. They come in here every morning for oat bran and yogurt. As if they couldn't buy that at the grocery store."

We all laughed. Kiki, Beatrice, and I did a quick perusal of the menu before making our orders. Kiki, heeding my warning about Francis's displeasure, ordered chicken soup and a garden salad. Beatrice, who didn't seem to care one lick about healthy eating, got a grilled cheese sandwich, french fries, and a slice of the devil's food cake that was on display at the counter. I myself decided to go in between and get the turkey club.

As we walked out of the diner with all of our food, Beatrice peeked inside the bag and noticed that they had given us each a slice of devil's food cake even though we hadn't paid for it. Kiki was overjoyed and looked expectantly at me, as if waiting for permission to dig in.

I laughed. "Our little secret, okay?"

* * *

The big, grassy lawn that was the entryway into the town's park was packed with picnickers. Kiki nimbly wove his way through the spread-out blankets and Tupperware containers of homemade egg salad to find us a spot squeezed in between two incredulous-looking families. He withdrew a large, rolled-up quilt from his backpack and he and Beatrice began to lay it out.

"What else do you got in there, Mary Poppins?"

"Always come prepared, Arthur."

I laughed as Kiki extracted three apples he had hidden away in his mystery bag, as well as three bottles of water. We laid out our food and started to tuck in. I hadn't realized quite how hungry I was until the first bite hit my mouth. From where we were sitting we could see the whole fair. There were rows of booths in a semi-circular formation. In the middle of the horseshoe was a stage and an area clearly partitioned off for three-legged races and beanbag tosses. I could see a petting zoo kept apart from the rest of the festivities, probably because of the smell. The highlight of the fair, though, was clearly the Ferris wheel. It was not so big, but it was big enough to excite Kiki, who apparently had never been on a ride like that.

As we ate, Kiki strategized. When it came to fairs, or amusement parks, music festivals, or anything like that, there were always two types of people. There were the free-spirited, "let the muses take us where they will" types who never really cared whether they hit all the rides or saw all the acts. They just lived in the moment, stress-free and jolly. Then there were the planners, who had mapped out the whole affair beforehand with timetables on when certain things would be less crowded and kept strict schedules. They wanted to do and see it all, as long as it was in an orderly manner.

Kiki was clearly the latter. He consulted his watch numerous times, turned to each of the families near us to ask which attraction was the most popular, scribbled down a basic schedule of where we should be and when; I was pretty impressed with his organizational skills. On his schedule, two o'clock was the end of lunchtime. Right on the dot, he started to pack away our things.

Other families all around us had started to drift off toward the booths. Even from the picnicking lawn I could see a long line of people waiting for the Ferris wheel to start its rotation. Kiki was eager to get there and tried to go on ahead of us as Beatrice packed away the picnic blanket.

"Woah there." I said, grabbing the collar of his jacket. "You're not going anywhere without me or Beatrice, okay?" Somewhere behind me, a woman gasped. I let go of Kiki's clothes.

"But I could go hold us a place in line."

"Yeah, well if Francis were going to be mad about our food choices for a day, he'd really lose it if he heard I let you go off on your own."

"Oh fine. But hurry!"

Just to tease him, Beatrice slowed down her motions, looking like a woman underwater. Kiki laughed and jumped on her, attaching himself to her side and pleading with her to go faster while also trying to grab the blanket out of her hands.

"Oh, like this is going to make me go any faster."

Once we finally got everything packed away, Kiki sped off like a mad person toward the Ferris wheel. Beatrice and I stumbled to keep up, shouting his name. When we finally caught up to him in line, he was talking to a burly, bearded man at the end of the queue. The man had a hand on Kiki's shoulder and a small crowd of people behind him. The line had become less of a line and more of an amoeba gathered behind this guy and Kiki.

"Stay behind me." I said to Beatrice as we slowed our gait to walk up to Kiki.

Beatrice gave me a confused look. She seemed like the she was about to say something when the burly man spoke. But not to me.

"Is this your friend, kid?"

"Yes, sir. Mr. Arthur Bean, meet . . . I'm sorry, sir, I didn't catch your name."

"Arthur Bean? This your kid?" The man finally regarded me. In fact, the whole crowd behind him, which was now also gathering behind me, looked hard at Beatrice and me.

"Not my kid, no. But he's a family friend. I'm taking him and my sister around the fair today."

"Just like I said, sir." Kiki said cheerfully, giving his shoulders a shrug. The man's hand stayed firmly in place.

"Then why were you chasin' him?"

"Oh, that's my fault, sir. You see, I ran ahead when Arthur asked me not to. I was just too excited about the Ferris wheel." Kiki's voice was as light and charming as ever, but I could tell by the slight tremor at the end, and the way his eyebrows were slightly furrowed, that he had not at all planned for this in his schedule.

"Is that right?" The man asked me.

"That's right. Kiki," I said, trying to keep my voice level, "Why don't we try out some of the other attractions first and do the Ferris wheel later? I bet the sunset would look pretty good up there."

"Oh, yes." Kiki glanced between the man above him and me. "Yes, I hadn't thought of that before. Sunset would be a much better time for the Ferris wheel." He tried to take a step forward, but the man's grip on his shoulder jolted him back.

"Hey!" Beatrice said.

"Why you trying to take him away so quick, huh?" The man's face had gone a little red. He looked on the verge of explosion.

"We are just trying to enjoy the fair. Could you please let go of him? We are all just here for some fun. Don't ruin that for the kid."

"Arthur . . ." Kiki's voice had gone small.

"Now don't worry, kid." The man leaned down, bringing his face close to Kiki's. Kiki grimaced and then his eyes flew open to look at me. "You don't have to go with this guy if you don't wanna. We'll help you find your mommy and daddy. Just tell us where they are."

I opened my mouth to talk, but Kiki beat me to it.

"My mother is dead and I don't know who my father is. Arthur and Beatrice are my friends. Please let me go." He started to cry.

Beatrice took one step forward. Out of the corner of my eye I could see her fists clenched at her sides. I put my arm out in front of her. If the look on her face was anything to go by, that move alone lost me major points in our game of reconciliation.

I moved forward instead, going until I was standing face-to-face with the guy, my torso right against Kiki's nose. I felt his small head bump into my stomach as his almost-tears became full-on sobs. I placed one hand on top of Kiki's head protectively and the other on the man's arm, the one that held Kiki in place. I stared at him, trying to look as hard as he did.

I had never been good at physical fights. I was naturally strong and pretty coordinated, but most of the time I lacked the commitment that usually made one successful in a fight. At the best of times, I was passive, calm, and levelheaded. At my worst times, I was lazy, cowardly, and apathetic. Thia used to say I just didn't have enough aggression to really fight someone.

But in that moment, seeing Kiki look so helpless and small and confused on a day that was supposed to be so amazing and magical for him ignited in me a protective furor that I'd never experienced before. My blood felt all hot, rushing to my face in angry gushes. I could have ripped the guy's face off if I hadn't had both Kiki and Beatrice with me. But everyone could see that I was out for flesh and just barely keeping it under control. The crowd behind the man had started to bunch together as if to shield themselves.

"Look," I started, voice hard but steady, "I know what you're thinking. Cute little kid like that with a guy who clearly isn't his dad. But this kid is a friend of mine. I'm not doing anything to hurt him, and clearly he wants to be with me. Now you're ruining a perfectly fine day for him, and you're making me angry on top of it. If you want this day to continue being nice, then you're going to have to let go of Kiki and let the three of us be on our way. All right?"

The entire time I'd been talking, my grip on his arm had gotten progressively tighter and tighter. I watched the sensation of pain overcome the one of pride that had previously seasoned his face. Truthfully, if someone had really wanted to take Kiki away from me, they could've. I had no legal relationship with him. Child services could have swept him off before I could get on the phone to tell Francis. The police could have come, shot both me and Beatrice, and then taken Kiki to "safety." But the man holding Kiki didn't seem to think as logically as me. Clearly, he hadn't expected to be so blatantly challenged.

His grip on Kiki's shoulder slackened. One breath later it fell entirely. As soon as he was loose, Kiki launched himself into my arms. I picked him up, walking away from the man and his crowd. Supporting Kiki's weight with one arm, I extended the other to Beatrice, who took my hand without question.

"It ain't right!" The man called out. "It ain't right! A kid like that shouldn't be with the likes of you. It ain't right!"

I could've sped up, made a run for it as we passed through the crowd of faces that had gathered behind me. But I had a crying kid in my arms and an angry girl holding my hand. Sometimes you just had to show strength for the people around you, even when you weren't feeling strong yourself. So I walked, slowly, steadily, through the crowd with my chin held high. I kept walking until we got to a bench behind a booth that sold homemade candies.

"I want to go home immediately." Kiki said, voice muffled in my shoulder.

I settled myself on the bench, rearranging Kiki so that he sat in my lap. Beatrice held onto my hand the whole time but remained standing. She glanced nervously behind us to check if anyone followed. No one had. The people in the candy booth were stealing not-so-subtle looks at us, but for the most part they seemed sympathetic, not hostile. Beatrice used her other hand to stroke Kiki's head. This made him look up at me. I was glad for that. I didn't have a free hand to coax him into retreating from the safe space that was my shoulder.

Once I caught his gaze, I said, "Kiki, what good would that do?"

Truthfully, I wanted to run back to the Hotel as quickly as possible. But there were two reasons why I couldn't let that happen. The first was entirely selfish. I didn't want to return to the Hotel hours earlier than expected with a crying Kiki and a rattled Beatrice in tow. That would not only put into question my ability to play babysitter for the day, but it would also instill a greater sense of unease about the town in general. If I could make it out of this day without either of those things happening, I would consider it a success.

The second reason was simple. I didn't want to ruin Kiki's day, at least not more than it already had been. The kid was intelligent beyond his years, but he was also slightly naive. He lived a sheltered life in an unusual setting. In my opinion, this made him a better person. He didn't think twice about the fact that Beatrice was transgender, or that he and I were different colors, or that Caleb was gay. He simply recognized that everyone around him was different and thought that was how it was supposed to be. If I let him run away at that moment, then maybe, just maybe, his opinions would change. Maybe he would start to question how easily he accepted people who weren't like him.

On top of all that, I wanted to be something more to him than just a babysitter. I wasn't sure if it was being around Grace again, or if it was the fact that Kiki was so young and so easy to love, but I felt myself experiencing unexpected paternal instincts. In order to protect Kiki, but also to teach him, I felt like staying was essential. If we ran away, not only would I appear to be a coward to Beatrice, but I would also be showing Kiki that simply ignoring problems was the only way to travel through life.

Neither Kiki nor Beatrice immediately understood why I wanted to stay.

"Arthur, maybe he's right. I mean . . . they were ready to fight us." Beatrice, whose voice was usually so strong and straightforward, quivered and petered off. Not two hours ago she'd basically told me to screw them all and not care about it. But after being confronted with real ugliness, she wanted to run. I wondered if maybe, like Kiki, this was the first time she'd ever experienced just how close-minded and cruel people could be. I found it hard to believe, having gone through what she had, but maybe she'd managed to escape some of the worst of people.

"Yes! Arthur these people are terrible. We can't stay and enjoy our time around them. I refuse to do it."

"Kiki, I know you're scared —"

"I am not scared! I am disgusted. I am furious. I am . . ." He broke off into a sob.

"Okay. And I understand that too. What those people did was just like you said, disgusting and infuriating. But if we run away now, they've won, haven't they?"

"Won what?"

"Just won. They want us out of their town. They want us to feel scared and they want us to run. But we came here to have a good time, didn't we? Should we let them take that away from us?"

"No . . . I suppose we shouldn't."

"And Beatrice, just because they wanted to fight us, does that mean we shouldn't fight back?"

"You're saying that we should fight them?"

"No, I'm not. I've honestly never been in a fight in my life, and I hope to keep it that way. But life is full of fights. Usually they aren't physical, but sometimes they are. All I'm saying is that you shouldn't let yourself be run over just because you're scared. Sometimes you gotta fight back. And in this case, fighting back just means showing them that they can't ruin our good time."

"But why would they even act like that in the first place? I just don't get it." Kiki asked, curiosity getting the better of him.

I grimaced. Maybe this was something that Francis had not yet touched upon in his lessons. Maybe it was something he never planned on teaching. I could've avoided it, or made something up, but the look in Kiki's eyes told me he wanted the truth. He expected it.

"You know . . . we look different, right?"

Kiki nodded. "Everyone looks different."

"Yes, but we look very different."

"Well yes. You're black and I'm white."

"Yeah, well see, really that doesn't mean anything. I mean biologically, scientifically it doesn't mean anything. We've got the same parts, organs and all. Our brains are pretty much the same. But culturally, it means a lot. Not to everyone, but to some people, the color of your skin means more to them than the person you actually are. Maybe some people in this town are like that."

"That's stupid." Kiki said.

"I agree. Unfortunately, that's how it is. Still, I don't think it should drive us away. We do that, and we are basically saying we agree with those idiots."

They were silent for a long time. Kiki rubbed furiously at his eyes until the tears stopped. Beatrice still gripped my hand tightly, but instead of glancing behind her, she considered me, seeming to be deep in thought about what I said. I could almost see it, that barrier she had built up against me crumbling down. It was as if I were seeing who she was for the first time. I couldn't help but feel the slightest twinge of self-satisfaction at this. Whatever I had done, without even realizing it, I had been forgiven by her.

"So what do you guys say? Shall we go forth into battle?"

Kiki grinned. I knew one of his favorite pretend scenarios was ancient Roman war. He hopped off my lap and held his hand above his head, fist clenched as if he were holding a broadsword in those tiny fingers.

"To battle!" He shrieked. It was so loud that the homemade

candies people startled and looked back at us. Once they saw it was simply Kiki being a normal little kid, they laughed a little, shaking their heads.

I followed suit, raising my own imaginary weapon, which was a spiked flail. "To battle!"

Beatrice, laughing slightly at the ridiculousness of it all, raised her fist slightly less enthusiastically and mumbled, "To battle . . ."

* * *

Our first stop was the homemade candies booth behind which we had been previously hiding. There were truffles dusted with some kind of gold sugar and lollipops with rainbows swirling into themselves. Homemade marshmallows with weird flavors like maple or bourbon and long strings of pale, pink taffy immediately caught the kids' eyes. One of the women running the booth let them try a chocolate marshmallow each and gave them a string of taffy, which they tested to see exactly how long it could stretch. Once it snapped, Kiki and Beatrice shoved some in their mouths and went wild digging through the wicker baskets and examining every piece before they placed it before the grinning woman at the cash box. She was clearly amused by their enthusiasm.

"Is she your daughter?"

I smiled uncomfortably at that. "My sister."

"Aha. I thought you two looked awfully alike. Got a sweet tooth, huh sweetheart?"

Beatrice didn't respond, not realizing she was being spoken to. An artfully sculpted chocolate bust of George Washington had caught her attention.

"Bea, she asked if you have a sweet tooth." I said.

"Huh? Oh yeah. Big one."

We walked away with a backpack stuffed full of candies. I allowed Beatrice and Kiki each five pieces to eat during the fair, and the rest they had to save until we got back to the Hotel. Then, I figured, how much candy they binged on was Grace and Francis's problem. With much grumbling and groaning, they finally picked out their five pieces and munched on them as we checked out the rest of the booths. I asked Kiki if he wanted to try riding the Ferris wheel again, but he shook his head and mumbled something about having lost the urge. I felt it was a great accomplishment just

106

having gotten him to stay at the fair in the first place. I decided not to push the Ferris wheel. There would be other times he could go on those kinds of rides. Absentmindedly, I started considering amusement parks I could take him to, maybe on road trips. I didn't even think about how weird it was that I suddenly felt so comfortable making plans like that, however loose.

What would've taken a less enthusiastic group of people an hour or two tops took Beatrice and Kiki upward of four hours, well into dusk. Now that she had let her guard down, I saw just how amazed Beatrice was by everything at every booth. She and Kiki paid great attention to all the various wares, even if they had no intention of buying anything.

At a ceramics stand, Kiki could not stop gushing over how intricate the designs were. Beatrice was thoroughly impressed by a caricature artist's sketch of former President Nixon. Luckily, both Kiki and Beatrice did not happen to notice the rather large painting of the confederate flag that was displayed on the right of the artist's booth.

Any booth that sold food was a huge hit with all three of us. And there were plenty of those. We could see a group of men setting up about a dozen barbecues and long plastic tables in preparation for the cookout that was going to be dinner, but that didn't dampen our appetites for all the other goodies on sale. Beatrice and I split a pretzel that was larger than both of our faces combined, dripping butter and mustard. Kiki buried his whole head into a pink cloud of cotton candy and came out with tufts of the stuff stuck in his hair and eyebrows. At a stand that sold homemade donuts, all three of us walked away with three donuts each, all in different flavors. We spent a long time sampling each other's and discussing the pros and cons of each donut's texture, flavor, and toppings or fillings. The general consensus ended up being that while the cake donut was a classic done right, the winner of the donut war was definitely the boysenberry jam-filled chocolate donut with vanilla sprinkles.

We made it a mission as well to gather gifts for the other guests back at the Hotel. Beatrice picked out jewelry for the ladies, and Kiki found books for Francis, Diego, and Thadeus. At a booth filled with antiques, I found a pair of old, elaborate cuff links that I thought matched Caleb's style. When we passed a booth that sold vintage toys, I got an old Rubik's cube for Sam, who I'd noticed enjoyed puzzles, and an old model rocket for Luke. Kiki even found a booth that sold homemade dog treats along with other baked goods and bought Zorro an assortment of savory snacks.

Eventually, tired and full and laden with brown paper shopping bags, we settled off to the side of the sports lawn and cheered along with the other spectators. We saw a pair of twins win the three-legged race by a landslide and a pair of newlyweds crush every other pair at the egg toss. Beatrice and Kiki seemed so enthralled by the games that it might as well have been the Super Bowl. Watching their faces, it was easy to ignore the pointed glances that were still being sent our way.

"Oh, there you three are!" A kind voice broke me out of my thoughts. Standing above us was Ms. May, and to her right was her husband, a short, stout, pleasant-looking man who smiled down at us warmly. "Mind if we join you?"

"Oh, not at all Ms. May. I'd forgotten that you were going to be here. We've had such an eventful day!" Kiki scooted closer to me to make room for the two newcomers in our little semicircle.

"Oh yeah, we heard." Her husband said. "I'm so sorry that happened. This little town breeds some pretty intolerant people I'm afraid."

"Oh . . . I wasn't talking about that." Kiki said, his cheerful demeanor slightly shaken by the reminder. "But I suppose that was eventful, yes."

"Oh, I'm sorry." The husband raised his hands up. "I just thought . . ."

"I think what Kiki was saying, Jeff"—May put a soothing hand on her husband's forearm—"was that they've had a lot of fun today. Isn't that right, Kiki?"

"The most fun! I've eaten so much I feel like I'm about to explode."

Ms. May laughed. "Us too. The fair can have that effect on people."

Ms. May, Kiki, and Beatrice fell into idle chatter, discussing their favorite parts of the fair and reviewing the rules of tug-of-war.

I turned to Jeff and extended my hand. "Hey, I'm Arthur. Nice to meet you."

"And you." Jeff gave a firm handshake. "May couldn't stop gushing about the two adorable kids she met at work today. She's been keeping an eye out for you all day, but I guess you've been busy."

"We have. I'm glad you found us though. It lets Kiki and Bea see that not everyone here is . . . well . . . how those other people are."

Jeff sighed and nodded his head, turning his gaze to watch the game taking place on the field. "Yeah. Well I'm glad to not be like them. I have a bit of firsthand experience with how close-minded these people can be."

"How do you mean?"

Jeff laughed a little. "Well I was born and raised here, but my mother was . . . damaged. She did drugs and drank too much and was pretty abusive I guess you'd say. To me and my brothers and my dad. Eventually she just sort of took off for good and my dad hired a woman to take care of us because he couldn't stop working. And that woman was one of the most amazing people I've ever known. My dad and her fell in love, got married after he found my mother and got her to sign divorce papers, and well . . . the rest of the people didn't take too kindly to that."

"She wasn't white I take it?" I asked.

"She was not. I think it was the first time a black person and a white person got married in this town. Anyway, the rest of my brothers got out of here as soon as they could, and so did I for a while. I met May at school in Chicago, but then my mom . . . um, my stepmom . . . god that sounds weird, I don't usually call her that." He chuckled. "My mom died kind of unexpectedly and my dad just lost it. So May and I have been here ever since, taking care of him."

"I'm sorry to hear that. How long have you and May been married?"

"Almost five years now. But we'd been together for six before that." Jeff smiled that kind of soft, goofy smile that only people in love knew how to use. I used to have that smile on my face whenever I talked about Thia. "We want to have kids of our own, but both of us don't want to raise them here. Wish I could move my dad back to Chicago with us, but that extreme of a change of scenery would just make things worse for him."

"What are you two talking about so seriously over there?" May asked, craning her neck to look at us with an expression of mock suspicion.

Jeff laughed at his wife's antics and leaned forward to give her a quick peck. "Oh nothing. Just getting to know each other a bit."

"Look!" Kiki said. "People are lining up for the food. Maybe we should go wait?"

Sure enough there was a long line gathering next to the barbecues. All of us stood up, patting down our bottoms to make sure no grass or soil stuck to our pants. We started to make our way over to the line, Kiki holding Ms. May's hand and talking animatedly with her and Jeff about something. Beatrice placed a hand on my arm, holding me back to allow the others to get ahead of us.

"Everything okay?" I asked.

"Ms. May said that Jeff is a contractor." Beatrice said. "Apparently he has a pretty big team of people . . . good people."

"Huh, is that so? Think he could help us out with the Hotel?"

Beatrice shrugged, but the smirk on her face showed just how happy she was to have helped in some way. It had been a worry of mine, especially after what had happened at the Ferris wheel. Up until that point, it seemed unlikely that we would be able to find a team willing to work on our place. Not only was our location inconvenient, it also offered up some special difficulties that other places wouldn't. Plus, it seemed like a lot of people would feel about us the way that crowd in front of the Ferris wheel had. I was grateful to know that not only were there decent people around, but also that those decent people could help us.

We spent the rest of our time at the fair breaking personal records of how many hot dogs we could eat. By the end of it, Kiki was so gorged and exhausted that he couldn't walk on his own. I scooped him up for the second time that day. Almost immediately, he fell asleep in my arms. My heart beat so violently that I could've sworn that the thumping against my ribcage would wake him up. All it took was that one move for me to fall in love with the kid.

May and Jeff walked with us to our car. It had gotten dark. Even though they didn't say it, I knew they were walking with us so we could feel a little safer. Even then, with the two of them beside us, I still had the feeling that we were being followed. I handed Kiki off to Beatrice as I turned to say goodbye to our two new friends. I took Jeff's card, as well as their phone numbers. They stood on the curb waving at us as we drove off.

The drive was shorter than I remembered, but maybe that was because I felt so content. At some point during the day, the stress of being in that small town had been replaced by the joy of the day's festivities. Beatrice sat in the back with Kiki, but she kept smiling at me every time I looked at them through the rearview mirror. Kiki snored softly in the back seat, and that pleasant sound was the soundtrack to the last moments of our day.

"We shouldn't tell anyone about what happened." Beatrice said as we disembarked the airboat.

"You mean at the Ferris wheel?" I asked.

"Yes. I think . . . I think it's better if they don't know. And maybe if we don't mention it, then Kiki won't remember."

I smiled down at the kid who, despite the noise and movement, had stayed sound asleep during the boat ride. I doubted Kiki would really forget what had happened, but I agreed with Beatrice. He didn't need to be reminded of it.

Francis waited for us on the porch. He was smoking a cigarette. Up until that point, I hadn't seen a single guest at the hotel smoke, except for Thad and his old pipe. As soon as we walked up the porch steps, though, Francis quickly dropped the thing and stomped it out with his boot. Then he kicked it off into the weeds that lined the patio and strode up to us with his arms outstretched to collect Kiki. I gave him over.

"You smoke?" My tone was teasing, but Francis didn't seem to appreciate the joke.

"Not around him."

We went back into the Hotel where Grace and Clancy were both standing, chatting in the foyer. Both of their faces broke out into warm, affectionate smiles when they saw Kiki cuddled against Francis's chest.

"Would you look at that picture?" Clancy said.

"Little guy's worn out." Grace ran a hand through Kiki's hair. "Did you guys have fun?"

"So much fun." Beatrice responded. "We ate all this food and the parade was so cool. We took pictures on Kiki's camera."

Beatrice tumbled into a full account of the day, attracting other guests from the library. Soon the whole group was circled around her, listening with rapt attention as she showed them the pictures of the parade floats, all the candies they'd tried, and the various sports that they'd seen. She told about Ms. May and Jeff, who she called her new friends. One by one, she handed out the gifts we'd gathered. As everyone gushed over how much they loved and appreciated what we'd gotten them, Francis snuck off to put Kiki to bed. I sidled away toward the kitchen for some water. All I'd had to drink at the festival was soda and a milkshake. A dull dehydration headache started to bloom in the back of my skull.

"There's leftovers in the fridge if you want them, dear." Mrs. K. said.

I felt my stomach churn at the idea of more food in my already overstuffed gut. "God, please no more food. I don't think I can eat for the next week."

"Yeah. We ate so much." Lowering her voice, Beatrice said, "Kiki had, like, ten hot dogs. It was amazing!"

After I poured myself a glass of water, I came back out to the foyer, but the crowd had dispersed. Suddenly, the exhaustion that had been lingering in my bones since the Ferris wheel burst to the surface and practically overwhelmed me. I looked woefully at the long staircase and considered for a while whether it would be too odd for me to settle down for bed on the hardwood.

Right as I was about to crawl into bed, someone knocked on my door. Grudgingly, I dragged my feet to the doorway and opened it.

Grace and Beatrice stood in the hallway, both in their pajamas. Grace wore a red flannel set, and Beatrice had on an oversized T-shirt with some unfamiliar band name.

"I just wanted to say good night." Beatrice said, stepping forward and giving me a short but comfortable hug. "And thanks for the amazing day."

"Oh. Yeah." I could feel my tongue getting tied at her show of affection. Her opinion of me had changed so abruptly that it was giving me whiplash. "I had a really good time too."

That response seemed to satisfy Beatrice. She shuffled across the hall to her room, shutting the door gently. Grace lingered, smiling at me knowingly. I wondered if maybe Beatrice had decided to tell Grace what had happened after all, and she was simply waiting for me to come clean too. My anxiety didn't last long, though, because Grace eventually smiled and leaned up to kiss me on the cheek.

"You were a hit today, Arthur." Grace said, squeezing my arms. "I knew you could do it."

"Really?" I laughed. "Because I didn't."

"You're too modest. You're a good guy. Don't be afraid to show it."

"Okay." Grace started to move away, but then I remembered Jeff. "By the way, I might have found a solution to our renovation woes." A yawn made the last word elongated and comical. Grace giggled.

"Good. Let's talk about it tomorrow. You're clearly exhausted."

I nodded and said good night. I'd never fallen asleep so fast in my life.

* * *

Thia sifted through the box of pictures, her legs tucked up underneath her. One by one, she pulled out old prints that had long been forgotten by everyone, even my father. I had taken the box, along with a few other random mementos, back to New York after my father's funeral. Mari wanted to sell everything in the house, and that was fine by me. But before she sent everything off to auction, I made my way through, collecting memories that were too precious to be sold. I salvaged his old Zippo with leopard print carved into the metal, and his old black-and-tan bowling shoes, and the two-dollar bill he always kept with him for good luck. Those and the box of photos was all I needed of my dad.

Thia had, of course, glommed on to the box of pictures first and was now on an avid search for embarrassing baby photos of me. Along the way, she'd stumbled across ones of Grace, Luke, Beatrice, Mari, my mother, and my father.

"This your kid?" Thia asked, holding up a picture of me as a teenager stiffly holding a baby Grace on her first birthday. Grace had her arms outstretched in the picture, attempting to snatch the sparkly pink birthday hat off my head. I had held her away from my body, attempting a grin at the camera that came off more as a grimace, a facial expression which I'm sure I mirrored as a response to Thia's question.

"That's my sister. You know. Grace."

"As a matter of fact," Thia said, setting down the photograph and returning her attention to the box, "I do not know her. I mean, I know of her. But we have not had the pleasure of meeting."

"Right." I said absentmindedly. While Thia lounged with the photographs, I was attempting to master a rather complex recipe for chocolate soufflé, a recipe I had failed every time I tackled it. I could cook, but Julia Childs I was not.

"In fact, I never met any of your family."

"Do you want to?"

"I wouldn't mind it."

"Well how about this? When you introduce me to your parents, I'll introduce you to my siblings." I'd never met any of Thia's family either, but she often said that was more for my sake than anything else. Her traditionalist Korean parents wouldn't appreciate her choice in a romantic partner. She was sparing me their judgmental gaze and thinly veiled racist comments. It didn't matter to me one way or another. In my experience, families could be a bit of a pain. I wasn't exactly chomping at the bit to spend two awkward hours over a "not-so-nice to meet you" dinner with my girlfriend's parents. I couldn't see why all of a sudden Thia felt the need to meet Grace or any of my kin.

"Yeah, well, I guess it'll be a while then." Her dry tone took my attention away from my soufflé for about twenty-eight seconds. I attribute those twenty-eight seconds to why that particular batch of soufflés came out tasting more like chocolaty dirt than smooth bites of cocoa heaven.

"Are we fighting?" I asked.

Thia laughed. It was a question I asked a lot. Sometimes it was hard to tell if Thia was simply being playfully standoffish or if she was actually upset about something. Probably a man of more intuition than I possessed would've been able to discern between the two without having to ask. But I found that, in general, the best way to start solving conflict was to at least know if you were in one.

"Not really. It's just . . . you never really talk to me about your family."

"Not sure if there's anything to talk about." I turned my attention back to my soufflés, probably to hide the blatant lie that I'd just told. In fact, there was quite a bit to talk about when it came to my family. Like how Luke had just been arrested for the third time that year, this time for vandalizing his school's gymnasium. Or how Beatrice was doing with her transition. Or how Grace was actually my daughter, not my half sister. But if Thia was allowed to be secretive about her past, then I was certainly allowed to be secretive about my family's present.

"All right." Thia said after a long pause. She'd dropped the subject much easier than I had expected, but I wasn't going to question it. Usually Thia knew when to push me on something and when not to. Maybe she'd simply caught on to the fact that at that moment the outcome of my soufflés was far more important to me than my family's history. "I don't want you to meet my parents. You know why."

"Yeah I do."

"But there are other people in my family I wouldn't mind you meeting if you could."

"Really?" That piqued my interest, drawing my attention once again from the soufflés. They were becoming a lost cause anyway.

"Yeah. I'd like you to meet my uncle someday. But he's in Korea. He comes to New York every once in a while, but usually that's for business. Even I hardly see him those times. He's a busy man."

"Yeah? What's he like?" I relished hearing Thia speak about her past.

"He's really nice. He's actually younger than my dad, but he's got this big sense of honor. When my grandfather died, my dad didn't want to take over the company. My uncle wanted to be a photographer. He took that actually." She gestured to a photo that had decorated every place Thia had ever lived in, as far as I knew. It was of an old woman laughing with a large batch of kimchi in her bare hands. She was bald. I thought she was a monk. It was a stunning photo. "But then my grandfather died and my uncle did what he thought was right. When I was a kid, I wished that he was my father. Visits to see him in Korea are some of my favorite memories. My parents used to just plop me on a plane and send me off. I didn't mind though. I liked it better that way."

"Wow. I'd like to meet him."

She smiled. "Maybe one day you will. Now are we gonna eat tonight or what?"

I had promised her I would make her soufflés when I got back from cleaning out my dad's house. His death also happened to coincide with the week of her birthday. I hadn't had time to put the usual effort into organizing festivities and buying an overabundance of gifts. Baking soufflés was the best I could do, but it turned out I wasn't actually very good at that.

"How's it going over there?" Thia asked.

"How would you feel about ordering cookies from that twenty-four-hour place instead?"

Thia rose from the couch and placed her hands on my shoulders. Leaning up on her toes, she pressed herself into my back and gazed down at the batter-filled ramekins. "They look pretty damn tasty to me. Let's just eat them like that."

"Sure. If you want your birthday gift to be salmonella."

She laughed, kissing my cheek. "I have full faith in your French pastries. But maybe let's order cookies just in case."

"Yeah. And Chinese food."

"Oh! And pizza from that new place down the street."

"Our bodega should still be open. Want to go out and grab some ice cream too?"

"Oh man. Best birthday ever." Thia said from the couch.

I turned, thinking she was referring to the binge fest we had just laid out for ourselves. Instead she held up a picture of me as a toddler. I was standing in front of the ocean in one of those pink Sleeping Beauty costumes that they sell at Halloween stores, glancing coquettishly behind my shoulder at the camera as my bare bottom peeked out of the bottom of the frills.

"Oh yeah." Thia said. "This one's going up on the fridge."

I laughed as I watched her place one of our zombie survival tip magnets over the picture to keep it in place. Now it was between one of those photo booth strips of her and I at Coney Island and a list of groceries that needed buying.

"What do you think? I reckon it fits right in."

"Oh you *reckon*, do you?"

She put on an effected twang, swiveling on her heels and

striding toward me with long, bowlegged steps. "That's right, cowboy. I sure do reckon so."

Swooping her up in my arms, I kissed her, and she kissed me back. We kissed for so long that the soufflés cooked over by six seconds, and whatever hope I had at saving them was lost. It didn't matter much, though. As long as I was there kissing Thia, even a deflated soufflé couldn't dampen my spirits.

You all right, dear?

"Huh?"

I had been staring bleary-eyed at Mrs. K. placing her soufflés into the oven for probably longer than normal. I'd slept long past breakfast and lunch. Apparently, so had Beatrice, and Kiki had only woken up at a normal hour because Francis wasn't going to allow another day free of studying. Now both Beatrice and I were huddled at the kitchen island looking as if we were both hungover. Mrs. K. had placed a couple of sandwiches left over from lunch in front of us, but both of us shuddered at the sight. We were still recovering from yesterday's overdose of treats.

"Why are you making soufflé so early again?" Beatrice said. Apparently she had asked Mrs. K. this question before, but I couldn't remember her even acknowledging it.

"Oh just practice for Grace's birthday party next week. You know how much she loves soufflé. They are particularly tricky to make though."

"You could say that again." I said. "Grace is having a birthday party next week?"

"Arthur," Beatrice said, "You didn't forget her birthday, did you?"

I waved my hand dismissively, using the other to pick up and examine a sandwich, and then toss it disgustedly back onto the plate. Lettuce and tomato dislodged itself from between the two slices of bread and skidded across the island.

"Of course not. I bought her present months ago."

"Really?" Beatrice asked.

"That's awfully sweet." Mrs. K. said.

I shrugged. I had just stumbled upon Grace's present one summer day before I'd quit my job. The woman I had been loosely seeing at the time insisted that I come with her to the Brooklyn Flea Market. Usually I avoided events like that because the number of hip people all milling about in one place looking cool and fashionable gave me anxiety. The only reason I really enjoyed those events was for the food. In fact, I was chowing down on a vegan hotdog covered with a ridiculous amount of tumbling toppings when I found it.

It was a pair of old ballet shoes in a glass case filled with dried flowers and ribbons. Grace hadn't done ballet in years. As she grew older, she became much fonder of less rigid styles of dancing, but she'd always kept her shoes. She said that ballet shoes had a certain aura to them. They were such delicate, light little things, yet they demanded sacrifices of blood and bone from their wearer, unforgiving if not used properly. I got it. Ballet had always seemed closer to torture than art for me.

One of my first thoughts when we'd collected my car those weeks ago was that the glass case might have shattered, and Grace's present would be ruined. Luckily, my duffel bag full of underwear cushioned it, and it remained unharmed. Some of the flowers were displaced, but I thought that just added to its sort of lonely appeal. The girl I was with was quite pleased by my choice, thinking that I was going to set it up in my own home as a decorative piece. She thought I was a lot cooler than I was. Then again, she was white and younger, and I had a distinct feeling that anything I did was cool in her eyes just because of the color of my skin.

"Did you get my present already?" Beatrice asked.

"Your birthday is like . . . almost a year away. And I sent you one for your last. Give a man some time."

"I want a guitar. Just in case you were wondering what to get me."

"I'll get you that for Christmas then."

"You're too easy." Beatrice laughed.

I shrugged my shoulders again and then groaned, letting my head fall onto my forearms. "Why do I feel like I spent the night with a bottle of Hennessy?"

"You two are acting rather intoxicated." Mrs. K. said.

"More like post-intoxicated." Beatrice said.

"You're too young to drink." I said.

"And you're too old to eat three cheeseburgers and a hot dog."

"You're never too old for that."

We all laughed. The swinging door at the side of the kitchen opened. Grace came in with Diego at her side. Zorro waited obediently at the threshold. Mrs. K. was not the biggest fan of dogs. She seemed pretty frightened of Zorro most of the time despite the fact that he was one of the stupidest, most lovable pups I'd ever met. Zorro was never allowed in the kitchen under the guise of hygiene, but I think Mrs. K. just wanted a space free of annoyances like dogs. It was probably the same reason why Thadeus was never seen in the kitchen.

"You two look awful." Grace said as she approached us, laying a soothing hand on both of our shoulders.

"Just like Kiki." Diego said. "Expect a scolding from Francis for letting him eat too much."

"I'd like to see him try to stop that kid once he sets his sight on food. He's like a python. His jaw dislocates, and the food is gone before you even have a chance to pay for it."

Grace giggled. "For such a small kid, he sure can pack it away. So, Arthur, are you ready to discuss what you mentioned last night?"

It took a while for my brain to register what she was talking about, but then I remembered Jeff's card still stuffed in the pocket of yesterday's jeans. The idea of trying to work out anything to do with renovations at that moment was not so appealing, but Grace had waited patiently for me to wake up, so I figured I could force my ass to move.

I went up to retrieve the card and met Diego and Grace in the library. Thadeus was there too. He had fallen asleep with a *Time* magazine splayed open across his chest. Some young musician was on the cover, peeking up at the camera through his perfectly sculpted bangs. Thadeus's reading glasses had gone crooked and were threatening to slide off his nose at any moment. I removed them and set them down on a table nearby before sitting down to talk to Grace.

She seemed utterly pleased not only that we now had some concrete information with which we could move forward, but also that there were people in that town that seemed somewhat kind and trustworthy. Of course I'd left out Jeff's history, because then it would require me to explain why he felt he should confide such personal information to a stranger in the first place. Beatrice had kept her word about not telling the others what had happened. I imagined that Kiki wouldn't tell either, if just to avoid remembering something so nasty.

Diego took the card from my hand and examined it, nodding. "You're absolutely certain he does good work?"

"No, not really. But we could call him and find out. He could come take a look at the place, give us an estimate. I mean . . . we already know it's going to be expensive."

"Maybe," Diego said, "Now that your arm is healed, you, me, Luke, and Sam could go around and make a list of things that we could do on our own. That way when we contact this man, we'll have a better idea of what it is he needs to help us with." I noticed Grace staring at Diego with an almost approving look. She must have liked his dedication to the Hotel.

"That sounds good. I should also spend some time fixing up my car."

"Oh, Clancy and Caleb could help you with that." Grace said, tearing her eyes away from Diego. "They usually fix up the other vehicles when they need it. Apart from Luke, they are probably the most skilled mechanics among us."

"Good. Because I've never been that good with cars."

"Do you feel up for a tour of the Hotel now? That way we can call this man tomorrow and get things started quickly. I feel like we've already waited too long." To emphasize his point, Diego tapped his foot impatiently, disturbing Zorro's head on his knee.

"I think I can make it. After all, it's only a food hangover, not a real one."

Grace smiled and nodded. "I think Luke is out by the dock fiddling with something on the airboat. I'll go get him."

"Do you know where Sam is?" I asked her.

"Wherever Caleb is, I suppose."

"I think I saw them in the ballroom." Diego said, already rising.

"I'll go get them." I said.

Surprisingly enough, I'd never actually been to the ballroom. I knew it was there, of course, but most of my time at the hotel was spent either in the library or in the kitchen. It wasn't a room that was much used by the other guests. Usually, the grand doors that led into it were shut, and none of us ever really had cause to go in there. Grace hoped one day that the Hotel's ballroom would be a sought-after location for weddings and parties. If it were as run down as the rest of the Hotel, it would be a long time before that dream became a reality. Then again, this whole thing was a bit of a long shot.

The doors to the ballroom happened to be open this time. Sure enough, both Caleb and Sam were in there. They stood about a person-width apart, both of their arms up as if they were leading a young lady through the box step. Caleb doled out soothing instructions to improve upon Sam's posture and form. Slow down. Chin up. Long strides. Raise your hand; this isn't a mating dance. Sam followed each of Caleb's instructions, mirroring his movements, eyebrows furrowed in concentration. I wished I had a camera at that moment. Caleb looked like a father teaching his son how to move before his first high school formal.

I lingered in the doorway, watching them and gazing around the ballroom. It clearly had been quite grand in its heyday. Large bay windows lined the walls, and above them swung impressive crystal chandeliers that were missing a few pieces and more than a few bulbs. The walls were covered with intricate scrollwork, painted a fading gold that accented the cream-colored walls. All of these carvings led up to a ceiling that perhaps had once been decorated with paintings of cherubs and gods, but now just looked like a rainbow swirl of fading paint. The hardwood floors that perhaps had once been polished and shiny were now scuffed and slightly warped, puffing up in certain places. Restoring this to its former glory seemed a far more daunting task than the other rooms.

"Are you spying on us good sir?" Caleb's voice brought me out of my observations. I looked back at the two of them and saw that Sam had now dropped his arms firmly to his sides and was staring red-faced at the floor.

"Don't stop on my account. Looked like fun."

"Care to join us?" Caleb raised one eyebrow playfully.

"Maybe next time. For now, Diego is determined to take stock of what needs doing around here. Sam, could you help us out with that?"

"What about me?" Caleb asked, feigning annoyance at being left out.

"I was hoping maybe you and Clancy could take a look at my car. Grace told me you two are pretty good with mechanical stuff, and I suck at it. Think you could help me out?" Somehow, my voice had regressed into a softer, more appeasing tone than it usually took on. I think subconsciously that was my best effort at flirting, something I tried to do whenever I wanted something. Caleb was not fooled, but he wasn't put off by my clumsy attempt at manipulation either. Instead, he just laughed.

"Oh you devil, trying to get me to do what you want by being all cute. Well it worked. You got the keys?"

I tossed them over and he caught them with ease. "Thanks. So Sam, what do you say?"

He didn't say anything, which was not surprising. Instead he just nodded and walked past me. I guess he assumed that I would follow. Caleb came up to me chuckling.

"You know, after dance lessons I might need to give my star pupil a few lessons on etiquette."

"I don't mind. Why were you teaching him to dance anyway?"

"Because he asked me to, and well, it would be pretty selfish if I didn't share my knowledge with others. After all, not everyone had the joy of escorting multiple ladies in various coming-out parties."

That last statement was said with the heaviest of sarcasm. Even though I knew about Caleb's past from Grace, he had never actually mentioned it himself. I figured feigning ignorance was the best course of action until the subject brought itself up naturally.

"I bet you were an amazing dance partner." I said.

"Oh, believe me, I was. I'll show you sometime."

"I wouldn't. Unless you want your feet crushed."

"You don't scare me, Arthur Bean." Caleb slid past me, chuckling slightly.

Luke, Sam, and Diego all waited for me in the foyer. Diego decided we should split into teams of two. He and Luke argued that point for a bit, Luke claiming it would be faster if we all just took different parts individually, and Diego claiming that a second set of eyes never hurt anyone. Sam and I just stood there watching the back-and-forth blankly. Blank was Sam's resting face. I was still a little checked out from before. I was inclined to agree with Diego simply because having someone else with me would've prevented me from lying down on the floor and falling asleep.

Eventually Luke conceded, mostly because Diego had started to use large SAT words and he got too confused to keep arguing. Usually when that happened, when someone tried to appear smarter than him, Luke would blow up, but today he just seemed annoyed. He and I teamed up to take the bottom floor, and Diego and Sam went off to the top floor. We each had papers divided into two sections, one for "Personal Fixes" and one for "Professional Fixes."

The whole survey ended up taking over two days to compile. There were three comprehensive lists for the upstairs, and four for the downstairs. Then we branched out and made more for the various shacks, the landscape, the garages, and the exterior of the

Hotel. I kept them in a file that eventually became overstuffed with invoices, blueprints, and bills. Needless to say, the "Professional Fixes" far outnumbered the "Personal Fixes." In the end, we came to the general consensus that while we could undoubtedly help Jeff and his crew, the only things we could feasibly do on our own were things like stripping the old wallpaper and deep cleaning. Like I'd originally thought, the Hotel was just too old and too neglected. It needed a massive overhaul. Luckily, when we called Jeff three days later, he seemed entirely up for the job.

* * *

All of the guests stood on the porch watching as I drove up in the airboat with Jeff and three of his best men. There was Roscoe, a large, stone-faced man with a lumberjack beard and a plethora of tattoos. He apparently was a master carpenter and landscaper. Vince was a self-proclaimed whiz with plumbing and electrical work, and Gabe was an ethnically uncertain interior designer with bright eyes that seemed to absorb the Hotel with glee. The five of us walked up to the group on the porch. I gave a silent prayer to whatever deity was listening that the guests wouldn't scare them off.

"Everyone," I said, "This is Jeff, Roscoe, Vince, and Gabe. They'd be the supervisors of the work done here if they decide to take on the job, is that right?" I turned to Jeff for confirmation. I had no real idea how construction teams like this worked.

"That's right. They each head up a team, and I supervise. Make sure everyone has what they need and no one goes over budget. Stuff like that."

"So," Roscoe said, skepticism heavy in his voice as he regarded the Hotel and its guests, "Y'all live here or something?"

"That's correct." Grace said, stepping forward but not leaving the porch. "I am the Hotel's manager, and the rest of the people you see here are either guests or employees." The word employees sounded like a lie coming out of her mouth, but she seemed to think it would make things easier to understand for the newcomers.

"Uh-huh. And y'all want to fix up *this* place?"

"That is correct." Grace seemed to be tired of Roscoe's attitude already, but she kept her voice light and pleasant. I had a feeling she was measuring up these men, calculating what use they'd be in her goals and how to act accordingly. It was a bit shocking to see Grace in this setting, but I had known for a long time that she had become a different person. It was only once in a while that I got a glimpse of just how different.

Everyone went around introducing themselves, except Sam who stayed silent until Caleb introduced him. After that, as Diego and I gave the team a tour of the hotel, the guests dispersed. Or at least they seemed to disperse. Really they were just not-so-subtly spying on us. We could see Luke and Clancy ducking into a room as we rounded a corner, Mrs. K. busying herself with some trinket as we walked by, Sam silently following us everywhere we went. At one point, Caleb arrived and engaged Gabe in conversation about interior design, and the two of them wandered away to the library so that Caleb could show Gabe the furniture we already had.

"It's terrible, Gabriel. Really. You have to save us from our inept design aesthetic." He placed a hand on the small of Gabe's back as they walked by, which made Gabe blush in a good way. I smiled.

By the time we finished showing them everything, including the shacks out back and the rest of the land, Roscoe had grown more and more skeptical, whereas both Jeff and Vince had looks of strained optimism. That seemed to be a poorer diagnosis than Roscoe's clear disbelief that this job could ever get done.

Mrs. K. set out a lunch feast for the guests and the crew in the kitchen. I could tell that Roscoe and Vince had never seen anything quite like it in their lives. Mrs. K. tended to cook on the Middle-Eastern side, embracing ingredients and spices most commonly found in those areas. Roscoe and Vince, who both had confessed to have never even left the state of Louisiana, seemed flabbergasted by the spread. They stood there in front of the table as the rest of us settled down to eat. Their eyes darted wildly from dish to dish. Eventually Mrs. K. had to give them an in-depth description of each plate before they even dared to serve themselves.

As soon as Jeff sat down, Kiki began to pepper him with questions about Ms. May and his business. As it was with everyone,

Jeff was absolutely smitten by the boy. It was only after Francis forced Kiki away from the table for afternoon studying that we finally got a diagnosis on the Hotel.

"I'd say it's pretty much hopeless." Roscoe said.

"I'm not so sure about that." Gabe, sitting next to Caleb, said. "This house has massive potential. With the right design . . . well it could be something magnificent."

"But before you even get to that, we'd have to fix everything that's wrong with it." Vince said.

"And there's a lot wrong with it." Roscoe stuffed an oversized piece of chicken in his mouth for emphasis.

"What exactly are the issues that you seem to think are so hopeless?" Grace's voice sounded kind and understanding, inquisitive even, but I could hear the hint of sharpness that lingered beneath the surface.

Roscoe made to answer but Gabe beat him to it. "Maybe Jeff should answer."

Vince nodded at the suggestion. Roscoe just shrugged and continued to stuff his face. He was a very unattractive eater. He ate quickly, shoving food in his mouth like he thought someone would steal it, and he didn't close his mouth when he chewed. Even though I somewhat agreed with him on the hopelessness of the Hotel, I was finding that I didn't much like him. Gabe seemed very nice and already had a lot of big plans for the place. Vince, although slightly awkward and maybe a little bit too interested in the ladies of the Hotel, didn't seem to be a bad guy. Roscoe, though, didn't seem to care much about anything. It was as if he'd been dragged there against his will. Maybe he was more like the people in that town than I'd thought.

"Well," Jeff started, "I think the biggest problem from what we can see is the mold and the sinking foundation."

"Mold?" More than one of us echoed.

"That's right. Louisiana is naturally damp. That breeds mold even in the most secure of homes. But this place is old and also in the middle of the bayou. The ground beneath it and the air around it is very moist, and it's been neglected for so long that that moisture has been allowed to seep in. Unfortunately, once mold really takes a hold, the only way to fix it is to get rid of the affected areas."

"And what are the affected areas?" Diego asked.

Jeff grimaced a little. "More than you'd like, I'm afraid. All of the shacks out back are beyond repair. My suggestion for them would just be to tear them down and start anew. But the real issue here is whether or not the basic structure of the place is sound. We already know that the foundation has sunk significantly on one side, but as far as mold infestation goes . . . well we're not sure. We can see a lot of mold on the exterior, but there might be a chance—"

"A very slim chance." Roscoe said.

Jeff nodded, unfazed by the interruption. "Yes. A slim chance that the basic structure can survive. If that's the case, we could strip away all in the infected areas, basically down to the bare bones, and start fresh. But if the foundation is affected by the mold . . ."

"We'd have to tear it down." I finished his sentence for him. It was what I'd been afraid of. The faces of despair around the table seemed to reveal that many of the other guests had also suspected something devastating like this. Nonetheless, we had all been hoping for the best.

"Not to mention y'all have been breathing mold for God knows how long. It's a wonder you're not getting asthma attacks every damn day." Roscoe leaned forward and helped himself to some more rice.

"Our health is just fine. Thank you for your concern." Grace said. I looked over at her. Her hands were clenched into fists.

"How would we know if this is really a lost cause or not?" Caleb asked. To the right of him, Sam's face had gone bright red, shaking as if he were just barely holding in his emotions. Next to me, Luke also vibrated. I gently placed my hand on top of his and squeezed it a little.

Jeff's face revealed how badly he felt for us. I found myself feeling so grateful that we'd met him at the fair. It was rare that I felt immediate trust in another person. But Jeff was so genuine in everything that he did that I could already tell that if I let him, the two of us could become pretty good friends.

"I can see how much this place means to you lot," Jeff said, shooting Roscoe a warning glance when he opened his mouth to say something. "We'd have to do a bit of work to get to the core of the problem. That would take maybe a week, tops. After that, we'll be able to give you a better assessment." He paused, taking time to look at all of us in the face. "I promise that we'll do the best that we can."

"That's very kind of you, dear." Mrs. K. said. Really very kind.

"And if it isn't a lost cause," Grace said, "What exactly can we expect in terms of time and money?"

"Well the money is going take some work on our part." Jeff said. "We need to go home and work up some plans and budgets and whatnot. I don't exactly feel comfortable laying out a precise number right now, but I can tell you that it isn't going to be cheap. As for the time, if the best happens, which I truly hope it does, then I can't see the project being finished in less than nine months. More, if you want us to do the landscaping and rebuild those shacks out there. It could be up to a year and a half easily."

"And would we be able to live here while all this is happening?" That seemed to be the elephant in the room. As soon as Grace asked it, every one of the guests' attentions piqued and their attention zoomed in on Jeff. I knew already that if this was going to make living in the Hotel impossible, Grace might throw away the idea completely. We didn't have anywhere else to go.

"It might be uncomfortable." Jeff said. "But if that's what you guys want to do, we aren't going to kick you out. Besides, Arthur said that a few of you are handy. We'd be glad for the free labor."

Everyone laughed at that. It made me happy to see that, even though everything seemed a lot bleaker than it had when we had woken up that morning, there was still some sense of humor rippling through us. It seemed like Jeff had won the guests over, if only somewhat. He and the rest of his associates left soon after lunch. The goodbyes the guests gave were much more cordial than the greetings had been. I noticed Caleb slip something into Gabe's hand as he shook it.

Luke volunteered to take them across the water, so I walked over to Caleb on the porch.

"New love interest? I gotta say I'm a little hurt."

Caleb laughed. "Oh I haven't given up on you just yet. But he's interesting . . . don't you think?"

"Sure. Handsome. Creative. What's not to like?"

"My thoughts exactly. And he seemed interested. Which is more than I usually get from my flirting."

I laughed. "Well I'm not sure if the Hotel is the best place to meet guys."

"Maybe not. But maybe Gabriel will prove you wrong."

"I certainly hope so."

Caleb turned to look at me then. He had this kind of cool, calculating expression that was so far from his normal look of smooth indifference. Then, slowly, a grin broke out across his face. He gave me a rather violent smack on the shoulder.

"You're a good guy, Arthur Bean. A damn good guy. I wasn't so sure about you at first. I'm not sure that you're so sure about yourself. But I see you now. And you're a good guy."

My face felt hot at the compliment. I certainly didn't feel like a damn good guy, but I was more than glad that Caleb thought that was who I was. Luckily, I didn't have a chance to respond to Caleb's praise. I imagined that if I had, it would've come out as blubbering and nonsensical as I felt in that moment.

"Arthur, my boy." Thadeus said, walking toward us on the porch. "Your sister wants to talk to you."

"Which one?" I asked.

Thadeus seemed confused for a moment, and then laughed at

himself. "Gosh sometimes I forget that you and Bea are related." He let himself fall into chuckles for a little longer before he straightened up and said, "Grace wants to talk to you. She's in the library."

I nodded, thanking him, and made my way inside. Just inside the foyer, next to the doorway, Clancy and Sam stood in a darkened corner, Sam backed against the wall and Clancy in front of him, one hand placed firmly on her hip. The image almost looked like a bully threatening the school nerd for his lunch money. But then I noticed that Clancy's free hand hovered just next to Sam's. They weren't touching. I'd never seen anyone touch Sam since that one time in the garage. But they were almost touching. It was the kind of closeness where you could feel the warmth coming off the other person, where the electricity of their skin made your hairs stand on edge. It was shocking to me to see Sam allow someone else to be so close to him. Even Caleb didn't get that privilege.

As soon as they noticed me, Clancy's hand retracted lazily into her jeans pocket. Sam shrunk somewhat further back into the wall. It was that moment when I knew I'd just walked into some private conversation. Awkward, ambiguous silence followed.

"Uh, hey. What's up?" I asked dumbly.

"Sam's nervous about that big guy." Clancy said plainly. I hadn't expected that she'd actually answer me honestly. I also hadn't known that Sam was capable of having a conversation at all, let alone with Clancy. Up until this point, I'd hardly seen Sam and Clancy interact at all. I had thought that Caleb was his only confidant.

"You mean Roscoe?"

"Yes."

"Oh . . . I mean he's definitely not the most pleasant guy in the world, but . . ."

"He has a tattoo, Arthur. A bad one."

"What kind of tattoo?" Clancy had a number of tattoos herself, so it seemed weird to me that she would care about Roscoe's ink.

"Slave flag." Sam said quietly.

"The Confederate flag?" I asked. My stomach was already starting to churn, but I found it hard to believe that after everything I knew about Jeff, he'd have hired someone with *that* tattooed on his body.

Sam simply nodded in response.

"I didn't notice it . . ." I said more to myself than either of them.

"Sam said his sleeve moved up when he was reaching across the table for food and he saw it."

"Okay. Okay. Um . . . I'll call Jeff and ask him about it." I said.

"Yeah. That's okay, right, Sam? You liked Jeff, didn't you?"

Sam nodded, but he didn't seem convinced.

"Trust me, Sam. If that guy believes in that kind of stuff, then he'll never step foot in this place again." I promised.

"Arthur?" Grace had come out of the library looking for me. Because of Sam's distress and what he'd told me, I'd forgotten that Grace was waiting for me.

"Hey. Sorry. I'm coming. You two okay?" I asked Clancy.

"We'll be fine. Thanks."

When I approached Grace, she jutted her chin in the direction of Sam and Clancy. "What was all that about?"

"Sam was just saying how he has a bad feeling about Roscoe." I decided to leave out the part about the flag until I could call Jeff and see if he knew anything about it. I really wanted to give Jeff the benefit of the doubt. I was inclined to trust his judgment on who he hired.

"Yes, well I think we all felt kind of skeptical about him. A feeling that appeared to be mutual." She settled herself in her usual chair, and I took a spot on the love seat that I usually shared with Beatrice or Diego.

"So what did you want to talk about?"

"I wanted to thank you."

"Really? For what?"

"For being here. And for helping us."

"Oh. No problem. Although I'm not sure how much help I'm being. So far all I've done is have a group of guys come here and basically tell us it's gonna take a lot of time and money to fix this place, if they can even fix it at all."

Grace smiled. "You know, Arthur, I've always felt a close connection to you. Even when I was a child, I always felt like you were so much more than a brother to me."

The fact that I didn't vomit on the carpet right then and there was a miracle only one of the saints could've produced. I willed my face to keep passive and my heart to stop beating so damn loudly.

Grace continued. "Our father was a nice man, but by the time I'd come around . . . well he was kind of done, wasn't he? I don't mean that he was cruel or neglectful. Just that he wasn't always present. Probably a big part of him died when your mother did."

I nodded, but I wasn't even sure if what she'd said was a question or a statement.

"And my mother . . . despite having three kids, she is just one of those people who never should've had children. She's selfish and spiteful and . . . well you know." Her face went dark for a second. Then she shook her head, expelling images of Mari from her mind. "I imagine my childhood would've been quite lonely had it not been for you."

"But . . . but I wasn't even there." It's true. Except for holidays and birthdays, I'd hardly been around Grace when she was growing up.

"But you *were* there. In all the ways that really count. And I just wanted to thank you for being here now. I'm sorry. I know how these kinds of deep conversations make you feel uncomfortable."

I laughed shallowly at this. Although it was true, it was not the emotionally raw nature of the conversation that was making me uncomfortable.

"Grace, I . . ." my voice had taken on that choked, stuttered quality that came before crying. I had been afraid ever since I came to the Hotel that a moment like this might come, a moment where my greatest secret, pretty much my only secret, would be revealed. At that time, I felt certain that Grace knew. How she knew, or how she felt about that fact I couldn't be certain. All I knew was that I felt far too many emotions to even begin to try and explain myself. I was terrified, frustrated, furious, hopeful, regretful, maybe even a little relieved. But before I could let those emotions spill forth in tears, Grace held up a hand to stop me from speaking.

"You don't have to say anything, Arthur. You don't have to apologize, and you don't have to explain yourself. For anything." Grace's voice was steady, and I could've told myself that she was simply talking about my absence as a brother. But something deep inside of me told me that she knew everything there was to know, and she didn't expect anything from me except for what she'd already asked: for me to be there.

If I were to have confessed my secret to her at that moment, it would've been messy and ill-timed. I wouldn't have been able to control myself enough to fully explain why I'd let things play out the way they had. So I took what Grace said at face value, and I allowed myself some more time to try and figure out everything that I'd shoved down for so many years.

So I just said the three words that too often go unsaid, or are uttered for the wrong reasons, but in that moment were the three most genuine and true words I'd ever spoken.

"I love you, Grace."

Grace nodded, smiling in that soft, knowing way. "I love you too, Arthur."

For the first time in my life, I let myself see how beautiful Grace was. It amazed me, and still does, that something like her could've been brought into existence because of me. I'd never done anything so wonderful. I have never done anything so brilliant since. And I knew that I would do anything to make her dream for the Hotel a reality. If I couldn't give her the truth, at least I could give her that.

Surprising her and me, I reached forward and pulled her into a hug. She tensed for a moment. Then she laughed and wrapped her hands around my waist, patting my back in the way a mom burps a baby. I could've stayed like that forever, and would have, if her phone hadn't rung. She pulled away from me. I caught a glimpse of the screen, but the name wasn't in English. It wasn't even written in letters that I could recognize. Grace smiled at me before she walked out the library, flipping the phone open and greeting whoever it was on the other line. I stayed there a little out of breath, wondering who else Grace had in her life who wasn't here.

"Why is this so hard for you?" Thia asked.

We were in a coffee shop just outside of campus. Usually it was crawling with grads and undergrads sipping espresso and shoving their faces into books or computers. The baristas were those friendly hipster types who treated each customer like they were some close childhood friend. Unless someone didn't tip. In that case, that customer would get drilled with passive aggressive stares and slightly off coffee drinks until they felt compelled to leave. Thia and I did not usually do our work in coffee shops. We didn't even go to the library often. We were both too susceptible to the stress of others to do any sort of meaningful work in public.

But Thia had said that we should show this kid a normal day in a college student's life, and that, she claimed, always started with a cup of coffee. It didn't for either of us, but it should for him, apparently.

Thia had signed me up to be a freshman mentor with her as kind of a joke. Although I think she actually liked the idea of some impressionable frosh hanging on her every word. I was slightly afraid she might play some kind of practical joke on her mentees, like convincing them that everyone jumped naked into the Union Square fountain on New Year's Eve. But Thia actually became one of the most sought-after senior mentors of the bunch. She was genuine and honest with the participants in a way that they hadn't heard before. I got it. Freshman orientation was a joke of idealistic, propagandistic dribble that left out a lot of the nittier and grittier aspects of adjusting to college life. I could imagine why Thia's straightforward advice was so popular.

I, on the other hand, had had only two mentees, both of whom had requested a new mentor after our first meeting. I'd already said that I got tongue-tied around people I didn't know. For the most part, I didn't have any pearls of wisdom to bestow upon freshmen. My college life was far from typical. When they asked questions about where to get free condoms, or what was the best time to avoid the rush at the dining halls, I could only come back with answers like "I buy my condoms at Duane Reade," or "I've never eaten in the dining halls."

So when I'd received notice that I had a new mentee seeking my futile guidance, Thia had offered to come with me. I'd told her that if she were there, then I'd probably just let her do all the talking. Then the freshman would want her as a mentor instead of me. But Thia insisted that she would merely guide, not interfere in any way. Besides, she said, she was meeting a friend nearby in a couple of hours, so my victim and I would be left alone soon enough. When I asked her who she was meeting, she just shrugged and said, "No one special."

"I'm just not good with new people." I said, picking at the lid of my coffee cup.

"You were good with me."

"Actually, I think you'll remember that you were good with me, and I was a bumbling mess. Not everyone's as understanding as you."

She laughed and kissed my cheek, squeezing my arm as she did. "That's true, but I thought that you were just so taken aback by my beauty that your brain just exploded a little."

"Yeah well that probably didn't help." I checked my watch. The freshman was fifteen minutes late. "How long am I obligated to wait?"

"Why, you got somewhere to be?"

"There's probably homework that I should do." It was a lame excuse. We were both deep in the throes of senioritis and were getting through our classes entirely on bullshit and charm.

"If you really hate this mentoring thing so much, why not just take your name off the list?" Thia took a long sip of her hot chocolate. Thia did not drink coffee. She didn't eat or drink anything that she didn't immediately think was delicious. She had enough natural energy to not need caffeine to get her through the day.

"Because I'm a lazy, masochistic loser who would rather suffer than walk across campus."

"But you love walking."

"Yeah I do."

Thia rolled her eyes. "Why don't we wait another ten minutes, and if he doesn't show up, we'll go get donuts and watch joggers trip over stuff in the park."

"I thought you had to meet someone." Just as I said it, an obvious freshman with wandering eyes opened the door to the coffee shop. Spotting me in the outfit I said I'd be wearing, he started waving enthusiastically. Thia just laughed and gave my butt a small tap as I stood to greet him.

Arthur? Arthur Bean?

"Huh?" I looked up from my coffee cup, startled. I'd been up all night the night before thinking about my conversation with Grace. Getting lost in thought in public spaces had always been a flaw of mine.

"You okay?" Roscoe asked, sitting down in the seat opposite me. We were in the diner where Kiki, Beatrice, and I had gotten our picnic on Veterans Day. I'd remembered that the waitress had been kind to us and given us extra cake. It seemed like a safe place to have a meeting like this. Unfortunately for me, when I walked in, the waitress from before was not there, and I recognized a number of the customers from the angry crowd in front of the Ferris wheel. I had been keeping my head down ever since.

"Yeah, sorry. Just didn't get too much sleep last night."

Roscoe shouted out an order for coffee and a slice of blueberry pie to the counter. "You not eating anything?"

"Nope. Mrs. K. keeps us well fed."

Roscoe laughed at this. It was the first time I'd seen him smile. He had a nice smile. It didn't match the rest of his face. "Yeah I bet. Thought I was going to go into a food coma after that spread. Never had food like that before. Course Gabe knew every dish."

I nodded. "Glad you liked it."

Roscoe waited until the waitress brought him his pie and coffee before he spoke again. "Gotta say I was a little surprised when Jeff told me you wanted to meet."

I held back a snort. It had not been my idea to meet Roscoe. I had called Jeff that morning to talk about the tattoo, but Jeff had insisted that Roscoe explain himself. He wouldn't say why, but my possibly unwarranted trust of Jeff led me to agree. Now I was regretting it. Not only was I in an uncomfortable place, I was also with uncomfortable people.

"Yeah, well I wanted to talk to you about something."

"Yeah I figured as much. Look, if this is about me not being so supportive of y'all's little renovation scheme—"

"It's not about that." I said quickly. This guy really rubbed me the wrong way. I was ready to peg him as a Confederate-loving, slavery-nostalgic lunatic and call it a day. But I promised Jeff I'd hear Roscoe out. If I stormed off right then, the chances of us fixing the Hotel went down severely.

"Okay. So what's it about?" He took a large bite out of his blue-berry pie, shoving almost half of the thing into his mouth.

"You have a Confederate flag tattoo on your arm."

Roscoe paused in his chewing for just a moment before nodding and swallowing. "I do at that. I ain't proud of it."

I blinked. "What?"

"I said I ain't proud of it. But I reckon you wanna know more than that."

"I guess I would." The conversation was not going the way I'd expected. I felt all of my indignation and fury begin to deflate.

"I got people in my family tree. People who fought in the Civil War, as Confederates. And people who owned slaves. Some were . . . good owners I guess, and some weren't. But I guess there's no such thing as a good owner. In the end they were all bad people." He took another bite of pie and chewed it slowly.

"Anyway, as a kid I didn't know they were bad people. It's kind of ridiculous, now that I know better. But in schools down here and stuff, we learn about the Civil War in such a different way. My whole family thought that our ancestors were heroes and patriots and all that bullshit. We thought the Civil War was about preserving southern freedom and culture. Slavery was hardly even mentioned. It wasn't until I got put away that I really got some sense knocked into me."

"You were in jail?" It wasn't surprising, but I just wanted to be clear.

"Yessir. Twice actually. First time around I fell in with some bad people because my pops told me they'd keep me safe. Second time around I got put on library duty with a black guy, we became friends, and then he got jumped by those bad people from my first time around. Didn't even make it to the hospital before he died. Spent the rest of my time there reading and trying to figure myself out."

Roscoe sighed. I thought I saw a hint of moisture lining the bottom of his eyes. "It ain't no excuse that I waited until a friend got murdered to find out what was what, but that's just how it happened for me. As for the tattoos, I ain't got no money to get them removed. I wouldn't even if I did."

"Why?"

"I was who I was and now I am who I am. My family don't talk to me because I started to argue against 'em, so I use my tattoos to remind me of how messed up I was. It's good to remember that. I mean, it's a struggle for me now, with so many people in the world. When I first met Gabe, I felt that kind of stupid hate people feel for someone like him. But it just takes one look at my tattoos, at my past, to remind me that what he is don't say anything to *who* he is."

"Damn." I laughed a little. "I was about ready to fight you before all this."

"Yeah, I don't blame you. Must be hard seeing something like that. You had family who were slaves?"

I probably should have been offended by the assumption. But it seemed to me that the way Roscoe worked things out for himself was by being curious and asking questions that other people thought shouldn't be asked. If that helped him to be a better person, I wasn't going to turn around and tell him it was wrong.

"Don't know. Probably. I've never looked it up, honestly. But you're right. I don't like seeing something like that." I gestured to his arm.

"I'll try and keep it covered up around y'all then. It ain't no trouble. And I'm sorry. I shoulda thought to explain it myself before you guys had to start worryin'."

"It's okay." I could hardly believe how civil this whole thing was going, but it made me feel better on so many levels. For one thing, it showed that my faith in Jeff's judgment was not misplaced. For another, it showed me that Roscoe, though doubtful of our ability to succeed in renovating the Hotel, was a person I could trust. There weren't a lot of people like him, people who started off as one thing and then, against all odds, became something completely different. And for the better at that. It couldn't have been easy for him. He already said he'd lost his family.

"Does your family still live around here?"

"Yep. They live in the next town over, but it's the same county as this one. My dad is the head of the school board. He also runs that little museum over there."

I choked on my coffee, spitting up a bit onto my white shirt.

"You all right?" Roscoe said.

I coughed again. "Uh, yeah. Just . . . is he a bald guy? Big beard?"

"Yeah that's him. Why?"

"Oh . . . I was in the museum a while back waiting for my brother to pick me up, and a man came up to talk to me. Think it might've been your dad."

Roscoe didn't respond immediately. Instead he finished his pie, chasing spare crumbs of crust around the plate. His brow was furrowed as if he was struggling with some deep thoughts. Just as the silence started to make me feel antsy, he took a large gulp of his coffee and said, "Is that so?"

"Um yeah. Could've not been him though."

"No, it was probably him."

The conversation ground to a halt. We both sat there with empty cups of coffee and darting eyes, until finally Roscoe coughed and extended his hand for me to shake. It was an awkward kind of gesture, but I couldn't blame him. I had no idea how to end this odd-paced, slightly immersive meeting.

As we left the restaurant, Roscoe cracked his neck and said, "Can I walk you to your car?"

"Oh, um, it's right there." Caleb and Clancy had done enough with my car that it was drivable, although still pretty dinged up. I'd parked it right in front of the restaurant where I could see it out of the windows.

"Smart move." Roscoe said. "Well, Jeff and the rest of us are working hard to figure out what to do with your place. Hopefully we'll have some good news for you soon. Though I doubt it."

I laughed. "Thanks, man. I'll see you around."

"Yeah. Get home safe."

An unsettling feeling began to worm its way around my stomach at his words. They were innocent enough, something you said to a coworker at the end of the day or to a friend getting into a taxi after a night out. Roscoe had proven himself to me. At least I thought he had. He had been honest and forthright about his past and his failings. I thought that was admirable. Not all of us could be so straightforward about our own downfalls, past or present. But as soon as I had mentioned Roscoe's father, he had shut up like an oyster protecting its pearl. And now, he was essentially telling me to watch my back.

I just nodded and got in the car, my hands shaking as I stuck my keys into the ignition. The whole drive back, my eyes kept darting to the rearview mirror, searching for something I couldn't quite pinpoint. My most paranoid self was convinced that I was being followed by the Klan, ready to lynch me the moment I stepped out of my car. Maybe Roscoe's father was a grand wizard or something heinous like that. But my more reasonable side said that the idea was absurd, that no one really cared about me even if they cared about my skin, and, if anything, they were just glad every time I left town. They probably felt the relief that other people feel at successfully removing a dark stain from an otherwise pristine white shirt. That thought didn't exactly make me feel any better, but it definitely did help me get out of my car and walk to the airboat without breaking into a panicked sprint.

My stress must have showed on my face when I arrived back at the Hotel. Beatrice and Clancy sat on the porch wrapped up in blankets and sipping some hot, spiced apple cider that Mrs. K. had been fond of making lately. They were giggling about something. The sight warmed my heart. Beatrice was probably closest to Clancy out of everyone else at the Hotel. Despite their pretty wide age gap, they seemed to understand each other in that deep, mischievous way that only best friends do.

When they saw me coming up to the porch, their smiling faces dropped and were replaced with looks of concern.

"Arthur?" Beatrice said slowly. "Are you okay?" She had been worried about me going into town alone that morning. She had even walked me to the airboat, trying to convince me to take her. Clearly the incident at the Ferris wheel still shook her.

"Oh yeah, everything's fine."

Thia's voice entered my head. *You're a terrible liar, Arthur Bean.*

"You're lying." Clancy said. "Was it that bastard Roscoe? What did he do to you? We should've sent Diego or Caleb or someone . . ."

"Because I'm black?" I'd meant it to come out as a joke, but it sounded a lot more strained and serious than I'd intended.

"Of course because you're black. The guy has a Confederate flag tattooed on his arm, dummy."

"He *what*? Clancy?" Beatrice's eyes had gone wide. Apparently that little detail had stayed a secret between Sam, Clancy, and me.

"I didn't want to worry anyone. Arthur said he'd figure it out." Clancy looked guilty. No one really liked to lie to their best friend.

"Arthur." Beatrice said. "How could you go off and be alone

with someone like that in a town like that? You should've taken me with you!"

Her voice was escalating to the point of shouting. Above us, a window opened and someone poked their head out, but I couldn't see who. Luke came skidding around the corner. Apparently he'd been on the other side of the house.

"What's wrong?" He said, fists clenched like he was ready to fight someone.

"Nothing, buddy."

"Arthur!" Beatrice said.

"Look, Bea." I knelt down in front of her so we were face-to-face rather than me looking down on her. "I know you're worried, but really everything was fine. Roscoe is actually a good guy. He just had a bad past. I can explain everything in more detail later, I promise, but right now I really just want to get inside and have some of that apple cider you two are drinking."

Beatrice hadn't been looking at me throughout all this, but once I finished talking she looked up at me sulkily. "You're treating me like a kid."

"Am not. I said I'd tell you everything, didn't I?"

"Yeah . . ."

"Well then, I'm not treating you like a kid. I don't even really treat kids like kids."

She laughed because she knew it was true. My interactions with Kiki were enough to prove that. Then again, Kiki was a kind of odd adult-kid hybrid, so it was easier to treat him like a man far older than he was.

"Fine. I trust you." She smiled a little bit, but then her face got hard again. "But if you end up doing something stupid, I'll kill you."

"Understood." I said. I stood back up, feeling my bones creak and crack. It was a strange reminder of my age that I still wasn't completely used to. "Now, where's that cider?"

"I'll get some too." Luke said, walking up to the front door and waiting for me.

146

* * *

J eff, Roscoe, and Vince spent the next few days tearing up stuff and making a whole lot of noise with not a whole lot of answers. Every time one of us asked how things were looking, the most we'd get was a sympathetic glance and a deflective answer. On the sixth day, Jeff asked if he could meet with us. Grace, Diego, and I met with Jeff in the library to discuss prices and timelines while Roscoe and Vince went around with tools for one final check. I think all of us were more than a little relieved at how quickly it was all moving along. Waiting was certainly not my strong suit. Impatience seemed to be a trait shared by my fellow guests as well. If we were doomed, we might as well know sooner rather than later.

The prices were high, so high that I felt like my eyes might bug out of my head like in Looney Tunes. Jeff looked extremely apologetic about that fact. He said they had tried to figure out a way to make things cheaper, but there was really no way around it, especially not if we wanted the quality that Grace had described. Grace wasn't fazed at all. She just nodded.

"We are willing to pay the price to get this place up and running."

Jeff raised his eyebrows skeptically. He'd clearly had enough dealings with customers to feel a certain distrust for anyone who didn't complain about money. Even if we couldn't do a thing to change it, he had clearly been expecting at least an attempt at negotiation. He quickly assumed a look of passive pleasantness and moved on with the other logistics.

I was still struggling with Grace's complete lack of concern about money. During the first two weeks, I'd been so curious about how everything in the Hotel got done with such apparent ease. Mrs. K., for example, always had an endless supply of ingredients, but no one ever went to town to get them. On top of that, I severely doubted whether the little Stop and Shop had some of the exotic ingredients Mrs. K. was so fond of. It wasn't until one of my more restless nights that I was able to finally solve the mystery of the magically appearing food.

I'd been staring mindlessly out my window late one night when I saw two shapes making their way down to the docks. They were only illuminated by one of those electric camping lights, but by silhouette alone I could tell it was Mrs. K. and one of the other women, though I couldn't tell who. They met another figure on the dock, someone who had come up in their own speedboat. Then the two nameless figures began unloading boxes upon boxes of stuff while Mrs. K. bent over to examine the contents of each. The next morning, we had a fresh supply of food.

But everything else went unsolved. I had tried dropping hints now and then about our financial security, but Grace just brushed it off. I eventually got tired of asking. I guess Jeff learned quicker than I did.

Halfway through Jeff's explanation of the timeline, there was a scuffling sound outside the library, then a bump, a yelp, and the sound of pounding footsteps scurrying off in different directions. Roscoe and Vince entered the library chuckling a little. Vince held Kiki's hand. Francis stood behind them in the doorway.

"We caught a couple of your friends eavesdropping. Scared 'em half to death when we came in through the front doors." Roscoe said, plopping himself down on the chair that was usually Thadeus's throne.

"Luke tripped and fell trying to get away." Kiki said, clambering into Vince's lap once he'd sat down next to Roscoe. "I hope he's all right."

"Luke is just about the clumsiest person I've ever met." Grace said. "He'll be fine."

"You're one to talk." I said teasingly.

"I, sir, am a dancer! By nature, we are graceful and lithe creatures." Grace pretended to be affronted, placing a hand on her chest like a woman scandalized.

"Didn't you bump into the doorway when we came in just now?"

"Oh, shut up." Grace laughed.

"So Kiki, what have you been up to?" It wasn't that I was surprised to see Kiki with Vince. Nor was I surprised to see him be so friendly. Kiki was just that way. He trusted everyone immediately. And why shouldn't he? He was a beautiful white boy with bright baby-blue eyes and wispy blond hair. He didn't have much to fear from this world just yet. But my newly emerging paternal instincts forced me to check just in case anyway.

"I was helping Mr. Vince and Mr. Roscoe look for mold. It really is fascinating stuff. They gave me this fun mask and everything! I looked like one of those doctors doing surgery. They said I could keep it."

"That's cool. Maybe we can use it as a prop in one of your plays or something. So," I said, turning to the men, "Did you find anything?"

Roscoe nodded. "But we're lucky. It seems like most of the structural damage is limited to the veranda and balconies since they are the ones most exposed to the elements. And they can be easily replaced without damaging the rest of the place. There are a few trouble spots inside the structure itself. The foundation, luckily, has stopped sinking, so with some creativity we might be able to have your hotel leveled. We should be able to fix everything without bringing the whole place crashing down."

"Yes," Grace said, "We would very much like to avoid any crashing down."

Roscoe laughed. "You got it."

"What about the plumbing, Vince?" Jeff asked. "Doable?"

Vince shrugged. "Oh yeah it's doable. I mean, this place is old school, but a lot of it's still functioning exactly the way it should be. I'd like to go in and reinforce what I can, but it shouldn't be too bad. Electricity is what has me worried, honestly."

"How so?" Diego asked.

"Well like I said, this place is old school. Clearly it used to be all gas lights and candles when it was first in use. But then modern days came, and, well, it seemed like the electricity was just sort of shoved in there in a hurry. There's a lotta wires that are wearing down, and that kind of stuff is more dangerous than mold, if you catch my drift."

"You think there's a risk of fire?" I said.

"Oh no." Kiki said.

"There could be. But never fear. Now that I'm here I can get in there and make sure that everything's up to snuff. I'd also like to set up a generator for you guys at some point later on. You're kind of off the grid here. Wouldn't be a bad idea to have some back-up power just in case."

"That would be lovely, Vince. Thank you." Grace said.

"Right so, if that's the case then the preliminary logistics we've set shouldn't change that much. Maybe a little bit more time and money for electrical work, but otherwise . . ." Jeff flipped through some papers, marking a few things with a red pen. Then he looked up and smiled at us. "Great. I'd like to get to work as early as next week. We'll need some time to gather everything we need and check in with our laborers, but the sooner the better really. Winter's coming. I'd like to get a majority of the outside work done before the weather gets too unbearable."

"Yes, sooner is better for us as well." Grace said.

"And feel free to put us to work as well. We're eager to help." Diego said. Grace shot him a smile.

"Oh don't worry. There'll be plenty for you to do." Roscoe said.

There was a brief pause as everyone let the task we were about to undertake sink in. There was a modicum of disbelief mixed in with the excitement and relief that buzzed around our heads. I myself still couldn't quite grasp what was about to happen. I had been so sure that it was a pipe dream, a completely ludicrous scheme. Life was like that a lot of the time. It always threw you for a loop.

I walked Jeff, Roscoe, and Vince out with Kiki still attached to Vince's hand. Jeff held me back for a moment as Roscoe climbed into the airboat and Vince said goodbye to Kiki, showing him a secret handshake that he appeared to make up on the spot.

"Arthur, I just want you to know that all my people who'll be working on the project are good. I know you were concerned about Roscoe, and I get it. But you gotta trust me on this one. They may be rough around the edges, but they are good."

"I trust you Jeff," I said, clapping him on the shoulder. "I have to say, you have no idea how happy you've made my family and friends."

"I'm glad to do it. You guys seem tight. It's nice."

"Thanks. So I'll see you next week?"

"Monday morning, bright and early."

I gave Kiki a piggyback ride back to the Hotel, hopping over puddles and sending him into fits of giggles with my Seabiscuit impersonation. As soon as we got to the veranda, Francis lifted Kiki off my back.

"All right young man, I think that's enough distraction for today."

"You're no fun, Francis." Kiki whined.

"Oh really? We were going to continue reading that Lincoln biography that you've been so interested in. But perhaps we'll continue our math lesson instead."

"No! No! I want to read the Lincoln. Math can wait."

I laughed to myself that Kiki's idea of fun was reading a seven-hundred-page biography on Lincoln. I followed Francis and Kiki into the foyer, about to head up to my room for a nap. I didn't make it far. A pair of arms reached forth from the dining room doors and tugged me inside. I stumbled, struggling to regain my balance, when strong hands stood me upright.

"So, word on the street is that everything is okay with the renovations?" Mrs. K. stood in front of me, flanked on either side by Beatrice and Sam. Thadeus stood off to the side with Luke and Caleb behind me.

"Yep. Everything's good."

"So . . ." Luke said. "Party's still on?"

I grinned. "Yep. Party's still on."

A soft cheer went up from everyone in the room, except Sam who just smiled. Grace's birthday party had been postponed because of the stress everyone felt about the renovations. Mrs. K. had been convinced that it simply wasn't time for anything like a celebration. Everyone else was inclined to agree. On the actual day of Grace's birthday, she'd whipped up a special brunch, and we gave small gifts. Most of them were lame and not the real thing. Even then we were still planning to throw her a big bash, so most of us were saving our real presents for that. I gave her a book of photographs of lumberjacks in their best flannel that I'd been planning to give her for Christmas as a joke.

Grace had also received a mystery package on the day of her birthday. She'd gone into town to collect the mail from our post office box like she did every week. When she returned, she had her arms full of the usual things: junk, bills, a *New Yorker* magazine, and the usual padded envelope that I had started to suspect was stuffed full with cash. But this time she also had a large box wrapped in rose-gold wrapping paper. I had been coming out of the kitchen with a sandwich in hand when I caught her trying to quickly scurry up the stairs.

"What's that?" I'd said.

She startled so badly that she dropped the box and the envelopes. I went to pick up the padded envelope when she lunged forward, snatching it from underneath my palm.

"It's nothing." She'd said before running off.

When she came back down that afternoon, she acted as if nothing had happened. So did I. The party, and my own niggling worries, kept getting postponed.

Now that the weight of worry had been lifted from us, party planning went into overdrive. It was the perfect way to celebrate Grace's birthday and to honor the start of the long-awaited renovations.

Mrs. K. had planned an elaborate menu of all of Grace's favorite foods, including the soufflés she'd been practicing in secret. Caleb was in charge of music, and the playlist included some of Grace's favorites, a few classical ballroom-style songs, and hints from the top forty. Beatrice and Luke were doing decorations in the ballroom, which meant an eclectic mix of tasteful blue-and-silver decor and props that seemed like they belonged at a six-year-old's birthday party. Thadeus, Diego, and I had set up a movie projector in the library so that the festivities from the day could continue long into the night. And Clancy and Sam were put in charge of keeping Grace out of the way long enough for us to get everything done.

Grace probably suspected something. She hadn't seemed disappointed by the lack of a party on her actual birthday, but she had seemed somewhat surprised, even if it was just the faintest hint. I had a feeling that birthdays and holidays were somewhat of a big deal for the guests, which made sense. From what I now knew about most of them, they hadn't had much chance for celebration in their former lives.

Caleb always said that holidays in his family were more about religion and repentance than they were about celebration. On Easter he had to go to confession for at least two hours; on Christmas his family dragged him to a never-ending sermon about the story of Jesus's birth that rivaled *Passion of the Christ* in racism and arrogance; even on Thanksgiving his family gave thanks to God for keeping them white, straight, and southern.

Mrs. K. hadn't celebrated any holidays or birthdays after her husband died. Thadeus's family had tried to put him into a nursing home just so they wouldn't have to deal with him, especially not on the holidays. Diego never mentioned his past, and the only birthday celebrations he consistently mentioned were Zorro's. Clancy—who had revealed her past somewhat to me in a drunken (on her part) conversation one night—had been a runaway since she was thirteen years old, escaping an abusive father and addicted mother. Almost all of her birthdays and holidays had been spent in shelters, on the road, or huddled somewhere trying to get warm. Overall, none of them were overly burdened with happy childhood memories.

Grace almost caught or half-caught us more than a few times in the following days. She walked in on Mrs. K. making soufflés for the umpteenth time.

"Oh, just perfecting an old recipe, sweetheart." Mrs. K. had said in a less-than-convincing tone.

Grace had almost discovered Luke in one of the coat closets filling a dragon piñata with candy. But when he had heard her coming, he'd shoved the thing under his bottom, crushing both the piñata and the candy. Grace hadn't really thought it was weird that Luke was hanging out in a closet in the middle of the day. Luke liked small spaces. It was one of his many quirks.

The Hotel was enormous, but for some reason Grace seemed to be everywhere and anywhere. I had noticed it before, her sort of ever-present attitude. Before, it had been comforting to know that someone I trusted was always looking out for me. But with party planning, it simply became a nuisance. Clancy had to walk Zorro twice as much as usual just as an excuse to get Grace out of the house. Those thirty-minute reprieves were when we got most of our work done.

On the day of, Clancy and Sam claimed there was something they needed to show Grace concerning Luke's truck. Clancy rattled off some mechanical jargon that seemed to confuse Sam as much as it did Grace, but the way she said it made the situation seem dire enough to require Grace's personal attention. Caleb had been smirking the entire time Clancy had been talking. When the three of them left through the front doors, I turned to Caleb.

"What did Clancy say was wrong with the car?" I asked.

"In layman's terms? She said the front tire had replaced the carburetor and the dashboard was leaking oil."

I laughed out loud. "Man, she's the only good liar among us."

"Tell me about it. But then again, she's had her practice."

I didn't ask what Caleb meant, partially because I knew that when guests of the Hotel wanted to reveal something about their lives, they did and never before. Also, I knew that there was just too much work to be done before Grace returned to get into any sort of deep discussion.

Impressively, Clancy and Sam were able to keep Grace out of the Hotel for almost three hours before, according to Clancy, Grace got frustrated with the whole thing. At first, Clancy had showed her pretty much every part of the engine, explaining what fictional ailment it was suffering from. Then she had moved on to a detailed perusal of the manual. Then she had forced Grace to get under the car on one of those rolling planks that mechanics used and given her a full lesson on the underside of a vehicle. Then, when Grace was finally beginning to lose patience, Sam had faked a rather elongated panic attack. Personally, I thought it was a pretty low blow, but then again, the idea of Sam acting out something like that tickled me a little.

Needless to say, when Grace stepped foot through the front door, her brows where firmly placed at a downward angle, her fists were clenched, and her mouth had drawn itself into a small, thin line. She was actually turning back to scold Sam and Clancy some more for wasting her time when we all burst out in a boisterous "Happy Birthday!"

Grace shouted and jumped back, knocking into Sam whose eyes went wide with very genuine panic at being touched. Luckily, Clancy seamlessly inserted herself between the two of them, wrapping Grace up in a hug from behind and whispering apologies into her ear. Sam took a second to recover before he sheepishly made his way over to us and allowed Caleb to put an obnoxious sparkly birthday hat onto his head. I thought I saw a few tears threatening to creep up in Grace's eyes, but she quickly hid them with a smile as she came over and thanked everyone.

The party quickly moved to the ballroom where Caleb began to blast his music, and Grace gushed over how incredible all the decorations were. Dancing, eating, and conversation ensued. Thadeus somehow managed to convince Mrs. K. to dance with him when a string of big band music came on. They looked like swing dancers from the roaring twenties, with Thadeus playing out all of the moves that a woman usually did. They both suddenly seemed much younger than their years.

Luke and Beatrice showed off their sporadic moves, battling each other for who could be the most uncoordinated and silly. Kiki jumped from person to person, wiggling like one of those blow-up car sales things. Francis settled into a much more subdued twirl around the dance floor with Kiki perched on his feet. I took Grace out for a few dances, trying to force the words "father-daughter dance" out of my mind. When things slowed down, Diego asked for Grace's hand, and Caleb seamlessly slid into my arms, leading me in a waltz. I laughed at him, but followed, playing the part of a dutiful dance partner. He was clearly a better dancer than me anyway.

I glanced around the dance floor to see who else had paired up. Luke was smushed up against Mrs. K., looking uncomfortable but also happy. Thadeus was schooling Beatrice in the proper execution of a box step. Francis had Kiki in his arms as they swayed from side to side.

Turning my head to other side, I was shocked to see Clancy and Sam together. They weren't touching, but their bodies were mere inches apart, just enough space to ensure that they didn't touch accidentally. Their hands hovered in place, Sam's next to Clancy's waist, and Clancy's just over Sam's shoulders. The look on Sam's face was something I'd never seen on him before. He looked shy, giddy almost, but there was something deeper there too. He looked the way someone did after they'd finally gotten something they'd wanted for a long, long time. He looked satisfied. And Clancy looked just about as open and calm as I'd ever seen her. Her focus was entirely on Sam. I felt somewhat like an idiot for not having seen it coming.

"They're cute, aren't they?" Caleb said. He had followed my gaze, joining me in observing Sam and Clancy. For a moment we stood still in the middle of the dance floor, just holding each other and watching.

"Is that why you were teaching Sam how to dance?" I asked.

"Yeah. He's a good student. He knew we were going to do something like this for Grace. He wanted to make sure he knew what he was doing when he asked Clancy to dance."

"How long have they been like that?"

Caleb didn't answer immediately. My question hadn't exactly been specific, but I had no idea how else to ask. To me it wasn't clear what they were to each other. They were just something.

"Sam, I think, has been in love with Clancy ever since he first saw her paintings. I'm not sure, but something about them really speak to him in a way that people can't. It's like he sees her through them."

"That's romantic."

Caleb laughed. "You're just a big marshmallow."

I smiled, not denying it. "What about Clancy?"

He made a thinking noise, one of those long, drawn out sounds from the back of the throat. "Not sure really. I think she loves Sam as much as she can. And she has problems with intimacy in that way." He meant the physical way. I didn't need much more explanation than that to see why they clicked. "I guess in that strange, messed up way, they are made for each other."

"Guess so. It's sweet, but also a little sad."

"Why is it sad?" Caleb was now looking me dead in the face. I realized how close our bodies were and decided that I didn't care. Of all the guests, I could say that Caleb was my closest friend. It actually felt kind of nice to be close to him like that, secure almost.

"I don't know. I guess it's been my experience when two people are damaged, things don't usually work out between them. There needs to be at least one person who's got their head on straight." I was thinking about Thia and I.

"What, so the sane one can absorb all the other's crazy?"

"Yeah. I guess."

Caleb nodded. "Sure, maybe that works for some people. But it doesn't sound healthy to me. I'd much rather be with someone just as messy as me. At least then we can make a mess together."

"And Gabe? Is he messy?"

Caleb smirked at me, but hidden beneath that ironic expression was a hint of genuine feeling. "He could be."

The music changed to something more upbeat then. Caleb laughed, suggesting that we get a drink.

"What?" I said. "You don't like to pop and lock?"

Caleb just laughed at me, and I followed him to the drinks table. The party had already been going on for a bit, but most of the alcohol on the refreshments table was still there. Everyone was so caught up in dancing or eating that they had hardly taken a sip. Looking at it, I realized that I hadn't drunk anything at all since I'd been there, and I hadn't been drunk since long before that. One look I shared with Caleb showed that he meant to change those facts.

Caleb shut off the music, which brought about noisy complaints from everyone on the dance floor.

"A toast!" Caleb said. "Come, everyone, get a drink."

"Sparkling apple cider for the young ones." I said, holding out two plastic champagne flutes to Beatrice and Kiki.

"I'm old enough to drink." Beatrice pouted.

I rose one eyebrow. "Grace, how old is Beatrice?"

"Nineteen." She said, retrieving her own glass of bubbly from Caleb.

"Uh-huh." I said with that deep fatherly tone that had begun to creep into my voice more and more lately.

"Grace!" Beatrice said.

"What?" Grace smiled. "You *are* nineteen."

"Yeah, but he didn't know that." Beatrice took the apple cider abruptly from my hand.

"Hey. I may not have been around for every birthday, but I still remember how old you are, young lady." I added a little extra paternal flair to that last part, putting on a pretend expression of sternness. It was becoming slightly easier, and less like pretend, but I decided to let that thought slip right out of my head.

Beatrice laughed at my acting, but she still mumbled something about getting drunk tonight under her breath as she walked away.

Once everyone was gathered with a drink in their hand, Caleb turned to me. "Arthur, would you do the honor?"

"What?"

"A toast, sweetie. Give a toast to your sister." Mrs. K. gave my shoulder a little nudge.

"I'm not so good with public speaking." I whispered ineffectively to Caleb.

"Oh it's just us, lad." Thadeus said merrily. Clearly he'd been one of the only guests to tap into the supply of alcohol already, if his rosy cheeks were anything to go on. "What's there to be afraid of?"

I sighed, and everyone laughed at my reluctance, none so much as Grace.

"My big brother. The wordsmith." She teased.

"All right. All right." I held up my hands. "Okay so, um, a toast. Okay."

"Any day now." Clancy said. Sam, who stood next to her holding his champagne flute like it was a weapon of mass destruction, laughed under his breath.

I shot Clancy an evil glance. "Fine. Okay . . . Grace is pretty amazing, right?" There was a murmur of agreement from the other guests. "I mean I knew that from the moment she was born. To be honest, she scared the shit out of me, even then." Everyone laughed. Okay so maybe this toast thing wasn't going to be so hard after all. Then again, I didn't say the real reason why infant Grace scared me so much.

"Even as a newborn, Grace seemed to know so much more than anyone else around her. And even as a newborn, she was clumsy as fuck."

"Language." Francis warned.

"Sorry. Anyway, yeah as a little kid she used to crawl around knocking into things and breaking all this stuff in the house. I used to call her our little wrecking ball." More laughter from the guests.

"But um, Grace grew up. She didn't become more coordinated, but she did become even smarter and even scarier."

"Jeez, Arthur, you're making me sound like some kind of clumsy evil genius."

I laughed. "Not what I meant. I guess what I mean to say is that Grace has always been this amazing thing in my life. She's so hard to grasp, but that's what makes her so beautiful. I think that I missed out on a lot when she was growing up. I missed out a lot of seeing how that little wrecking ball became this amazing woman I've gotten to know this last few weeks. I mean, she is amazing right? She's taken you all in and given you a place to belong. She's dragged me out of my sorry existence and given me purpose again. She's . . . well she's just great. And I'm not so good at expressing that sometimes, or just expressing stuff in general. But I got to say that I'm really proud of her. I'm proud of all of my family, but I know that none of them would've gotten to where they are without Grace. So I'm proud, and happy, and I'm talking too much so can we just drink now?"

Everyone laughed and clapped and praised me for such a wonderful speech. I felt so awkward that I hardly waited for everyone else to raise their glasses before I'd downed mine. The champagne felt like a million tiny party poppers going off in my throat, but it was nice. I wanted another glass. I noticed Grace wipe away tears once I'd swallowed my second drink.

"Please don't cry."

She laughed, watery eyes shining. "Sorry, Arthur. You're just going to have to deal with it." And then she gave me a big hug, wrapping her arms around my neck and pulling me down until my chin rested on her shoulder. I clumsily wrapped my arms around her waist, feeling ridiculously large pressed up against her petite dancer's form. "You're a good man, Arthur Bean." She whispered in my ear. "No matter what happens, just remember that."

She pulled away grinning and wandered off to mingle with some of the other guests before I could even question her somewhat ominous words. I definitely needed another drink.

Caleb turned the music back on and people proceeded to dance and drink and eat even more. Eventually Mrs. K. insisted that we head into the dining room so we could partake of the incredible meal she'd labored over for days. As we walked there, she gave Grace a full description of just how much blood, sweat, and tears she put into every dish. When we got to the dining room doors, Mrs. K. stopped us, taking a deep breath, before opening the doors with a flourish.

If I had thought that Mrs. K.'s other meals were impressive, then this one was otherworldly. I couldn't fathom how in the world she had managed to do all of this and get it all set up on the table without any of us noticing or helping. But there it was, a magnificent spread of all of Grace's favorite foods, filling the air with the most intoxicating aromas I'd ever experienced.

There were dishes piled high with Italian sausage and peppers, fried chicken sandwiches, fluffy biscuits and jam, and honey-baked ham. There was macaroni and cheese, avgolemono soup, Thanksgiving stuffing, roasted brussels sprouts, and, oddly enough, Fruit Loops accompanied by a frosty pitcher of milk. There was a massive chicken Caesar salad and too many kinds of bread for me to count. I felt as if I'd been transported to medieval times, when every banquet involved such impressive feasts. Maybe it was my slightly tipsy brain talking, but I knew that this meal was going to be the best one I'd ever eaten.

Even though all their mouths were clearly watering, all the guests hung back until Grace had made her way, somewhat in awe, around the table and filled two big plates. Once she was seated in her regular spot, we descended on that table like a wake of vultures feasting on a rotting corpse. I could hardly choose what I wanted, trying to distinguish between what I should get first and what should be saved for later. I just piled everything on and grabbed a few more things with my bare hands.

Dinner was filled with laughter and even more alcohol. It was clear that people were descending into a haze of drunkenness, but it was pleasant and warm, not the frantic kind of drunkenness that usually accompanied parties. It was comfortable, even if my stomach swelling under the constraint of my belt was not.

The soufflés were brought out, along with fresh whipped cream and a raspberry coulis that smelled like springtime. Many of us were more stuffed than we'd ever been before, and yet we devoured those soufflés like men and women starved. Then, when we all moved into the library for the movies, we continued to stuff our faces with the various kinds of popcorn that Mrs. K. had made for the occasion. Kettle corn, caramel corn, buttered popcorn, salted popcorn, cheddar popcorn—I thought that if I weren't twenty pounds heavier the next morning, then I must be some kind of alien.

I'd specifically picked out movies that I knew Grace liked, even though one couldn't exactly call them party movies. After the first one, Francis took a sleeping Kiki off to bed and then returned, finally taking a bottle of wine and gulping down a large portion of it. Besides the champagne for the toast, he hadn't had anything to drink all night. I wondered if maybe Francis had once been a man of many vices, but had been forced to suddenly control them all once Kiki came under his care. I wouldn't be surprised. It seemed to me that a kid like Kiki could cleanse any person of their sins.

About a quarter of the way into *The Manchurian Candidate*, our third movie of the night, more than half of us had fallen into unattractive, deep sleeps. Caleb's head hung off the back off his armchair, his mouth gaping wide and a steady stream of drool running down his chin. Giggling to myself, I took out my phone to snap a potential blackmail picture.

Clancy and Sam were snuggled up on the love seat together, their heads and fingertips almost touching. Luke and Beatrice had splayed out on the floor like two starfish, and in the armchair next to them, Mrs. K. snoozed with a sleeping Thadeus curled up in her lap like a toddler. Francis was propped up against the wall by the fireplace, his expression as stern in slumber as it was in wakefulness. Only Grace and I remained awake, along with Diego who was watching the movie with an abnormal focus, muttering some-thing to himself in an accent that did not sound entirely Spanish.

Grace hadn't drunk nearly as much as the rest of us, but she still swayed happily back and forth on the couch, musing about how handsome men were back then. I just nodded, finding it too hard to make my tongue do much more than lay heavy in my mouth. My vision was starting to blur in and out, and the sounds from the projector sounded little more than babble to me.

Slowly, my eyes began to shut, and my body, heavy with too much food, sank further and further into the couch until I felt I was falling—down, down, down.

"You never could hold your alcohol, Arthur Bean." Thia said.

* * *

I was reminded quite rudely of the exact reason that I hadn't allowed myself to be drunk in such a long time. When you're in your twenties, a hangover is nothing more than the meager price of a good time. When you're as old as I was, a hangover is the stinging, brutal remembrance that your body is slowly starting to become useless.

It was the sound of someone retching that finally pulled me from the profound, alcohol-induced unconsciousness. I tried to open my eyes but found them crusted together with some unidentified substance. Even if they hadn't, though, my eyelids felt far too heavy for me to lift them on my own. Even Atlas couldn't have pried them from my eyeballs.

I lingered for a while in a hazy limbo between waking and sleeping. There were sounds all around me. Some I could pinpoint, like the groan of someone stretching, or Kiki's giggle. Some I had no idea what they were and didn't care very much either. It wasn't until the acrid smell of coffee began to waft into my nostrils, accompanied by a slightly warm sensation tickling the tip of my nose, that I finally convinced my eyes to open.

Grace stood in front of me, looking far too put together and pretty for someone who had stayed up until four in the morning drinking wine, stuffing her face with popcorn, and watching old movies. She held a mug full of coffee under my nose and a plate with toast and crackers next to my face. I grumbled something in the way of greeting, but she just took advantage of my mouth opening to pour some coffee into it. I spluttered and coughed but managed to swallow most of it. It was black, sugarless, and scalding, but it did the trick.

Once I took the mug and plate from her, she shuffled off to rouse other guests who still slept in the library. My vision was fuzzy, but I could see Kiki's blurry form playfully tugging at Francis's arm as he continued to sleep against the wall. Beatrice was gone, but Luke still lay splayed out on the floor and was apparently unmovable, if Grace's fruitless efforts to wake him were any indication. Mrs. K. had disappeared in the night, but Thadeus was now awake in the chair in which he had slept, head in one hand while the other held shakily on to his own coffee. Clancy was gone, but Sam was awake, staring up at the ceiling with a dopey look on his face that made me think he was possibly still drunk.

The whole scene was somewhat familiar. After all, it looked no different than waking up at a friend's house after some massive party. But it was the cast of characters that made the thing so hilarious. A child trying to wake up his guardian, a young girl playing mom to people far older than her, an eighty-something-year-old man looking like he regretted every choice he'd made in the past few hours, and my brother convincingly playing the part of Rip Van Winkle. The laughter came out of my mouth before I could stop it. Once it did, the rumble it caused in my chest and belly was so painful that I immediately stopped.

For most of us, the rest of the day was spent sleeping, vomiting, eating excessive amounts of leftovers, or downing excessive amounts of water. All of us discussed our own hangover cures and how they were better than anyone else's. Clancy tried to shove a greasy egg, cheese, and bacon sandwich into my mouth. She only stopped when I started to look like I might throw up. My preferred hangover cure was silence, stillness, and coffee. I didn't move from the couch or say anything to anyone that wasn't entirely necessary.

It wasn't until Zorro started to bay mournfully at a squirrel through the window of the library that I felt the need to move. Once I stood, the pounding in my head became worse, but the feeling of nausea got better. I hadn't eaten the crackers and toast that Grace had brought me in the morning. By that point they would've been stale and unappetizing. I figured that the kitchen would have something to offer in the way of hangover food.

Apparently I wasn't the only one to have that thought. Clancy was there, shoving leftover mac and cheese into her mouth and washing it down with apple juice. I was surprised she had any room left in her stomach after last night and eating throughout the day. Francis and Kiki were there as well. Kiki was abnormally quiet, but that might have been because of Francis, who was practically falling asleep on the counter. Beatrice sat next to Kiki, eating off of his plate occasionally. He shot her wicked looks, but that didn't stop her.

I gave a weak greeting to everyone and began to rummage through the refrigerator. The cool air felt like a blessing on my overheated skin. I realized that I'd been sweating all day. It was a little bit cold in the Hotel, but my body was trying to purge my sins through sweat. I probably smelled pretty bad and decided that a shower would be the next step in my recovery.

I ended up taking out all the starchy things I could find and piling them into a bowl. My hangover meal ended up being a strange concoction of Thanksgiving stuffing, biscuits, a fried chicken breast, and various breads with butter, honey, and jam. I didn't even bother to heat any of it up.

"That looks disgusting." Beatrice said, before sticking her fork into my stuffing and taking some for herself.

"You know, there's a lot of food in the fridge that you could eat." I said, although I didn't really mind. Now that I had the food in front of me, I doubted my ability to eat it.

"My back hurts from sleeping on the floor. Don't wanna move."

"Yeah. I'm sure all that wine I saw you sneaking didn't help either."

"Am I in trouble?" Her tone of voice showed that she didn't really fear retribution.

"If you're gonna drink, I'd rather you do it around us." I said. "But that doesn't mean I approve." I tried putting a forkful of stuffing and chicken in my mouth. My eyes bulged out as my tongue attempted to push the food to my teeth to be chewed. The whole thing was like a mushy bowling ball in my mouth. I'd never experienced such a lack of coordination with my mouth before. I managed to swallow, but then slid the rest of my food over to Beatrice. She happily took it.

I shuffled out of the kitchen to the stairs. They seemed far more massive then they ever had before. The task of walking up seemed just as impossible as trying to climb Mount Doom. For a long time I just stood there, staring with my mouth agape until someone floated by like a ghost in the corner of my eye. Suddenly understanding how stupid I must have looked, I forced my right leg to lift itself and my left leg to follow it. It felt like the longest climb anyone ever made. At the top of the stairs, I wished I'd had a flag to set down and mark my victory.

The shower felt too hot, then too cold. I couldn't find the middle ground between the two, so I settled for scalding over freezing. Someone in college once told me that sweating out hangovers was the best way to deal with them because then all the toxins got released from your body. I'm not sure if I believed any of that bullshit. Everyone seemed to have their own hangover cure that was specific to them and no one else. But being pelted by boiling-hot water definitely made me feel more like a human, if only because of the adrenaline that rushed through my body at the fear of being burned alive.

I didn't exactly wash myself as much as just let the water rinse over me. Once I felt like I'd been sufficiently scorched, I dried myself off with a towel that felt too rough on my skin and crawled naked beneath my covers. The sheets were itchy and heavy and hot, but they also made me feel like I was being pleasantly smothered into sleep. I was just about there, just about to achieve that restful bliss, when someone knocked on my door. I groaned loudly. My visitor took that as permission to enter.

"Hey there. Going to bed already?" Grace said.

"It's only like eight thirty, dude." Luke said, following her into my room.

"I'm tired." I wasn't able to form a more complicated explanation than that.

"All right. Well before you drift off, set your alarm for six forty-five at the latest." Grace said. "Jeff called and said his crew would be here by seven."

I scrunched my eyes closed. "Seven's too early." I sounded like a spoiled, whiney child.

"Yeah, well, there's a lot to be done. Think you can handle it?"

"Yeah, sure." Already my eyes were starting to droop closed. There weren't many times in my life when I felt so exhausted that I'd fallen asleep mid conversation. Part of being an adult was staying awake even when the only thing you wanted to do was sleep. "But we're all children here."

"What'd he say?" Luke asked Grace, who had decided to set my alarm clock for me. "Oh gross, are you naked?"

Ever since I was a kid, I had this recurring dream. It was half nightmare, half epic, and every time I dreamed it, it would affect me for days afterward. It was always the same every time, to the point where I'd memorized it and could recount it perfectly while awake. But it was never lucid. Whenever I was in it, immersed in slumber, I had no idea I was dreaming. The dream was my reality. When I was a kid, when it used to happen at least three or four times a month, I had a hard time distinguishing which reality was the truth.

It always started like this: I lay facedown on a pile of fallen autumn leaves. They smell cool, earthy, and slightly sweet, like maple syrup. Their edges scratch my skin, leaving little red lines of blood across my arms, legs, and face. I'm wearing a red-and-white striped T-shirt and a pair of denim shorts. My feet are bare. My hair is done up in cornrows the way it was when I was five.

I try to look up, but realize that some sort of weight is holding me down. I can breathe, but every time I do, something evil flows into my lungs and stays there, breeding darkness inside me. I feel its wicked tendrils curling around my organs. After a few minutes, I start to sink. The leaves cover me, embrace me, pull me under, until finally I'm standing in my father's diner in front of the stove. All six burners are going. Only the flames aren't blue and red and orange. They are black and green, Disney cartoon creations of evil magic. I stand up straight, staring at the stove. Then I begin to walk backward as if I were walking forward. My head stays facing the stove, but my legs twist and crack and move in ways they never should.

I walk like that until I'm outside the diner. Then my body rights itself. I'm no longer on solid ground. I'm on a river raft. My clothes have changed too. I'm wearing a rough shirt with a lace-up collar and brown burlap pants. On top of my head is a frayed and holey straw hat. I look down at my hands. They are rough and cracked, almost broken. Clearly they've done hard work. On each side of the river, a fire rages. This time it's red, too red, uniformly red. It looks more liquid than flame.

People shout to me from the shore. People shout to me as they are burning. Some ask for help. Others call me names. Some people need me. Some people hate me. I don't save any of them. I keep rowing my raft until the river ends abruptly at a rickety old house held on stilts above the flowing water. I leave my raft and climb the ladder to the house's porch.

Hanging in front of the door are human teeth and a naked, brown voodoo doll with pins in its eyes. It's dangling from its neck, swinging in the wind. I feel hot and the smell of burning flesh permeates the air. The fire is nowhere to be seen. From inside the house, I hear the hateful murmuring of angry people. I know I should walk away and go back to the diner where I'm safe, where people love me. Instead I knock on the door. The teeth rattle together.

There's a pause. I realize that I'm not breathing. Then the door shoots open, knocking me back. A roaring blackness bursts forth from the empty chasm. Its tentacle fingers reach out and grab me, dragging me inside. Whatever scream I might have let loose gets swallowed whole. Then the door slams shut, and I wake up.

For as long as I could remember the dream was exactly like that. Every time. Up until this point, I'd never told anyone about it. Even in the days that followed it, when I jumped at every shadow and refused to go near the stove at the diner, I would simply tell people I'd had a nightmare and say nothing more. I'd always thought that telling other people your dreams was narcissistic and boring. But that night, at the hotel, as I fell into a painful slumber, the dream changed.

This time, when I step outside of the diner, I'm not on a raft. I'm on an airboat, and instead of the rough, primitive clothes, I wear all white. A crisp, white polo shirt buttoned up to the top and pressed white slacks that one might wear to a Labor Day party in the Hamptons. Not that I'd ever been invited to something like that. Black skin does not scream "white party."

I'm on the airboat, but it isn't moving. It's still tied to the docks.

There's still that unnaturally red fire, but it's only on one side of the river now. It's localized around one spot. It rages and spits and twists around an antebellum house that looks as if it were built yesterday, crisp and new. The house itself isn't burning. If I look closely, I can see silhouettes of people in the windows, wailing and clawing to get out. But the house isn't burning.

There are still screams for help coming from the house. Shrieks of women and children and men. And from the other side of the river, a continuous chant. It feels hateful and heavy and other-worldly, but I can't hear what it's saying. I can't turn my head to see who is screaming. I can't move my legs forward toward the house. I'm forced to gaze helplessly at the fire as it rages.

Suddenly everything stops. A great whooshing sound engulfs the flames and sucks them up until all that is left is charred earth and the house, perfect amid all that destruction. I can no longer hear the screams of the people inside. Somehow, I know that they are dead.

The paralyzing inability to move is lifted, and suddenly I'm set free to run toward the house. Teeth hang over the front door, but no voodoo doll. There's no sound coming from within. This time I don't hesitate to yank open the door.

There's a sudden intake of air, as if the house were breathing. Then, like a tongue, flames explode toward me in a single, uniform column and drag me into the house, burning alive. The door slams shut.

"Arthur! Arthur!" Thia shouted, grabbing me by the shoulders. "Wake up Arthur! You're having a nightmare. Wake up!"

I bolted upward, waving my hands wildly out in front of me. I roared incoherent nonsense, clawing at whoever held me. Cold, sticky sweat caused the sheets of my bed to cling to my back. My hand connected with something hard, and I felt something catch under my fingernails. There was a shout. The hands that held me let go. Another pair take their place, forcing me on to my back once more. Another pair of hands grabbed my arms, another pair grabbed my legs, and I realized that my eyes were still closed. I forced them open.

Sam stood at the edge of my bed, a hand covering the right side of his face. I could see blood escaping between his fingers. Clancy stood in front of Sam, touching him, holding him by the arms as Sam looked at me with utter confusion in his eyes. Diego was on top of my chest, and Luke was at my legs. They were holding me down. Behind Sam were Mrs. K. and Thadeus. Thadeus held Mrs. K as she looked at me, mortified. In the doorway, Beatrice stood with a hand over her mouth, and Francis stood next to her, holding a trembling Kiki in his arms. Caleb was nowhere to be seen. Grace sat on the bed next to me.

I wasn't making noise anymore, just breathing heavily, winded by the dream and by Diego's weight on my chest. Caleb rushed in with a glass of water in one hand and a bottle of pills in the other.

"Arthur?" Grace said quietly. "Arthur, where are you?"

I blinked twice before croaking out, "I'm here. I'm sorry. I'm here."

Grace nodded curtly, once to Diego, once to Luke. They released me. Immediately I raised my hands in front of my face. One had blood on it. Torn skin stuck out from underneath the fingernails. Horrified, I looked at Sam.

"Sam . . . I'm . . ."

"You scratched his face. You tore it up!" Clancy shouted without looking at me.

"Clancy . . ." Caleb said.

"He tore up his face!" She said again. Sam just shook his head violently, but I couldn't tell if it was because he was hurt, or confused, or because he thought Clancy was behaving badly, or because he thought I had. Either way, I realized that Sam was the one who had been holding me at first, and I had hurt him.

"I'm sorry. I didn't mean to." I choked on my own voice. I

could still hear the chanting from my dream. I told Grace that I was there with them, but part of me was still in the dream.

"Katherine," Thadeus said, "Perhaps you should get some things to tend to Sam? I'll help you." He led Mrs. K. out of the room. Clancy and Sam followed.

"I'm sorry." I called weakly after them. Sam turned around for a second, but Clancy tugged him forward, and he was gone.

Caleb was suddenly at my side, sitting on the bed next to Grace. "Take these." He held out two small pale pink pills and the glass of water.

"What is this?"

"Sleeping pills. It's only ten."

I shook my head. I felt like I'd been under for hours. I thought we were deep into the night, maybe even entering early morning. I'd hardly been asleep for more than an hour, but in the dream, it had been an eternity.

I looked at Grace. I'd never taken sleeping pills in my life, but my dad had taken them a lot after my mother died. Sometimes he would take too many and become a zombie at night. I didn't want the pills, but I knew that I wouldn't fall asleep without them. Would the pills stop me from dreaming?

"It's all right. Just take one."

My hands trembled as I took one pill from Caleb's hand. He brought the glass of water to my lips himself. He must have thought that my hands weren't steady enough to hold it, that I'd spill. I swallowed. Even though the pill was tiny, it felt like a cannonball going down my throat. It landed in my stomach with a heavy thud. For a moment, I thought I was going to vomit it right back up again.

"I'm sorry." I mumbled.

Caleb's hand was in my hair, twisting one of my curls it lightly. "That's all right."

"But Sam . . . he touched me?"

"He was the first one to hear you screaming." Beatrice said from the doorway. "Then he started screaming for us. When we came in he was holding you by the shoulders, shaking you and yelling for you to wake up."

"I hurt him." The trauma of my dream combined with the surprisingly rapid effects of the sleeping pill were making it too hard to form complex sentences.

"You didn't mean to." Diego said.

It was true, but that didn't make me feel any better. Truth was not always a remedy for pain. The truth was that, whether I had meant to or not, Sam had touched me, and I had hurt him. It had probably been the first time in God knows how long he had willingly touched another human being, and he had bled for it.

I was being dragged back down into unconsciousness by the pill, its heavy fingers like hooks in my eyelids. I was so terrified that if I fell asleep then, all I would dream about was the blood between Sam's fingers.

"I see your brain working, Arthur. Just let go." Grace said.

"Just let go." Thia said.

I didn't dream again that night.

My father had not been a morning person, despite running a diner for most of his working life. He was always grumpy in the mornings, short and easily annoyed. The waitresses and cooks knew to step lightly around him until he'd had coffee and the clock struck ten. Sometimes, it felt like he wasn't even there in the morning, like his body was on autopilot. I'd call out his name, and he wouldn't even skip a beat.

That morning after the nightmare, my alarm went off, and I suddenly realized why my father was like that. My eyes opened begrudgingly. My legs and arms started to take me through the motions of the day, but the part of me that made me, well, *me* wasn't there. The soul—or whatever you wanted to call it—was still in the grips of the pill, being held captive in that deep, dark, unconscious world of no memory. It didn't even struggle. It accepted the fact that, when it was ready, the pill would release it.

Unfortunately, the pill decided it wanted to keep the conscious me for a little too long. It wasn't until the construction crew had broken for lunch that I felt myself returning. The morning had been a haze of shattered images and weak utterings. I'd greeted Jeff and the others, stood through introductions of the rest of the crew. By lunchtime I'd forgotten every one of those names. I'd been coherent enough to listen to Jeff's plan for the day and assist in finding certain things, like the bathroom. The guests in the Hotel had approached me slowly, one by one, to check on me, or, in Clancy's case, to apologize. They soon realized that I was not myself and backed off.

I knew in the back of my mind that I had some explaining to do. I had to apologize to Sam, and I had to thank Caleb, even though right now I was feeling more resentful of his little helper than I was feeling grateful. I had to assure Beatrice and Luke and Kiki, and I had to simply appear normal in front of the others. That was probably the most important. Even though they knew better

175

than anyone that the appearance of normalcy was just an unso-phisticated mask we used to fool others into leaving us alone. But perhaps, in this particular moment, it would make them feel better. At least that's what I hoped.

I caught Sam at lunchtime munching on a carrot that seemed fitter for a horse than a human being. He had a large bandage covering the cheek where my nails had torn his skin away. He stood against one of the dining room walls, far away from the crowd, eyes darting between the various interactions that took place. I noticed that Sam did this a lot. It was as if he were studying us, compiling anthropological evidence about the little tribe we'd created. But it seemed more likely that any studying Sam did concerning us was simply born out of the confusion he felt about human interactions in general.

He must have felt me coming though. Before I said anything, his eyes snapped rather abruptly over to me. At first, I thought he was going to shout. Instead he smiled, and said, "Hey."

I tried not to show how taken aback I was. "Hey."

"You're awake now?" Sam's voice was deep and pleasant. It had an almost lyrical quality to it made all the more beautiful by its rarity of appearance. I was certain that if Sam spoke more often, I wouldn't have been so captivated by the sound of his words.

I laughed a little. "Yeah. Took me a while, but I'm here."

He nodded, that soft smile still decorating his face, but he didn't say anything more. He was waiting for me to say what he knew I had come there to say.

"I'm really sorry." I said. "I . . . that dream sort of, um . . ."

"It scared you." Sam finished my sentence for me. It was simpler than how I might have put it, but it got the job done.

"Yeah. In the dream something had been grabbing me, and then I felt you grabbing me . . . why did you grab me?" I hadn't meant to ask that, but it would be a lie to say I wasn't curious. Sam never touched anyone, not even Clancy.

Sam nodded. "I don't know. I saw that you were scared, and seemed like maybe you were in danger. Like having a seizure or something. So I grabbed you. I forgot about everything else. But then you scratched me, so I let go. I didn't mean to scare you more."

"God no, Sam. That's not . . . I just was still dreaming that's all. I never meant to hurt you. You know that I wouldn't . . ."

"Yeah I know." Sam said. "I had to tell Clancy that about a million times before she finally calmed down. That night was the first time she'd ever touched me, or the first time I'd ever let her touch me." His smile grew a little wider, reaching up to his eyes. "It was nice, even though she was freaked out."

My head was still swirling with how much Sam was talking, and now he was admitting feelings to me. It was so unlike the silent, shy Sam that I knew. He noticed my look of confusion and smirked a little. "Don't get used to it."

"Okay. So, um, you and Clancy . . . do you think—"

"No." Sam said, cutting me off. "I don't think that will change anything. She tried holding my hand again this morning and . . . I didn't like it." He sighed. "I wish getting scratched up was all it took."

I didn't know what else to say, so I didn't say anything. I expected that Sam would do what he normally did too, but instead he kept talking. All I could do was listen.

"My dad had this kind of intense OCD that he never really got treated. He thought everything around him was dirty, including me. He used to scrub me so hard when I was a kid that I would bleed, and then he'd pour rubbing alcohol all over me because the blood was dirty. When I was a baby it was cool because my mom was around, but then she left us and, well, it went on for years like that. Then a teacher at my school caught on and called child services. I was put into the foster system after that, and never heard from my dad again. Guess he thought I was better off without him."

"Jesus." I said. Because what else was there to say to something like that?

"Yeah. Caleb gets it because his dad was a piece of shit too."

177

The curse sounded foreign coming out of his mouth. "Then again, it wasn't my dad's fault. He was sick. But still."

"Yeah. It seems like it's too hard to be a good parent. Some people just shouldn't have kids."

Sam looked over at me with a serious look in his eyes. He opened his mouth to say something, seemed to think twice, and closed it. Then, a moment later, he opened his mouth again and said, "Yeah. And some people are meant to be parents but aren't."

Before I could respond to that, Diego called to me from the table. Sam took that as his cue to walk away. Clancy saw him leave and followed. I watched him go too, feeling slightly winded by the whole conversation. I'd come to be so used to Sam being silent and nervous that to hear him speak so confidently about something that would be difficult for even the most loquacious of people was nerve-wracking. It made me question everything I knew about this Hotel, the guests, and my place in it all. Then again, maybe this was just what being trusted felt like.

The rest of the day was spent slightly more productively. I managed to make my way to all the guests and disperse any worries about me that might have built up. Mrs. K. seemed particularly traumatized by the whole ordeal. She said it reminded her of her husband's nightmares. He'd had PTSD before people knew that PTSD was something a person could have, and the nighttime was always the worst. She cried, saying that she hoped I wasn't suffering from the same illness. I assured her I wasn't. In my mind there was nothing from my past that had traumatized me. My mother dying, Mari in my bed, Thia disappearing, those were just things that had happened. Maybe I hadn't dealt with them, but I never thought about them as traumatizing. Maybe I should have. Then again, I didn't want to be a victim, so I didn't make myself one.

Beatrice, too, had been especially frightened.

"I thought you were dying." She whispered.

Luke said that I'd reminded him of how he got when things

were bad. I didn't let it show how much that mortified me. I loved my brother, but I didn't want to be anything like him.

Everyone else seemed to take my account of the night and my apologies at face value. Only Thadeus asked what the dream had been about. I lied. I told him I couldn't remember.

Grace seemed by far the most lighthearted about the whole thing, which surprised me a little. I wasn't expecting sympathy from anyone, and I definitely didn't want to be coddled. But still, it had been dramatic. If our lives had been a soap opera, my fingernails scraping off bits of Sam's face would've been the cliffhanger to keep viewers salivating until the next episode. But Grace acted as if it had all been commonplace. She even made a joke, one that I found distinctly unsettling.

"Some people think dreams can be prophetic. Think you're a psychic now?" The way she laughed made it clear that she didn't believe in any of that stuff. I didn't really believe in the paranormal either, but I also didn't want to be that dumb kid in the horror movie who doesn't believe and ends up killed for it.

For the rest of the day, I hounded Vince with questions about fire safety and the likelihood of an unexpected accident.

"Well if it's unexpected, and an accident, how am I supposed to give you a proper likelihood?" He asked.

For that whole first week, while the workers started on the very beginning of what was promising to be a long and exhaustive project, I was wracked with remembrance. I didn't dream again, but the memory of the nightmare was enough to keep me up at night. As soon as I lay freshly showered in my bed, the fear of it crept into my eyes and forced them to stay open. I stared at the cracks and stains on my ceiling, heard the wind moan on the bayou. I thought I could smell the fire. Sometimes it smelled so real that I feared I had never left the nightmare. Or that I was having a stroke.

Everyone seemed to catch on to my weariness and general discomfort, but none of the guests said anything. It was a fine line we walked between utter honesty and carefully avoided stress. We were there for each other in a way that only families could be, and, in the way that only families could be, we identified and anticipated each other's moods and moves with expert precision. This created an open atmosphere where you never had to worry about other people's perceptions of your actions. Everything was blatantly obvious to family. Perhaps that's why no one approached me. They knew I was suffering, and they knew why. They assumed that there was nothing they could do and, well, like families can be, they selfishly averted any extra responsibilities. In a way I was grateful because I couldn't imagine how it would be to try and talk about what I was feeling. The part of me that was slightly hurt that no one seemed to show concern got buried under exhaustion and my own brand of avoidance.

Only Jeff and Roscoe approached me.

"You're looking really tired today," Jeff said. "You don't have to help us out if you don't feel up to it."

"You haven't been reading the local news, have you?" Roscoe asked.

"Huh? No. Why would I read the local newspaper?"

"I was just wondering. News makes people stressed sometimes." Roscoe was not a very convincing liar, but I decided to let it go.

"I guess that's true. But I'm just tired. I haven't been sleeping well these past few days." Jeff and Roscoe didn't seem convinced, so I added, "I just keep thinking of everything that needs to get done and making all these lists in my head of stuff to remind you guys of."

"Oh." Jeff smiled welcomingly. "Well next time write them down, and we can talk about it. Hey Arthur, could I talk to you for a second?" Jeff took my arm and steered me away from Roscoe, waving him away to continue whatever work he had been doing.

"What's up?"

"Nothing really. I just wanted to know if you and some of your friends would be interested in having dinner with May and me?

She loves to cook, and she was thinking that she should return the favor of you all feeding me and my crew so well."

May hadn't been to the Hotel yet, but she'd been sending letters with Jeff, and Beatrice or Kiki had been sending letters back. The three of them had their own little club, and the letters were always top secret. Once I caught Beatrice and Kiki huddled over a pad of paper scribbling furiously. When they saw me come into the library, Beatrice threw her body on top of the letter as if it were a grenade about to go off.

To be honest, the idea of having a dinner party with Jeff and May sounded nice and, well, normal. It'd been a long time since I'd just hung out casually with people I considered friends. But then, the idea of wrangling all the Hotel's guests, bringing them into town, and shoving them all into someone else's house seemed like it could only end in disaster.

"That sounds really nice, Jeff. But I'm not sure if everyone would be up to it."

"Oh not everyone has to come. I mean, everyone is more than welcome."

"Even Roscoe?" I figured the reason Jeff had pulled me away from him was because he didn't want him knowing about the dinner party.

Jeff smiled sheepishly. "Yeah well, you've seen how Roscoe eats. May just hasn't taken to him, and I see the guy all day. He won't mind."

"Well I'll ask everyone tonight. Did you have a day in mind?"

"What about next Friday night? We'll finish up work early, and then whoever wants to come can follow me into town."

I almost asked if we needed a chaperone, but then decided it'd sound unnecessarily catty. "Sounds great. I'll let you know tomorrow, yeah?"

"Yeah, man, and get some sleep."

* * *

Caleb fussed over my wrinkled button-down, trying to smooth out the lines with the palms of his hands. Eventually, he grew too frustrated and threw his arms into the air.

"If you had just let me iron this earlier . . . You don't have any other shirts?"

"Caleb," I said, grabbing my blazer from the bed, "Relax. It's just a casual dinner party, not a reception at the White House."

"Still you don't have to show up looking like a slob. Wrinkled shirt and no haircut."

"What, not a fan of the 'fro?" My hair hadn't quite reached Soul Train proportions, but it was well on its way. I just hadn't had time to get it cut, and I doubted whether the hair salon in town would know how to deal with my hair.

"I don't mind large hair. I am from Georgia after all. But I do mind the fact that you don't take care of your hair. I mean honestly . . . it's all different lengths. There're little bits of gray too."

"I don't have gray hair!" I said, whipping my head around to look in the mirror behind me. There were maybe four gray hairs visible amid all my black curls. Even that was enough to make me feel old. I turned back to look at Caleb, who was now concerned with the crease in his own pants. "You're just being mean to me because you're nervous."

Caleb laughed a shallow, unconvincing laugh. "What do I have to be nervous about?"

"Oh well you know. A certain handsome interior designer is going to be joining us this evening. And he hasn't been around the Hotel that much."

Caleb gave me the side-eye but didn't deny it. Instead, he continued to fiddle with his pants until I came over and took his hands into mine.

"Seriously, why are you so nervous about this?"

Caleb seemed reluctant to talk, which was not something that happened often. I could feel his hands trembling slightly in my own. He took a deep breath and looked off to a spot behind me.

"I've never asked anyone out before." His voice was small and timid. It seemed like every day the guests at the Hotel revealed a little bit more of themselves to me, and every time it threw me for a loop. Caleb was a bit younger than me, but not by much. It was evident that he liked to flirt with everyone. It seemed odd to me that he wouldn't have a natural way with men. If Thia hadn't come along first, I might've been interested in more than friendship with him.

"Oh?" I said, not wanting to push him, but feeling like I needed more information.

Caleb gripped my hands hard as if to steady himself. "Yeah I mean . . . I was in the closet for so long. And then I was in that . . . place. I'm not a virgin, but like . . . I've never properly dated or had a boyfriend or anything like that. Most of the guys . . . I don't know. They were either, um, experimenting, or they just weren't interested in anything more." He sighed. "And I get it. I'm all fucked up, and I get weird when things are too real." He took a pause to look down at his feet. "But I really like this guy." He finally whispered.

I smiled, even though I mostly just felt sad seeing exactly how damaged Caleb was. He'd never talked about the conversion therapy, or really about his life before the Hotel. I knew about those places though. He didn't have to tell me that they were horrific and traumatizing. Still, he put on such a confident act that it seemed almost unbelievable to me that he would feel so insecure about something so simple as asking someone out. Then again, it'd never been my strong suit either.

"Hey." I said to get his attention. He looked up at me cautiously. I smiled warmly at him. "You can do this. Gabe seems like a good guy, and not exactly the casual sex type. He's obviously interested if the daily phone calls are anything to go off of. And I'll be right there the whole time."

"God," Caleb laughed, "I don't need a babysitter." His sarcastic tone couldn't hide the look gratitude on his face. He let go of my hands, and I let him.

Beatrice stuck her head in through the crack in my bedroom door. "Hey. You guys almost ready? Jeff's waiting by the dock."

I nodded. "We'll be down in a second." When she left, I turned to Caleb and said, "So are you going to let me pick my own shoes, or do you claim dominion over all my style choices?"

Caleb laughed a full, genuine laugh. "Please, like I would allow you to wear those disgusting trainers to a dinner party."

A lot of the guests had declined Jeff's invitation. Mrs. K. claimed the noise the airboat produced was too much for her nerves, and Thadeus, although clearly thrilled by the idea, decided to stay home and keep Mrs. K. company. Diego, who had been working harder than any of us to help the construction crew, just wanted to rest, and both Sam and Clancy visibly shuddered at the idea of such socialization. Kiki and Beatrice, of course, were thrilled, and Francis agreed to come and meet the woman Kiki was so infatuated by. Grace decided against attending as well, which surprised me a little. Grace had never been one to be rude. In fact, when she was a kid, she had been overly polite at times, forcing herself to do things just to save face if nothing else. It seemed out of character to me that she would pass on a friendly invitation by the man who was helping her achieve her dreams.

When I asked her why she didn't want to come, she said, "I have a phone call I can't miss. You know that."

I did know that. Or at least I knew that every Friday night at exactly nine o'clock, the phone rang and Grace disappeared into her room to talk to her nameless friend. No one ever mentioned it. I only asked once who it was that kept calling her at the same time every week. She told me it was a friend from college. It was a vague and unsatisfying reply, but I knew I wasn't going to get anything more from her than that.

When Caleb and I walked down the stairs, everyone was dressed up in their Sunday finest. We looked ready to go to an awards show. Kiki wore a darling little suit and a rubber ducky bowtie. Beatrice had pulled out another one of her secret dresses, this one a little more formfitting than the one she'd worn on Veterans Day. Luke and Francis both wore clean, unwrinkled shirts and crisp slacks. Luke looked especially out of place in his clothes. His hands kept tugging at the belt around his waist as if it were too tight, and one sleeve of his shirt was rolled up more than the other, which Caleb quickly fixed.

Jeff was waiting for us by the airboat when we came out.

"Don't you all look sharp." He said, laughing a little bit. I realized how awkward we must have looked to him. Up until this point, he'd only seen most of us in our natural habitat. Now we were braving the wild in the only attire we seemed to understand to be fit. I decided to take heart in our ridiculousness. At least it was consistent.

Half of us split between my car and Jeff's, with Jeff's pickup truck taking the lead. I noticed Francis staring out the window quite intensely as we passed through town. His bodyguard mode had been activated. When we turned onto Jeff's street, a confederate flag hung just below the American flag outside of one house. All of us except Kiki flinched.

Luckily, Jeff's house was not only far away from that first house on the block, but it was also the picture of pleasantness. Even under the streetlamps, I could see that the white fence surrounding the flower-filled front yard was impeccable. A charming little flagstone path led up to the front door, which was painted hunter green. May had left the door unlocked. Jeff announced us when we made our way in.

The smell of garlic and tomatoes and olive oil enveloped us. A soft crackling sound emanated from the kitchen where May also had an old Ella Fitzgerald record playing. The house was warm. Everywhere we looked, votive candles added a soft glow. The table had been set with plain white dishes and mismatched utensils. In the center of the table was a short flower arrangement, and every place setting was accompanied by a glass for water and one for wine.

May greeted us in her apron, a slight sheen of sweat lingering at her hairline. Her face was flushed by the heat of the oven. She smiled brilliantly when she scooped Kiki up into her arms, cooing about how adorable he looked. I was struck by how beautiful the scene was, how domestic and calm. Jeff was a lucky man.

Introductions were made, and May directed us to the coffee table in the living room while she finished making dinner with Kiki and Beatrice's help. The table was adorned with plates full of cheeses, charcuterie, breads, crackers, and fruits. Privately, I thought that May could almost give Mrs. K. a run for her money. Caleb sat next to me, but he was fidgety, eyes darting from the food on the table to the windows in front of him. I offered him a slice of baguette with Brie and cranberries on it. He took it but didn't eat. He stayed frozen with the amuse-bouche in his hand.

I held back a chuckle. "So, is Gabe the only other member of your crew joining us tonight, Jeff?" I asked.

Caleb's head snapped rather dramatically to look at me, which caused the food in his hand to go tumbling onto the carpet. Mumbling apologies, he hurriedly scooped up the debris and placed the ruined bite on a napkin.

"That's all right, Caleb. This is a house that's meant to be lived in. We encourage spillage." Jeff laughed heartily and popped a strawberry in his mouth. "And to answer your question, Arthur, yes Gabe will be joining us. He is notoriously late, but he has the best taste in wine, which is probably why May always invites him to these kinds of things. She can cook, but when it comes to wine she doesn't know a chardonnay from a merlot."

"Ah, so he's just late then?" I said, glancing at Caleb who was trying to pretend like he was more interested in the prosciutto than the conversation. Jeff didn't need to answer my question. Four soft knocks sounded on the front door.

Jeff stood. "Strange. He's usually much later than this."

Out of the corner of my eye, I noticed that Caleb had frozen again. He quite literally looked like a statue carved to depict a perfect example of panic. He held his breath, hands clenched on top of his thighs, eyes trembling as they stared into nothingness. It was sort of like seeing an android before they booted up, still, silent, yet somehow present. Francis, who had just come in from the kitchen, raised an eyebrow at the sight of Caleb.

I put my hand on his shoulder. "Caleb, it's going to be—"

"Roscoe?" Jeff's voice carried from the foyer. "What in the world are you doing here?"

"I'm sorry, Jeff." Gabe's calmer voice said. "He just showed up at my place as I was about to leave saying he needed to talk to you and that you weren't picking up your phone."

"I don't need you apologizing for me!" Roscoe said, voice wavering in a barely controlled whisper.

"Look, Roscoe, I'm sorry I didn't invite you, but we are just about to have dinner, and May—"

"I don't give a flying fuck about your wife's lasagna, Jeff. I need to talk to you, alone."

"Can't it wait?" Jeff sounded exasperated, like these kinds of outbursts were commonplace for Roscoe, but by the tone of his voice, I had a feeling something was off. Luke also seemed to be somewhat on edge by Roscoe's appearance, and Caleb, stirred out of his malfunction, stared curiously toward the front door.

"No, man. Now. I promise it won't interrupt your little party. But I gotta say this now."

"All right. All right, um . . . here. Come to the garage. Gabe, you can take those in to May and tell her I'll be five minutes, okay?"

Gabe rounded the corner from the foyer into the living room. Caleb's head immediately whipped forward again. The front door closed.

"Hello, everyone!" Gabe said, smiling pleasantly as he walked into the room with three bottles of red wine, bottlenecks clutched between his fingers. "Good to see you again. I'll just give these to May then be right back out." He went to the kitchen.

"You see!" Caleb whispered harshly as if this was somehow all my fault. "He hardly even looked at me."

Before I could even think of a response to that particular piece of ridiculousness, Gabe reentered the room, took the seat closest to Caleb on the love seat, and leaned toward him, placing his hand on Caleb's arm.

"It's great to see you again, Caleb. I've been looking forward to this ever since Jeff told me you were coming."

A furious blush rushed into Caleb's face, but remarkably he managed to keep eye contact for a few seconds before looking away. "Yeah. Me too."

Luckily for Caleb, Gabe seemed to find his bashfulness endearing, and they fell into a lighthearted conversation about a movie Gabe had seen recently. Gabe's hand remained on Caleb's arm the whole time, and every now and then I noticed his thumb gently stroking the fabric of Caleb's shirt. Smiling, I stood up, grabbing a few more hors d'oeuvres, and made my way to the kitchen. Francis got the hint and followed, but Luke remained seated where he was, picking at the charcuterie platter.

"Hey Luke," I said.

"Huh?"

"Why don't you come in here and help get everything out to the table?"

"Oh yeah, okay."

I couldn't tell if Caleb would thank me or hate me for clearing the room. Glancing back, his face seemed caught between gratitude and anger, but then Gabe said something that caught his attention and all that was left on his face was infatuation.

"Arthur," May said, "Would you mind checking on Jeff? The lasagna is just about to come out of the oven, and I really don't want it to get cold." She had Kiki on her back, and she was bent over the counter in such a way that he could grind perhaps too generous an amount of pepper onto a vibrantly colored salad.

"Sure, but Roscoe seemed pretty serious about talking to him alone."

May scoffed. "That big lug has ruined enough of my dinner

parties with his terrible table manners. I won't let him ruin this one by taking up all of Jeff's time."

"All right. I'll be back in a second."

I tried to make my way through the living room as inconspicuously as possible, but I could've been a woolly mammoth crashing through the house and Gabe and Caleb wouldn't have noticed. In the time that we had been in the kitchen, their hands had intertwined and their faces were within mere inches of each other. They both smiled softly and giggled at what the other said. That blush was still staining Caleb's face, but it was softer now. It just added to the glow that surrounded the two of them. I laughed to myself. Guess Caleb didn't need me after all.

The night was dark. There weren't too many streetlamps in the neighborhood, but a dull fluorescent bulb was lit over the door to the garage. I made to knock on the door before I entered, but then there was the sound of something falling. I stopped. Against my better judgment, I shifted so that I could no longer be seen through the window, and I listened.

"Jesus, careful, Roscoe. Honestly. You're like a bull in a china shop."

"It's not broken, Jeff. Don't worry. And if it were, you know I'd buy you a new one."

"Yeah. Yeah I know. You're a good guy, Roscoe, and I get why you're so worried, but I'm telling you that kind of stuff just doesn't happen anymore."

"And I'm telling you it's happening right now. How else can I convince you?"

"You haven't talked to your dad in ages. Why, suddenly, would he be telling you all this stuff?"

Roscoe paused. "He didn't exactly tell me . . ."

"Roscoe . . ." Jeff's voice had a tinge of trepidation in it.

"Look, it's not breaking and entering because I still have a key to the old man's place."

"Roscoe, you promised you'd stop going there."

"Hey! He has the only things that are left from my mother. I can't take 'em because he'd notice, but . . . look that isn't the point. The point is—"

"Okay. Okay." Jeff had clearly heard enough, and nothing Roscoe was going to say would convince him. "Your dad's a powerful man around here. Everyone knows that, and I'm sure that if he wanted to, he could shut the whole thing down. But I really, really doubt that he cares, Roscoe. I really do. If anything, what we're doing will just help the economy around here."

Roscoe let loose a startling guffaw. "Economy? Economy! Please, Jeff, you know that my dad doesn't give a shit about the economy, especially not if it means messing up his perfect little town with people he don't care for. And he's not the only one. Let me tell you, they can do a lot worse than just shut us down."

"But they won't, Roscoe. Really. They won't."

"You're a damned fool. You know that. You think everything's peaches and cream when the real shit is staring you right in the face."

"Then what do you want me to do about it?" Jeff raised his voice slightly. He sounded like he'd had enough. I knew that I had. The whole conversation was making my stomach churn, even though I had no clear idea of what they were talking about. All I knew was that May had made a delicious meal for us. I didn't want to lose my appetite all because of Roscoe's apparent paranoia.

I knocked on the door. Another something came crashing down, and the door was yanked open. Jeff stood there looking relieved that someone had come to rescue him, but also annoyed because Roscoe seemed to have knocked over a very expensive-looking drill.

"Hey, sorry to interrupt." I said. "But May says dinner's ready."

Jeff smiled. "Oh, you're not interrupting anything. I was just about to come back in." He started to make his way out of the garage and then cringed slightly. For a moment, he seemed to have a rather gruesome internal battle over whether to do the polite thing and invite Roscoe to join us, or to just let him clean up the mess he'd made and send him on his way. Of course, being the excellent man that he was, Jeff went with the former. Roscoe somewhat grudgingly accepted the invitation, and the three of us went inside.

* * *

At some point during the dinner party, Caleb and Gabe had disappeared together, but Caleb came back home with us. In the car, with Luke and Beatrice sleeping in the back seat and Francis and Kiki coming back with Jeff, I decided to tease him a little bit.

"Seemed like things went pretty well between you two. I'm surprised you didn't go home with him instead of us tonight."

Caleb chuckled shyly. "I was tempted. It's been a long time since"—he paused, glancing back in the mirror to assure himself that the other two were still asleep—"Well you know . . . but . . . I kind of want to take it a little slow. Maybe go on a real date before any of that stuff happens."

I had been expecting something snarkier than the honest answer he gave me, but it made me feel secure to hear Caleb talk like that. It felt good to be so trusted by him, and it felt good to see him so happy. "Sounds like a good plan. Did you guys set a date?"

Caleb nodded. "He wants to take me on a picnic. Not in town, but someplace special, he said."

"Sounds romantic."

"Yeah. I guess it does."

"Caleb and Gabe sitting in a tree." As much as I appreciated Caleb's openness, the whole conversation was starting to veer into a slightly too intimate territory. Being the master avoider that I was, I decided some childish teasing was the best way to lighten the mood.

Caleb didn't seem to mind. He laughed and whacked my shoulder. "What are you? Five?"

I just chuckled. By the time we got to the airboat dock, Luke and Beatrice were so deeply asleep, laden with cheese and tomato sauce, that Caleb and I couldn't rouse them. Caleb ended up carrying Beatrice bridal style into the boat, and I slung Luke's limp form over my shoulder like a sack of potatoes. Neither of them woke up. Francis joined us with a similarly knocked-out Kiki, and we all said a quick goodbye to Jeff.

When I crawled into bed, I half expected to be kept awake by the worry that Roscoe and Jeff's conversation had set into my stomach. It wouldn't be the first time that my thoughts ran rampant at the most inconvenient of times. But as soon as my head hit the pillow, I fell into a deep, deep sleep. A long, dark, nothingness.

"Have you ever thought about having kids?" Thia asked.

My head shot up, and I choked on the beer I was drinking. Spluttering, I tried to come up with an answer that didn't come off as completely douchey, while also conveying my absolute unwillingness to continue this line of questioning. Thia and I had just moved from friendship to romance. On top of that, I already had a kid. Not that Grace was really mine apart from what biology dictated. But still, that was enough for me.

"You want kids?" I eventually replied. When in doubt, answer with a question. It was a cowardly tactic of diversion, but I didn't mind being a coward now and then.

She had been laughing, watching me squirm in indecision, so it took her a few moments to collect herself before she leaned forward and kissed me. I was still at the point where Thia's kisses always took me by surprise. In fact, I'm not sure if I ever grew out of that phase.

"Not really." She said. "I'm not sure I'd be the best mother."

I frowned. I couldn't exactly argue the point because I'd never given it much thought, but Thia was a good person, if not a little selfish and unpredictable. She'd be as good a mom as any, I thought.

"Why do you say that?"

She shrugged, taking a sip of her beer. She liked the dark stuff, Guinness and this one called Petroleum, which was accurately named for its taste.

"I guess I'm just too . . . not selfish. I mean I am selfish but, you know, I give a lot to the people I love."

"I know." She'd certainly given me a lot.

"I think it's more that I'm not brave enough."

I couldn't help but laugh at that. Thia was the most fearless person I knew. I said as much.

"Being fearless and being brave aren't the same though, are they? Besides, I'm not fearless. I'm afraid of a lot of things."

"Like what?" I was genuinely curious. Thia knew that I was afraid of thunderstorms and bats and the Teletubbies. She knew that I always slept on the hotel bed furthest from the door and that I never willingly went into a basement or attic alone. She knew that when I had watched *Suspiria* for the first time, I had gotten so scared that I peed my pants. She knew all my fears, but the only thing I could think of that she was afraid of was cockroaches.

"Well not many, like, concrete things. Stuff like clowns and serial killers don't bother me that much. But I guess . . . not knowing stuff, not feeling like I'm in charge of my own destiny, not feeling like I can control other people . . . god that last one makes me sound so manipulative."

"I understand."

"Of course you do. You understand everything about me. It's annoying." She laughed. I was glad that she thought I knew her so well, because I felt utterly bewildered by her more often than not.

"So you think that because you wouldn't be able to fully control your kids, you'd be a bad mom?"

"No." Thia said. "I think the fact that I would *want* to fully control them would make me a bad mom."

"Oh." I agreed with what she was saying, but I sure as hell wasn't going to say that. Luckily my phone buzzed on the counter, delaying whatever further conversation Thia had in mind. However, when I looked at the caller ID, I felt the familiar feeling that the universe was playing some kind of joke on me.

"Hey, Grace." I said. "What's up?"

"Grace? Your sister?" Thia said. "Let me talk to her." She made grabby hands for my phone.

"What? Why? No." I said, smacking her hands away lightly. "Huh? Oh no, Grace, not you. Keep going."

"Oh you're no fun." Thia pouted.

Bright light glared beneath my eyelids. Groaning, I threw my arm over my face, attempting to block out whatever tried to rouse me. I remembered closing my curtains last night before I'd fallen asleep. They were those heavy blackout kind, thank goodness. Still, some kind of light was on in my room. Curiosity got the better of sleepiness.

Squinting my eyes open, I saw that the floor lamp in the corner of my room had been turned on, and someone was hunched over the desk there. Raising myself up in my bed, I croaked, but couldn't form a name. Whether it was sleep or fear that kept me from speaking, I couldn't say, but I knew that I was terrified.

When the figure turned around and I saw Grace's face, relief swept over me like a tidal wave so strong it almost knocked me back into my pillows.

"Jesus, Grace!" I rasped. "You almost gave me a heart attack! What are you doing? What time is it?"

"Sorry." She said. "It's early, not yet six."

"What are you doing then?"

"Oh . . . I just noticed that you had these pictures on your desk the other day, but I didn't get a chance to look at them."

I had gone searching for a long-forgotten tie two days ago in preparation for the dinner party. I dug through every pocket and every crevice of the luggage I'd brought with me to the Hotel to no avail. The tie was forever lost, like a left sock or Jimmy Hoffa. However, in my search I'd stumbled across a Ziploc bag filled with old Polaroids from my youth. I hadn't even remembered packing them, let alone bringing them from my father's old house to New York, then to Iowa, then back to New York. Maybe they'd been in that suitcase since my freshman year. It was pretty old.

I hadn't looked at them yet myself, except the one on top,

which was taken at one of those awful Christmas displays with the fake Santa and the fake elves and the fake snow. Grace sat on Santa's lap, and Santa was hugging her around the waist, presumably asking what she wanted for Christmas. I stood off to the side, glaring at the Santa out of the corner of my eye, hand extended to take Grace's. I couldn't remember what had pissed me off so much, but maybe I was simply creeped out by the charade of it all.

"Here." I gestured for her to sit down. "Let me take a look at them too."

She smiled and joined me on the bed, sitting cross-legged and spreading the photos out in a fan in front of her. Carefully we picked through them, lingering on certain ones, passing over others. We silently examined the reminders of my childhood as if they were artifacts in a museum. As time passed, I noticed that Grace kept coming back to one photograph in particular, staring at it for a longer time than any others.

"What you got there?" I asked.

"I think it's your mom." She said, handing the photograph to me.

I took it. Sure enough, it was a picture of my mom. She sat in her favorite chair in our old living room, her legs tucked up underneath her bottom. On her lap was a thick, cable-knit blanket and an open book with a title I couldn't read. There was a cup of something still steaming on the floor next to the chair and a box of tissues next to that. My dad stood above her, his hands on her shoulders. He was smiling down at her. It was the kind of smile he was never able to manage after she died. She was smiling up at him.

I remembered taking this photo. It was right before we really figured out what was wrong with her. My mom had been sick. We thought she had the flu, so my dad and I stayed home to take care of her. She hardly ever got sick. It was probably my last genuinely happy memory of her. We ate grilled cheeses and chicken noodle soup and played poker and watched *Friday*. It was a perfect day.

Grace ran her thumb underneath my eye. It was only then that

I realized I was crying. I couldn't remember the last time I'd cried. I definitely couldn't remember the last time I'd cried because of my mom. Even after she'd died, I'd felt empty and scared and alone, but I hadn't cried that much. When I had finally accepted that Thia was gone, dead or deliberately missing, I hadn't cried even though I'd felt an anger so pungent that it made me black out at times. I just wasn't much of a crier.

"Sorry," I sniffled. "I haven't seen a picture of my mom in a while I guess."

"What was she like?" Grace asked. I blinked at her, two huge tears escaping from my eyelids and rolling down my cheeks. "Your . . . Dad never talked about her, and there weren't any pictures in the house when we were growing up. I think he put them away when Mari asked."

"Oh yeah. I remember they made her feel weird." Mari had never cared that my dad was still in love with my mother because Mari had never been in love with my dad. But for some reason having my mother staring at her through picture frames was a little too much like being haunted.

"You don't have to talk about her if you don't want to." Grace said.

"No. No you should know I think." For a brief moment, I became unfathomably sad at the fact that Grace would never know her grandmother. "She was . . . she was really incredible. Dad was, you know, a good guy, but my mom brought out the best in him. She brought out the best in everyone. And she was so down-to-earth. Even when I was a kid, she never lied to me. She always talked to me like I was smart enough to understand, and when I wasn't, she would explain it to me. She just . . . seemed to have life down. And she was so kind and loving. Everyone knew they could trust her."

"She sounds amazing." Grace said.

"Yeah. In some ways you remind me of her."

"Really?"

"Yeah. You even kind of look like her."

Grace took the photograph back and looked at it again. She tilted her head to the side, fingers coming up to caress a stray curl that had escaped from her nighttime braid. "Yeah. Yeah, I guess I do. Her hair was much curlier though."

I laughed. "Yeah. She had wild hair, but she loved it. Whenever we'd watch music videos or awards shows, she'd get so annoyed with women who straightened their hair or wore wigs or whatever. She thought that curls were something to be cherished, and changing them was a disservice to beauty. She could see the beauty in everything, except for straightened curly hair."

Grace laughed. "She sounds like quite the woman."

"Yeah she was. Everything changed after she died."

"I would've liked to have known her. I would've liked to have known you before she died."

There wouldn't have been a Grace if my mother hadn't died. I'd never really thought of that before. If my mother were still alive today, maybe I would be living with a wife and kids of my own, kids who knew I was their father. But looking at Grace then, and thinking about Beatrice and Luke, I thought that maybe, even in death, my mother had given me three irreplaceable gifts.

I coughed, scrubbing at my eyes to stop the tears. Finally I looked up at her and said, "So was there a reason you needed to look at these pictures so early in the morning?"

"Not particularly. I think I just . . . well sometimes you're so secretive. I just wanted to glimpse into your past, I guess."

I smiled. "We all have our secrets."

Grace nodded. "Yeah. I know I do." I also knew that she did. I could think of at least five glaring secrets Grace was keeping from me. For example, the secret of her failed engagement. At first, I had believed the story of things ending amicably, but as time went on, I started to find the explanation less than plausible. Then there was the question of who was funding her pipe dream, and how Grace even knew him. Or her. But for some reason, I felt that if Grace were keeping secrets from me, then they were things I didn't want to know in the first place. It was self-preservation.

Grace and I went through the pictures until the sun started to peek through the edges of my curtains. Usually I would've begrudged her the lost hours of sleep, but somehow I didn't feel tired at all. The construction crew worked only in the morning on Saturdays, and so we both got up and made our way down to greet them.

In all my life, I'd never had a proper Christmas tree. My mother was allergic to pine, so we always had one of those plastic ones with the fake snow on the needles when I was a kid. After my mom died, we never had a Christmas tree at all. In New York, Thia and I had more of a shrub than a tree. Even though we decorated it with ornaments and lights, it couldn't compare to the behemoth that Luke, Sam, and Diego were struggling to get through the door.

The past month had gone quickly. Jeff and the others were dedicated to their work and were completing tasks a lot faster than originally projected. There had been a bit of worry the week after the dinner party. Almost ten workers quit the project for reasons that Jeff only vaguely explained. Luckily, he was able to find more in just a few short days. According to him, there were always men desperate to work in the South.

The Hotel was starting to actually look like it could be something, and it was having an effect on the guests. Caleb was light-footed and grinning half the time, but I think that had more to do with his new boyfriend than the construction. Gabe came to the Hotel almost every day, even though he still wasn't needed. On weekends the two of them would disappear on some romantic getaway. It was sickeningly sweet seeing the two of them in the honeymoon phase of a new relationship.

Sam and Clancy also seemed more open in their relationship, if you could call it that. Mrs. K. didn't rebuff Thadeus quite as often or as harshly. Beatrice had even caught the attention of one of the younger workers, a nineteen-year-old taking night courses at a community college while he cared for his sick mother. He seemed like a good kid, but my big-brother protectiveness made me too wary to be too encouraging. Still, she seemed happy, and they laughed a lot together.

Kiki thrived off having so many people around to indulge in

his fantasies and stories. All of the workers were utterly charmed by him, as was everyone else who got within shouting distance. Francis seemed to take the construction as an opportunity to teach Kiki some real-life lessons about physics and business, so even he was a little less stoic. Diego also seemed to enjoy having more than us few around. It meant that he could regale the construction workers with stories about his life in Spain, which I'm sure he knew by now that none of the other guests believed.

All in all, the good feelings were growing, piling one on top of the other until they culminated to this: an oversized pine tree stuffed through a door that was clearly too small for it, leaving emerald-green needles in its wake. Luke and Diego shouted at each other from either end of the tree, heatedly debating the best way to achieve their goal. Sam just stood calmly in the middle of it all, supporting the weight of the tree against his chest. Eventually Luke lost his patience and gave the tree a hearty shove from behind, sending both Sam and Diego toppling to the floor, but finally getting the latter half of Christmas foliage into the foyer.

"Jesus, Luke!" Diego shouted, that Midwestern twang seeping into his speech the way it always did when he was upset. "You could've killed us!"

"But I didn't, and now the tree's in. Where should we put it?"

"You have to put a base on it first." I said from my spot against the wall near the library.

All three of their heads whipped around to me. "A what?" Luke said.

"A base. It won't stand up if it doesn't have a base. And probably some wire to keep it upright too."

"Dammit!" Luke shouted, kicking the sawed-off trunk.

"Don't take it out on the tree." Sam mumbled.

The next day a base and some wire were acquired. It was unanimously decided that the massive tree would be placed right in the middle of the foyer, halfway between the front door and the stairs leading to the second floor. No one mentioned that it was the only place the tree could feasibly fit. I had to admit it looked pretty handsome there.

Jeff lent us a few ladders we could use to decorate the highest parts, but even those weren't tall enough. Kiki ended up having to place the star on top of the tree while being suspended over the second-floor landing by Francis. In the end, the tree looked like it had rolled around in boxes of old Christmas decorations. I couldn't have imagined it any other way.

The whole construction crew was going to have two weeks off for the holidays, so as a present, all of the guests decided it would be best to throw an extravagant holiday party. Mrs. K., of course, took to the idea immediately and began to plan out a menu fit for a banquet at Buckingham Palace. I couldn't even begin to describe some of the dishes she came up with, but there was more than enough for everyone and each of the flavors brought the feeling of celebration. Decorations got strung up around the Hotel in a slightly more organized fashion than they had on the tree. Soon, the entire foyer, library, dining room, and ballroom were decked out with hanging mistletoe, red and green ribbons, and sparkly images of Frosty and Santa. As far as I knew, there weren't any Jewish people on Jeff's crew. But Caleb and Gabe had found an oversized menorah at a thrift shop on one of their romantic weekend adventures, so we set it up next to the tree. None of us actually knew which night of Hanukkah it was, but Kiki said six was a lucky number, so six candles were lit.

All of the crew wandered in with their friends and families, looking quite in awe of the place they'd known only as a source of income suddenly transformed into a Christmasy wonderland. Presents were set under the tree. Mulled wine and eggnog was handed out generously. Many of the workers had children of varying ages accompanying them. Kiki was soon leading a gang of youngsters in a search for Narnia, and Beatrice and her new love interest sat around the fire in the library chatting with some of the teenage offspring of the crew. Jeff brought May, of course. May and Grace hit it off immediately. Jeff and I watched from the side as the two of them cackled at one joke or another, hands on shoulders and forearms.

"You've really got something here." Jeff said. "It's tight. Does it feel like this every day?"

I laughed. "Well there are certainly fewer decorations, but I guess so."

"It's pretty amazing."

I didn't thank him because in truth it had nothing to do with me. It was all Grace. Somehow she had found this place, found the people, found me, and put us all together like brand-new, unbent puzzle pieces.

Mrs. K. had decided against a sit-down dinner due to the sheer number of people. Instead everyone walked around with red and green paper plates piled high with finger foods and other traveling delights. It wasn't odd to see a construction worker with a plate of food in one hand and a glass of alcohol in the other, uncertain how to go about consuming everything laid out for him. I myself stayed away from the alcohol, the memory of the birthday party hangover still too poignant in my mind. Instead, I watched as people swung around the ballroom floor, looking like the perfect picture of holiday merriment. Caleb and Gabe showed everyone up with their salsa dancing skills, tossing each other around the dance floor and sliding back and forth. Eventually they got so worn out that, laughing hysterically, they made room for other couples to show off their skills.

They walked up to me, Caleb's arm securely tucked around Gabe's waist, and Gabe's cheek resting on Caleb's shoulder. If there were any better example of being fresh in love, I couldn't think of one.

"Man, what a party!" Gabe said, which earned him a kiss on the forehead.

"You two look like you're having fun." I smiled.

"Loads. Although I'm a little worn out from dancing. This guy takes no prisoners." Gabe slapped Caleb lightly on the chest for emphasis.

"Nonsense. You were the one wearing me out." Caleb laughed. It was such an adorable scene that I almost wanted to walk away from it and let them fully bask in the glow of their infatuation. "So Arthur," Caleb said, "Anyone catching your attention?"

I laughed. "Pretty much everyone is spoken for. All the taken workers brought their wives, and I'm pretty sure the single ones are as straight as boards."

"Never know unless you ask." Gabe said.

"Besides, one of the workers brought his sister. She's about thirty. Just the right age for you."

I knew whom he was talking about. She was a pretty woman with a good sense of humor as far as I could tell from conversations overheard in passing. But the idea of trying to strike up any kind of flirtation with her was the furthest from my mind. Maybe it'd just been so long since my last romance, or maybe I was just too content being alone. Either way, I didn't see the need to try and make anything happen that wasn't going to happen naturally. I was happy, for the first time in a long time. I didn't need anything more.

"You don't like sex." Thia said.

We were lying fully clothed in our bed, watching a Korean drama that Thia was inexplicably obsessed with.

"That's not true. Why would you say that?" My eyes were glued to the screen, afraid to miss a single subtitle. Okay, maybe I was a bit obsessed with it too.

"It's no big deal. It's just . . . you don't really initiate stuff that often, and when you do it's like all about me. It's like you don't want me to pleasure you or something."

I flinched a little at her words. It was true that sex didn't pass through my mind as often as it might for another person my age. I didn't like to admit it, but my experiences with Mari had made me somewhat fearful of sex. The time with Mari that had felt the best for me was the time that made Grace. Not that I regretted having Grace, but sex didn't carry the same mindless appeal to me after she was born.

"I like when you pleasure me. I guess I just get too caught up in my head. And part of the thing I love so much about sex is . . . making you feel good."

"Same for me. I like making you feel good."

"Oh." I felt bad. I wondered if this were something that Thia had been keeping under wraps this whole time, or if she'd just recently thought about it. Either way, I was clever enough to know that sex problems were usually the beginning of the end for a relationship.

"Don't feel bad." Thia said. "I'm not unhappy with the sex. When we have it, it's really, really good."

"But you want to have more?" I asked.

"Not necessarily more . . . just . . . I guess it makes me feel a little insecure when I'm the one always initiating. Makes me feel unsexy I guess."

"God, I'm sorry. That's not what I think at all. I guess sex just makes me a little nervous still is all."

"That's okay. It's okay to be nervous." I knew by the tone of her voice that she really meant it. "But, if you can manage it, maybe try to start things up with me more often. If I don't want you to do anything, I'll tell you to stop. Okay?"

"Okay." I leaned forward and kissed her. It wasn't just the kind of light peck you gave a partner after a deep conversation, or even the sweet kiss to show someone that you loved them. It was the passionate, all-encompassing, fiery kind of kiss that made a tightness curl in your lower belly. "Like this?" I asked her, pulling away only slightly.

"Yeah." She cupped her hand around my neck, pulling me on top of her. "Like that."

"Arthur?" Caleb said.

"Huh. Oh sorry, got distracted. Yeah she's all right I guess."

"Just all right?" Caleb sounded exasperated by my lack of interest.

I laughed and clapped him on the shoulder. "Yeah, man, don't worry about it. I'm fine being just my single self."

"That's too bad." Gabe said. "Caleb and I were hoping to find you someone so we could go on double dates."

I laughed again, this time a little more loudly. "Really? Why don't you go on double dates with Jeff and May?"

"We do." Caleb said, clearly annoyed. "But it's not the same. You're my best . . ." He cut himself off and looked wide-eyed at me. When I didn't flinch, he continued. "You're my best friend. I want to do that kind of stuff with my best friend."

I couldn't help the huge grin that spread across my face, nor could I help the swing of my arms as they reached out to pull Caleb into a crushing hug. I wasn't drunk, but Caleb's admittance made my head feel dizzy nonetheless. I don't think I'd ever been anyone's best friend, except for maybe Thia's. It felt good.

"You're my best friend, too." I said. Off to our side, Gabe cooed at the sweet display of friendship love.

"All right. Enough with the sappiness." Caleb pushed me away playfully. "You may be fine being all single and stuff, but I'm more than happy with my boyfriend, so I'm going to get him a drink. You want something?"

"No I'm all right. You two go ahead." I watched fondly as the two of them walked off hand in hand.

Getting tired of watching people dance, I made my way into the foyer. A seething group of little kids had gathered around the base of the tree and were sifting through the presents indiscreetly. I walked around behind them, crossing my arms over my chest in feigned consternation.

"Hey you lot! Just what do you think you're doing?"

All of their little bodies jumped in unison. Some of them dropped whatever they had in their hands and scrambled off to find their moms and dads. Others clutched their pilfered presents to their chest, whipping their heads to give me a look that said, *Don't you dare take this away from me.* Others still made a poor attempt to hide behind the tree, peeking their little faces out from behind the ornaments.

"We were just looking!" Kiki said, clearly playing the role of leader in his little start-up gang.

"And what would Santa say about you guys being so naughty this close to Christmas?" It felt thrilling to play the part of a disapproving father figure.

Kiki rolled his eyes with sass. "No one believes in Santa Claus. He isn't real."

"What?" A little girl with ribbons holding up two perky pigtails looked at Kiki with big, wavering eyes. I gave him a look, and he grinned goofily.

"Just kidding?" He said.

"Oh. Okay!" The girl said, relieved, before she skipped off to find her parents.

All the kids who had stayed set down the gifts and wandered off too. Only Kiki remained, holding a small box wrapped in shimmery blue paper in his hand. I reached out for it.

"Come on. Hand it over. We'll all open presents together."

"Oh you're no fun." He said, plopping the box in my hand. Before he ran off to find his new friends, he wrapped his arms around my waist and looked up at me, smiling. "Merry Christmas! This is so fun!" He only let go once I ruffled his hair.

The box in my hand felt light, almost like it held nothing but air. Lifting up the little card that was taped to the paper, I saw Grace's name inscribed on the inside, along with the message, "To the most powerful woman I know, something as beautiful as you are." I was surprised by the message. I wondered who among the guests or workers would write something so sweet, so romantic. The handwriting looked somewhat familiar, but I couldn't place it. Before I could examine it further, the box was snatched out of my hand and Grace appeared at my side.

"Hey no peeking!" She said, looking slightly more flustered than present pilfering should have caused. I think maybe she had had a bit more to drink than she was used to.

Still, I laughed sheepishly, somewhat embarrassed to have been caught doing the same thing I'd scolded all those children for not two seconds ago. "Sorry. It's for you."

"Oh. Yeah I know. It's from a friend." She said vaguely, pocketing the present. "I had put it on my nightstand, but I guess Beatrice slipped it under the tree."

"What friend?"

"Just an old friend."

I frowned. Evasiveness was becoming an unshakeable part of Grace's personality, but my attention was quickly drawn away. In the doorway to the library, underneath a sprig of mistletoe stood Beatrice and her boy, kissing lightly. The group of other teenagers stood behind them, hands in the air, teasingly jeering. When the two pulled apart, both of them blushed, Beatrice smiling shyly, and the boy scrubbing the back of his head. They wandered off to the dining room together, holding hands as their friends hollered after them.

My chest grew tight. It was a cute kiss, not vulgar. It was respectful. Still, it made me feel strange to see it. I turned to Grace.

"Does he know?" I asked.

"About Beatrice you mean?"

"Yeah." I never wanted to voice it to Beatrice because I didn't want to offend her or make her feel like something was unnatural about her. But it had been a worry in my mind since she had started taking interest in the kid. Not everyone was like the people in the Hotel. I wanted to try and protect her from the ugliness of others for as long as I could.

"He does actually. Beatrice told him up front. She's really brave, that girl."

"Yeah she is. And he was . . . ?"

"Obviously," she said, gesturing to the spot where they'd just kissed, "He didn't mind."

Relief flooded over me. "Oh. Good. Good."

Grace grinned at me. "You're a good man, Arthur Bean. You're a good dad."

I laughed. "What?"

But she just shook her head and walked away. Something about what she had said nibbled at the back of my mind. In fact, there had been quite a few words of hers recently that had struck a chord in me, but I had been ignoring them thus far. Still it seemed ridiculous now for me to ignore the possibility that maybe Grace knew more about her parentage than I'd thought. Mari had sworn to me that she'd never tell her, but it wasn't exactly like Mari was the pinnacle of trustworthiness. And there were other ways she could have found out. If she did know, what did that mean for us?

Pulling myself out of the depths of my spiraling anxiety, I brought myself back to the moment. That beautiful moment of cheer and food and drink and home was enough to assuage my worry, at least for a little bit. Because if I could live in this moment, then any moments going forward might not seem quite so bad.

"Merry Christmas." I mumbled to no one in particular. Then I followed my rumbling stomach into the dining room.

* * *

New Year's was a much tamer affair with just the guests of the Hotel, Gabe, and Beatrice's new boyfriend. Diego had managed to set up an old television in the library that looked like it could've been from the sixties. We all watched as the ball dropped.

Who was going to kiss whom had been arranged days before. When the ball dropped, Thadeus swooped Mrs. K. into a sloppy yet endearing kiss that lasted for a little bit longer than anyone else's. Beatrice and her boyfriend kissed as well, but kept it tame. My blood pressure was extremely thankful for that. Diego gave Grace a quick, friendly peck, which she accepted jovially, and then he leaned down to receive sloppy kisses from Zorro. Sam managed a kiss on Clancy's lips that lasted almost two whole seconds before he pulled away red-faced and babbling. Kiki kissed Francis on the cheek, and then, seeing Luke sitting in the corner watching all the kissing going around, did the same for my broody brother.

Caleb and Gabe of course kissed like the perfect couple they were. "One for my boyfriend." Caleb said and then, turning to me, pressed a firm but friendly kiss on my lips. "And one for my best friend."

I laughed. "Dude! Gabe is standing right there."

"Oh please, you think I'd just up and kiss you without asking his permission first?"

"Couldn't leave you without a kiss on New Year's." Gabe said, totally unfazed by the scene. I was suddenly struck by how lucky Caleb was to find someone like Gabe. I felt overwhelmed by happiness for him.

"Just don't get used to it. The other 364 days of the year, these lips are reserved for one man and one man only."

I chuckled. "I'll keep that in mind."

We had kept the decorations from the Christmas party up for the entire week leading up to New Year's Eve. On New Year's Day,

210

we started taking them down. I wasn't really sure why, but I was sad to see all that kitsch and festivity fall from the banisters and walls. My more rational side told me that everyone was a little depressed at the end of the holidays. After all, we had to return to eating normally and working normally and living normally. No more sugarplums and elves on the shelves. But my more morbid self built up a worry in my gut that felt far too poignant to be ignored.

The niggling in my stomach turned out to be almost prophetic.

Two weeks into the New Year, I had taken on a much more active role in the renovation of the Hotel. In fact, almost everyone had some part to play. It was as if we were part of the crew. Jeff joked often that he should be paying us salary for the number of tasks we took on.

Diego, Sam, Luke, Clancy, Caleb, and I were all strong and able-bodied, so we helped with a lot of the lugging and sawing and hammering. It got to a point where if one of the crew leads needed something done, they'd come to one of us first. After all, we had a large personal investment on the success of this renovation. We probably worked just a smidge harder than the rest of them. Thadeus wasn't much help where physical labor was involved, but he made sure that everyone was fed and watered, passing out lemonade and snacks like his life depended on it. Of course, every day, Mrs. K. provided a magnificent lunch for everyone. Beatrice helped her with that, at least when she wasn't helping her boyfriend with whatever he was doing for the day. In the mornings, Francis kept Kiki confined to the library so he could work on his studies. In the afternoons, usually during the last two hours before everyone went home, Francis would supervise while one of the workers taught Kiki some real-life construction skills. I couldn't count the number of screws or nails that had been put into place by his little hands.

Grace was the only guest who wasn't working constantly. She made her way around every once in a while, chatting with everyone and making sure things were going okay. But for the most part she locked herself up in her room. Beatrice said she was mostly on the phone and writing letters and checks and stuff. But Beatrice couldn't care less about Grace's secretive business dealings. My curiosity, on the other hand, was only growing.

I now knew where the food came from, an organic wholesaler based in Austin. I knew that about every three months, the guests at the hotel gathered around the one computer we owned and ordered clothes, or whatever else they wanted, off the internet. This was how Francis received materials for Kiki's lessons. I knew that all the guests who took regular medication received three-month supplies from a remote pharmacy. How they got their prescriptions refilled was still another question waiting to be answered.

I'd figured out a lot just by observation and careful digging. But I still didn't know where the money came from, and I didn't know to whom Grace was talking. Those were the two things that I felt I should know. But I didn't. I couldn't figure it out. For an amount of time after New Year's, I stopped trying.

The whole process of renovating the Hotel had taken on a kind of symbiotic feel. We all fed off of each other's energies. Every day Jeff marveled at how quickly things were getting done. Optimism grew like weeds among the guests at the Hotel, and every night we lay down to bed looking forward to being one day closer to our dreams.

A shriek from around the backside of the Hotel brought all those dreams crashing down. Luke and I were on the porch, taking a break with Vince and two other workers. We gossiped over fresh lemonade and scones that Mrs. K. had made that morning, talking about goings-on in town. Vince mentioned that a big group of men had traveled in from all around the South in recent days and were shacking up at various prominent locals' houses. Another worker speculated it had something to do with the town's Founder's Day celebration, which was that coming weekend. Before Luke or I could respond, the screaming shocked all of us out of our contentment.

The glass of lemonade in my hand slipped loose and shattered on the porch as I shot off in the direction of the noise. The shriek had been long and drawn out, pulling at my lungs until I felt I couldn't breathe anymore. Then it broke down, disintegrated into frantic sobbing. More screaming joined it, multiple voices yelling at each other or for each other. The front door to the Hotel swung open. I just narrowly missed getting smashed in the face by it. I skirted the open door and the people coming out of it, jumping off the porch. Suddenly Zorro was at my side, baying to alert everyone that something was wrong. Something was terribly, terribly wrong.

When I finally swung around the back of the Hotel, my feet slipped on the mud. I landed hard on my knees. Catching my breath, I looked up. I almost wish I hadn't.

The first thing I saw was red. It was spilling over the wooden boards. It had splattered onto two of the workers who now stood there with dumbfounded expressions on their pale faces. It had pooled in rivulets on the marshy ground. All of it still spurted forth from Kiki's hand.

Kiki was shrieking, sobbing, asking for help, using his free hand to claw around and try to grab some kind of savior from thin air. His face had gone ghastly white. I knew he was seconds from passing out. Sure enough, seconds later, he did, slumping over the board he had been nailing. His face rested in a pool of blood inches away from his injured hand. It looked like a dead animal nailed to a wall.

Francis roared at the two workers with the blood on their clothes. Other people had created a circle around the scene, with Mrs. K. shoving her way forward to examine Kiki's hand. Jeff and Roscoe both stood with her, mumbling frantically to each other. Grace appeared behind me and put a hand on my shoulder.

"We have to get him to the hospital." She said.

Up until that point, I had been frozen. With her words ringing in my ears, I sprang into action.

"Mrs. K.!" I said. "Can you get the nail out of his hand without hurting him more?"

"I—I think so. It just went through the fleshy part. Thadeus!" She screamed.

"Yes!"

"Get me my things. I need alcohol and gauze and tape. Now!" And then, turning to me, she said, "He needs to go to a real doctor, Arthur. He needs stitches, and there may be nerve damage or worse."

I nodded. "Just get him ready to go, and I'll get him there."

"I'm coming with you!" Caleb said. "You'll need someone to drive."

I nodded. "Thank you."

Francis had gone quiet watching us all work. Silent, panicked tears were streaming down his face. His fists were clenched so hard that his knuckles had turned white. As Thadeus reappeared with Mrs. K.'s supplies, I put my body in between his and Mrs. K.'s.

"Francis. Francis, Kiki needs you. You have to come with us."

From behind me, I heard Mrs. K. ask for Luke and one of the workers to hold Kiki down. Even though he was limp and unconscious now, the pain of having the nail removed would undoubtedly and cruelly wake him. She counted down from three. On three Kiki let loose a pained scream. Francis lunged forward. I caught him around the waist, but he managed to push me forward so my sneakers made grooves in the mud.

"You're hurting him!" Francis shouted. I squeezed him tighter around the ribs until eventually he stopped. Mrs. K. ignored everything else that was happening and set to work on quickly cleaning and wrapping the wound. I glanced behind me. The gaping hole in Kiki's small, pale hand was wider than I thought it would be. Through it I could see the pulsating muscles still pushing out blood. The sight of it almost made me vomit all over Francis's broad chest.

Francis attempted to move forward again. "Diego!" I shouted, but it was Roscoe who eventually came to my aid. He wrapped his big arms around Francis's chest, pulling backward until his movement was halted. The confederate flag tattooed on his arm flexed in my face with every move that Roscoe made.

Grace suddenly appeared at our side. Without warning, she slapped Francis hard across the face. Suddenly everything and everyone froze, except for Mrs. K. who blindly continued her work, and Kiki who had woken sobbing and whimpering.

"Kiki needs you. He needs you, and he needs us. Now get yourself together and get him to the doctor. Now!"

Francis blinked twice and then nodded. Roscoe and I took that as a sign to release him.

"He's ready." Mrs. K. said. Francis took three calm steps forward and collected Kiki's limp form from Beatrice's arms. Her white T-shirt had gained a blood-red Rorschach blot.

Before Francis could walk off toward the airboat Caleb had already run to get started, Mrs. K. grabbed his arm, her arthritic fingers curling around his forearm like a harpy's claw. "It's going to hurt him, but you have to keep pressure on that wound. He's bleeding a lot. Keep pressure on it until you get to the doctor."

Francis cringed but nodded. Scooping up Kiki's hand, he pressed it hard against his chest, flattening his own hand over it. Kiki cried out, but Francis did not let up. I followed them to the boat. No one else said a word.

The car ride into town passed by in a blur. I was glad to have Caleb there because the red staining my vision would've made it hard to drive. Francis refused to let go of Kiki. No matter how much he squirmed or how distressed he sounded, Francis did not release the pressure on Kiki's hand.

"What happened?" Caleb finally asked when we just began to enter the furthest outskirts of the town.

"I turned around for one second. I should have been watching. I should have been fucking watching." Francis said. It was all the answer either of us was going to get.

May was on the sidewalk in front of the clinic waiting for us.

She waved her hands frantically over her head when she saw us driving up Main Street. People on both sides of the road stopped to watch as the four of us emerged from our car. Their hard, white faces glared at us as we rushed to her.

"Oh my god." She said, ushering us inside. "I was at home when Jeff called and told me what happened. I came in straight after that. We're all ready for him."

The blur set in again. Kiki was taken out of Francis's arms. The rude doctor that had taken care of my arm was there, rolling Kiki away from us on a stretcher. Francis tried to follow but was stopped by another nurse. For a moment, I thought he would protest. Then May laid a hand on his shoulder, whispered something in his ear, and he crumpled. Guided by May, he collapsed into a plastic chair. The door to the waiting room burst open, and Gabe rushed inside. He immediately embraced Caleb. Caleb buried his face into his boyfriend's shoulder.

"Jeff called me. Oh, my darling. What happened?" He said softly, stroking Caleb's hair.

"I'm not sure." Caleb said, lifting his face to give Gabe a grateful smile.

"It was an accident." May said.

"Of course it was." I said, my voice coming out slightly harsher than I had meant it to. May didn't seem to mind. She just pulled me into a hug. I let myself be coddled. Caleb and Gabe shared a brief kiss. The receptionist behind the desk let loose a grunt of disgust. The sound sent needles down my spine.

We waited for two hours without any word. Every half hour, May's phone rang and she told Jeff that there was nothing to report. Two minutes before the two hours was over, two men walked into the waiting room and settled themselves in front of the reception desk, speaking softly to the young woman who sat there. Then the doctor emerged in surgery scrubs and beckoned us forward. I noticed as we came that her eyes flickered anxiously over to the two men at the desk. I chose not to look at them. Not now.

"As far as we can tell," the doctor said, her words laced with disapproval and malice, "The boy is going to be just fine." Francis let out a sob he'd been holding in. Gabe slung the arm that wasn't holding Caleb's waist around Francis's wide shoulders. The doctor sneered at the action but didn't comment on it. "Luckily the nail went through the fleshy part between his thumb and forefinger. It missed all the bones by some miracle. I don't think there will be any nerve damage. We've cleaned the wound, given him a tetanus shot, and stitched it up." She paused here, and we all waited with bated breath. "And I'm going to have to contact child services."

"What?" I said.

"You can't . . ." Caleb said.

"Maeve, are you sure that's really—" May started.

"Necessary?" The doctor raised her voice. "Yes I think it is. This is the second time this child has come to my office in the insufficient care of this man." She gestured harshly to me. "This man who is obviously not related to him in any way."

"But this is his legal guardian." I said, pointing to Francis. He nodded shortly. "This was an accident, nothing more. Kiki is well taken care of."

"Well if that's the case," the doctor said, "Then you have nothing to worry about. But I must insist you stay here until child services arrives."

"Where is Kiki?" Francis said.

"He is resting."

"Where is he!"

"Now, now, now," a smooth southern drawl said, "Easy there big guy. This kind lady just saved that kid's life, I reckon. Is that any way to speak to her?"

The man from the museum, Roscoe's father, came wandering toward us, a sickening smile on his face. A thinner, more weaselly but equally sinister-looking man stood behind him, arms crossed against his chest, eyeing Caleb and Gabe with a predatory gaze.

"Mr. Bloomington." Gabe said, his voice trembling. He tightened his grip on Caleb, who looked confusedly between his boyfriend and the two men in front of him.

Francis produced a few papers from his pockets. "I have the papers detailing my guardianship of that boy right now. You have no right to keep him from me." He must've carried them around with him all the time. I never saw him go back into the Hotel for anything.

The skinny man took them and examined them for a brief moment. Then, sneering, he ripped them in half and tossed them to the floor. May scrambled to retrieve them, but the man stomped his muddied boot on top of them, narrowly missing her fingertips.

"Now, now. Let's not get nasty." Roscoe's father said.

"Nasty?" Francis said. "You think simply because you tear up a *copy* of my legal documents it suddenly negates my rights? That child is my responsibility, and I will be taking him home. Now."

Roscoe's father regarded Francis for a moment with an amused expression on his face before turning to me. Out of the corner of my eye, I noticed May sneak past all of us to the back of the clinic.

"You must be Arthur." Roscoe's father said. "My son's told me all about you."

Despite my certainty that he was lying, I couldn't help the sense of betrayal that crept its way through my body. I didn't say anything.

"So let's see here. We've got a nigger,"—an icicle stabbed through my chest—"two fags,"—Caleb and Gabe reeled backward defensively—"and a retard,"—Francis didn't seem to understand that he was the retard—"all raising a child?" Roscoe's father laughed. "And all in that fire trap down in the bayou? With a whole group of other freaks? Heard you even got a towel head in that circus of yours. No. I don't think that will do."

"Francis?" Kiki's weak voice cut the tension. All of us turned to see May walking out, holding him in her arms. The doctor began to protest, but May just pushed past her to place Kiki gently in Francis's arms.

"Oh my boy," Francis said. "Oh my boy, I'm so sorry."

"It's not your fault." Kiki said. "I moved my hand when you all told me not to. I'm sorry."

"No, no, no." Francis gently stroked Kiki's blond hair, which had matted down with sweat and worry. "No, my boy. We all make mistakes. You have nothing to apologize for."

"Francis?"

"Yes, my boy?"

"Take me home. Please."

Francis made to move forward. The skinny man blocked his way. Caleb, Gabe, and I moved to Francis's side. Kiki buried his head in Francis's chest. The doctor grabbed May by the arm. Roscoe's father laughed. For a breath, I felt sure that this was it for us. I felt sure that Kiki would be taken away, that Caleb and Gabe would be beaten until they couldn't move ever again, that I would be strung up by my neck in the town commons like strange fruit, that Francis would be caged and displayed for entertainment. Then, Roscoe's father stopped laughing. Everyone backed down.

"This won't be the last we see of each other, I'm sure." All of us, May included, began to walk away. "Oh, and May?" We stopped as a unit but didn't turn. "Make sure your husband's little construction company is up to snuff. After an accident like this involving a minor, there's sure to be some repercussions."

The crowd of angry faces that had gathered outside the clinic had grown. A quick glance around told me all I needed to know about them. There they stood, shiny white faces, crisp, clean polo shirts and khakis, hands shoved into pockets . . . all staring. The new-wave racists. We all got into the car as quickly as possible, Gabe and May too, and drove away.

* * *

Everyone was silent. The dinner set before us on the table was just leftovers from lunch, everything lying sad and untouched. None of us looked at each other but we were all aware of what was buzzing through our heads. Even though no words were being spoken, the thoughts in all of our minds were deafeningly loud.

Francis had immediately ferried Kiki away to his room after we came back. He let people in, but he wouldn't come out. Only Mrs. K. and Clancy went in to see him. At some point while we were gone, Jeff had sent everyone home with instructions to not come back for another whole working day. They'd be paid, he said, but the proper inquiries needed to be made. Only Roscoe and Vince remained of the crew when I pulled the airboat up next to the dock.

Jeff rushed forward when he saw that May was with us. She had been shocked into silence the whole ride back. In my mind, I wondered how it must feel for her to be faced with the ugliness of people who looked so similar to her. I wondered if she was really surprised by what had happened or if she was simply ashamed that she had even the smallest part of something so vile. When she laid eyes on Jeff, the shock subsided into sobs.

"What happened?" Roscoe said, striding toward us.

"Why don't you ask your father?" I spat at him, shoving my way past as I followed Caleb and Gabe inside. I immediately regretted it, but the feeling of betrayal was too great. I couldn't avoid the pettiness boiling in my gut.

After that, all of us gathered in the dining room, surrounded by this uncharacteristically ordinary display of food. Caleb relayed everything that had happened. Initially, all eyes had fallen on me for explanation, but my roiling anger threatened to spill out into the world at any moment. I wasn't going to aid the spread of my own hatred through words I could not at the moment control. I sat

220

stubbornly under their gaze until Caleb put a hand on my shoulder and spoke for me.

Once the story was finished, I finally gained the courage to look at the others. Faces were pale, gaunt, looking like ghosts of their former selves, paintings exposed to light and rain, fading, dripping away. Beatrice let out a soft sob. Her head fell onto Luke's shoulder. Luke didn't move at all. He had shut down. So many of them had.

"I'll talk to him." Roscoe said. "I'll stop this." It seemed so wrong, so deeply, irrevocably wrong that the first one to offer a solution to a problem that was distinctly ours was not only not one of us, but the son of the man who had threatened us. He made to stand up, but Thadeus's arm shot out from beside him. With strength that none of us knew he had in his stringy, bone-thin arms, the old man forced Roscoe back into his seat.

"Sit down son." He said, his voice level and even. I could suddenly see the military man that he had once been. "I think you have some explaining to do."

Roscoe's eyes darted from face to face. He looked like a man under interrogation for a great crime. In a way, he was.

"My father is a bad man." Many of us held back a scoff at that overly simplistic prologue. "He . . . he used to be a member of the KKK." A sharp intake of breath took the wind out of the room. Even the fire in the hearth flickered. "But . . . he never really cared what organization he was under. He's been a member of so many of . . . those types of things. I guess now he considers himself to be alt-right . . . or a white nationalist. I don't know. It's been so long since I've really spoken to him."

"So you haven't been telling him about us?" I asked. His father had said that Roscoe had mentioned me. I needed to know whether it was true or not. I needed to know whether my judgment of his character was so misguided that it had caused this.

"I swear to you I haven't. I understand why you wouldn't believe me. Because of this." He rolled up his sleeve and showed his Confederate tattoo to the whole table. Those of us who had seen it before just stared. Those of us who hadn't visibly cringed. "But I'm not the man my father wanted me to be. I just don't care about that stuff . . . the stuff he thinks is so low and so evil."

"Being black." Luke said.

"Being gay." Caleb and Gabe both said.

"Being Muslim." Diego said. All of our heads turned to look at him. He shrugged his shoulders but didn't say anything more.

"Being trans." Beatrice whispered from Luke's shoulder. Gabe, reaching his body across the table, took her hand and squeezed it. I was surprised that she let him.

"So what is it, exactly? What is he planning to do?" It was the first time Grace had spoken. Her face had been set deep in thought. All the while she'd been sporadically tapping her fingers on the dining room table as if she were trying to communicate in Morse code.

"He wants you guys gone." Roscoe said.

"Clearly. But what is he planning on doing to achieve that goal?"

"For starters, he wants to shut Jeff down. Make it so he can't finish this place. He's already made sure that no one else anywhere nearby would take on the job. Before we even started, he threatened Jeff to cut it off."

"He did?" I looked at Jeff.

Jeff shook his head. "I'm sorry. I didn't take him seriously. I should have. I should have known."

Roscoe continued. "Then he wants to scare you guys out of living here. He's invited people . . . bad people from these organizations all over the South. Told them that you're threatening us, and he's told them that . . . that you all have kidnapped a young boy and are holding him hostage here."

"Kiki?" Beatrice said. "But . . . that's ridiculous."

"After what happened at the Veterans Day festival, that's what everyone believes."

"What happened at Veterans Day?" Sam asked.

Beatrice and I both winced but said nothing.

"What happened?" Clancy was on the verge of shouting. I told the truth, if only in a cowardly attempt to stop from being shouted at.

"Good god." Thadeus said.

"How could you keep something like that from us?" Caleb asked. His words stung me.

"We didn't want anyone to worry." Beatrice said. "We didn't know it would come to something like this."

Suddenly Grace shot up out of her chair, the sound of wood scraping against wood making a wicked sound that set all of our hairs on end. "I need to make a call," she said before leaving the dining room. None of us had the time to say a word.

"Look, I don't know how far my dad's willing to go, or what exactly he's going to do to y'all . . . but I think from now on you should stay out of town. If you need something, ask one of us and we'll get it for you. But if you set foot in that place . . . it can only end badly." Roscoe said.

"And what about us?" Vince asked. "What about Gabe? He lives there. He's got a house and everything. Do you think he's safe?"

"Gabe will stay here." Caleb said. "I mean . . . if you want to. Please want to."

Gabe regarded his boyfriend for a good long while before nodding. "I don't much like the idea of running away."

"And I don't much like the idea of losing you." Caleb said.

"Okay."

"I have a question." Luke said, his voice wavering between sullen and furious. "If you haven't spoken to your father," his eyes were all fire when he turned to look at Roscoe, "then how in the hell do you know all of his top-secret plans?"

Before he could answer, Luke burst forward out of his chair. Beatrice, who still rested her head on his shoulder, fell backward and hit her head hard on the back of his chair. I could hear her teeth clack together. Roscoe fell backward with a cry as Luke, flailing and wild, landed on top of him. The words *liar, liar, liar* fell in a steady, angry rhythm from Luke's lips as he pummeled Roscoe's sides and face. Roscoe was arguably the stronger of the two, but Luke moved so fast and unpredictably. The carpenter couldn't get his bearings.

"Liar!" Luke howled, his hands finding their way around Roscoe's meaty throat. Within seconds, his face had gone purple. That seemed to snap everyone else out of their stupors.

Diego, who was closest to the two on the floor, tackled Luke from the side and knocked him off of Roscoe. Roscoe shot up, clawing at the air as he struggled to regain his breath. Diego and Luke struggled on the ground for a moment until Luke brought his head crashing into Diego's. The headbutt knocked Diego unconscious. Luke then crawled on hands and knees toward Roscoe who immediately began to scramble backward on his bottom. Just before Luke got to him, I managed to wrap my arms around my brother's chest. Throwing my weight backward, I flung us both to the floor. I wrapped my legs around his torso and tightened my arms around him. He struggled. He probably could've gotten free had Clancy and Jeff both not thrown their bodies on top of him. The weight of the three bodies made me feel as if my ribs were going to crack. Still, I held on.

"Buddy, buddy, buddy." I said, trying to keep my voice as steady as possible. "Calm down, Luke. Calm down, buddy. Listen to me."

"He's a liar!" His voice was muffled underneath Clancy's chest. "He's a liar!"

"I'm not." Roscoe said, his voice hoarse and disbelieving. "I haven't talked to him."

"Then how did you know?" May asked. She seemed unfazed by her husband caught up in a writhing mass on the floor. "How did you know, Roscoe?"

"My cousin!" He said. "My cousin told me. We were in prison together. He kept up with my father's stupid ways. But I saved his life in there, so he owes me."

"You hear that, buddy?" I could already feel the fervor seeping out of my brother's limbs. "He's not a liar. No one is lying to you."

Four deep breaths later, Luke went completely limp. Clancy and Jeff lifted themselves off him, but I continued to hold him like that on the floor, shifting him a little so he lay on his side, face buried in my chest. Glancing over, I saw Beatrice helping a dizzy-looking Diego off the floor. I stroked Luke's hair and sat us both up carefully. We stayed like that on the floor together, everyone staring at him.

"I'm sorry." I said to Roscoe. Luke couldn't say it, but I knew he felt it.

Roscoe just nodded.

"I'll tell the crew not to come back for the rest of the week." Jeff said. Everyone looked at him, feeling utterly hopeless. "I know it's not what we all want. Trust me, none of us want this. But I have to make sure everything is done by the book. Now that a minor has been injured on one of my sites . . . it'll just make it that much easier for Roscoe's father to get what he wants. It's the only way."

"That won't be necessary." Grace said. It was no wonder she had managed to reappear without our notice in the midst of all the commotion. But there she stood, looking infuriatingly calm. For the first time in my life, I felt anger toward her. How far must she have come from the girl I once knew to stand there in the middle of despair and act as though nothing were wrong? I wanted to shout at her, but Luke still lay fragile in my arms. I kept my mouth shut, but found I couldn't look at her as she continued. Probably a lot of my anger came from a place of shame. I was ashamed for having let her not know me as her father, and I was ashamed for having not been there for her for every moment, good or bad.

"Mrs. K.," Grace said, we are going to have a guest joining us at the hotel late Wednesday night." It was Monday. "Will you prepare a room for her?"

"Ah . . . I . . . sure." Mrs. K. said.

"What guest?" Clancy said, suspicious.

"I think it's high time," Grace said, "that you met the woman who made all of this possible."

* * *

E arly Tuesday morning, after a long, sleepless night, I found Diego and Zorro in the library. Diego clutched a mug of coffee in his hands, but I could tell it had long since gone cold. Zorro stared mournfully at his master from his position on the floor, occasionally nudging at Diego's bare feet with his big, wet nose. I was struck by how helpless animals must feel in moments like these. Without words to console their loved ones, and with only the basest understanding of what caused such turmoil, how could they possibly hope to help? The poor creature must have been miserable.

"How's your head?" I asked, sitting down across from him, placing myself right in his line of sight so he couldn't ignore me.

"Fine. Thank you." He'd given up on the Spanish accent. A fully Midwestern twang now seasoned his speech.

I paused. There were subtler ways for me to present what I was about to ask him, but I'd had it with subtlety. Grace had been subtle this entire time. It was clear that the harmless secrets she kept were not so harmless after all. Whoever was coming had a part to play in all this, yet she was absent. Grace had allowed that. Not that I could blame her. I had my own massive secret kept from her. All the secrets were beginning to make my stomach churn.

"You're not from Spain. Are you?"

"I'm from Minnesota. But my parents are from Afghanistan. Refugees."

"Why did you hide that from us?"

"Force of habit." He said. "After 9/11 . . . once I left Minnesota, I tried to make everyone believe I was something I wasn't." He finally looked at me. "It was safer. I felt safer. Not that it stopped people from assuming. Not that it stopped my father from being beaten half to death by neighbors he'd known for years, and my mother going crazy with paranoia. But still . . . I tried."

"Diego—"

"Mateen." He corrected me. "My real name is Mateen."

I smiled softly at him and extended my hand. "It's very nice to meet you, Mateen."

Mateen smiled at me in slight disbelief. "Nice to meet you too, Arthur Bean."

We both just sat there for probably too long of a time, holding each other's hand and smiling at each other. From the rooms above us, we began to hear the stir of people waking. It was a sluggish, unenthusiastic sound. No one wanted to rouse themselves to the waking nightmare we had suddenly entered.

"What's going on here?" Caleb asked. Mateen and I dropped our hands and turned to look at him. He was already dressed and had a suitcase in his hand.

"Caleb? What the fuck?" I asked. The panic I felt at the sight of that suitcase was too powerful. I knew Caleb was upset about what had happened. After dinner last night, he had made it clear to me that keeping secrets like we had with Veterans Day did not sit well with him. Still, I never once imagined that any of us would try to leave.

Caleb seemed surprised by my greeting. "What?" Then, following my gaze to the suitcase in his hand, "Oh this? This is for Gabe. We are going to go to his house and get some of his things . . . the earlier the better, we think."

I breathed out a huge puff of air that I'd been holding. With that breath came more than a few tears. Caleb dropped the suitcase and came to kneel in front of me. Gently he wiped away my tears with his thumb, laughing gently.

"Silly man. I'm not going anywhere." He paused, waiting until I looked him in the eye. "Honestly, where else would I go?"

I nodded. "Sorry. Just stressed."

"As you have every right to be."

"Are you sure it's safe for you and Gabe to be going into town now? Should some of us come with you?" Mateen asked. I realized in that moment that I was the only one who properly knew his secret. Surely, after the dinner last night, some, if not all, of the other guests suspected. But to them, he was still Diego, the man with the fake Spanish accent. I was the only one who knew him as Mateen.

"I think if more of us go it'll be worse. We want to be in and out quickly and quietly. Roscoe is meeting us on the other side of the river. He'll take good care of us."

"I'm surprised Roscoe wants anything to do with us after Luke nearly choked him to death." I said, watching Caleb as he went back to collect his suitcase, which had popped open when he dropped it. I was relieved to find it empty.

"Turns out that man has quite a forgiving nature."

Gabe appeared behind Caleb, giving us a short greeting. "You ready to go, babe?" He asked.

"Yeah. Are you sure you're okay to do this? I can go on my own and get you some things." Caleb said, his voice all fondness and concern.

"As if I want you rifling through all my things. A man has to have some secrets." He laughed, but it was shallow. Gabe was scared. They both were. "I'm just glad to have you with me."

"Okay." They kissed. "We'll be back before lunchtime. Promise."

I watched the two of them go with a deep sorrow in my chest. In my mind, voices screamed at me to follow them, to protect them, to not let them go. But I found that I could do no more than listen as the heavy front doors of the Hotel slammed shut behind them.

"They'll be fine." Mateen said, accurately sensing my worry. "I had no idea that the two of you were so close. Seems sort of an odd pair."

I smiled. "Just crept up on us I guess. So, any idea who this new guest of ours might be?" The question had been plaguing my mind all night. I knew nothing about the person who funded all this, except that she apparently had limitless amounts of cash and didn't quite care how it was spent. And that she was a woman.

"No idea. I guess we'll find out."

Then we just sat there in silence. Zorro moved so he could lay his head on Mateen's lap. Finally relinquishing his ice-cold cup of coffee, Mateen began to scratch behind his dog's ears. This earned him a pleased rumble, and I laughed. That was the last quiet moment we were afforded. I didn't even think to cherish it.

When lunch came and went, and Caleb and Gabe had not returned, I was overwhelmed with dread. We had all set ourselves up in the foyer, practically burning down the front door with the intensity of our gaze. Kiki sat in Francis's lap, chewing his lip and watching me as I paced back and forth.

"Arthur, please." His voice was so small. Mrs. K. had some low-dose painkillers that she'd been giving Kiki, but she only gave him a half a pill at a time. He was young, and she didn't want to do anything that might harm him more. I imagined that the pain in Kiki's hand was still quite bad.

I stopped to look at him. "Sorry kid, I'm just nervous."

"What will we do if they don't come back?" Luke asked. No one answered him. There wasn't an answer to be given.

Silence and worry threatened to suffocate us when the doors of the Hotel finally opened and Caleb and Gabe walked in, followed by Roscoe, Jeff, and May. I practically fell in my rush forward. Once I was in front of them, I pulled both of them into a crushing hug.

"God damn it. Where have you been?" I asked. When I pulled away, my heart felt as if it were in a free fall from my chest to my butt. Gabe had a large cut along his cheek and tears spilled out of his eyes. Caleb looked unharmed, but he was visibly shaking.

"What happened?" Grace moved forward. "Tell us what happened." Her voice was too forceful. It made the two of them flinch.

"Grace!" I said, but before I could rebuke her more, Gabe spoke.

"My house . . . they've ruined it. Everything . . ." He choked on his words and couldn't continue. Caleb gripped him around the shoulder.

Roscoe stepped forward. "They lit a fire in the front yard. Burned everything he had . . . and then they'd . . . they'd written really disgusting things on the wall in . . . pig's blood, I think."

"Oh Jesus." Mrs. K. said.

"We have to call the police then! That's illegal." Thadeus said.

"I'm afraid we did." Jeff said. "That's what took us so long. They aren't going to help us."

"Said there was no evidence . . . that Gabe brought it on himself for hanging out with criminals. They hit him." May's voice was even, but beneath it was a barely contained fury that radiated off her body. I hadn't pegged her for the type to get that angry, but I could see now how mistaken I was. In her hand was a plastic shopping bag. She reached inside and withdrew a small prescription bottle with Kiki's name on it. "Antibiotics. Don't ask me how I got them." She handed them to me and I gave them to Francis.

Grace laid her hand on Gabe's shoulder. "Don't worry. This will all be solved once our guest arrives."

"And what the hell is she supposed to do?" I hardly recognized the sound of my own voice. Everyone stared, breathless as I allowed every frustration that had been building up inside me— probably since Thia had disappeared, since my mother had died, since Mari had stolen my innocence—shoot out in a targeted attack. "What secrets are you keeping from us, Grace? You're not telling the truth. You haven't been ever since I got here. What the hell is your friend going to do to save us?"

More words were said. More eruptions of venom, but I blacked out as I spoke. I'm not sure if I believe possession to be a real thing that could happen to people, but that's the only way I could describe my behavior in that moment. A vengeful spirit had entered my body and manipulated me into saying every hateful, cowardly thought that had ever entered my mind about Grace and her actions.

When I finally finished, I immediately felt ashamed. I shrunk into myself. The gaze of everyone on me was heavy. I couldn't tell if those gazes were shocked, disapproving, understanding, or simply sad, but I felt them. Boy did I feel them.

"I understand your frustration, Arthur." Grace finally said, her voice level but tinged with tears. "But I caution you to show more respect to our guest when she arrives!" Then Grace left, storming up the stairs as others scrambled to make way for her.

I stood hollow and frozen in the middle of the room before I felt a hand on my shoulder. Jeff. He didn't say anything. That was the good thing about Jeff. He knew when there was nothing to be said. It wasn't a talent that many people possessed. Eventually he let go. Eventually we all did.

I wanted to lock myself in my room. In fact, what I really wanted to do was to get in my car and drive away for good, do the thing that I was so afraid that Caleb was about to do that morning. I wanted to disappear, just like Thia had, and let my whole history be washed off the planet with only a handful of people to even remember I'd existed. I wanted to be free.

Instead, I bit my tongue hard as a way of punishment for my thoughts, so hard that I tasted the warm iron of blood. Then I apologized to everyone who was left to hear me. They all accepted immediately. A few even revealed that they shared my frustrations about how Grace was acting. That didn't exactly make me feel better. Grace considered these people to be her family. She'd never said as much, but I knew it to be true. We all considered her to be our captain, the leader of our gang of misfits. I wasn't exactly pleased to hear that a mutiny was afoot, even if I were the one who might've vocalized it. Then again, Grace was not a dictator. She owed us answers. But we weren't going to get them. At least not until the mysterious guest showed up.

Roscoe left soon after my eruption, saying he had to talk to his cousin. Caleb and Gabe went up to Caleb's room to sort through the last remnants of Gabe's life, the ones that had escaped the town's fury. Thadeus followed them with Mrs. K.'s first aid kit. Kiki said he was hungry, so Mrs. K. went to make him some food, and Francis, who hadn't let the kid be alone since the accident, followed the two of them into the dining room. One by one we all dispersed until it was just Jeff, May, and I left in the foyer.

"Were you with Caleb and Gabe?" I asked them.

"No. Not at first, but Roscoe called us and we went as soon as we heard." Jeff said.

"It's disgusting." May said. "How can people be like this?"

Jeff regarded his wife with a great deal of sadness. I realized how hard it must have been for him in that moment. He had been the one to bring her here. Maybe she had never wanted to come. Even though they'd made a happy life, one could only be so happy when surrounded by so much ugliness. She wanted to have kids. She wanted a community where she could trust that her kids would be raised well. And not just by her, but by the people around her too. She wanted a life free from hate.

"Arthur," Jeff said, "My father is sick."

"What?" I said. The information seemed to come out of the blue. Since the Veterans Day fair, I hadn't heard anything more about Jeff's father. I assumed he was in some kind of nursing home nearby, because he hadn't been at the house. I felt like such a selfish idiot for never once asking about him.

"Yeah. He's dying actually." Jeff said. His voice was level, but May reached out to take her husband's hand.

"Jesus man, I'm so . . . I'm so sorry."

Jeff smiled and nodded. "Thank you. But I think it's for the best. He hasn't wanted to be here for a long time. He knew he was sick for a year and now . . . well it's too late. If that's what he wants, then I won't try to convince him otherwise. But he was the only thing that was really keeping us here, and now after everything that's happened . . ."

"You're leaving." The words were dumbbells dragged out of my throat. I didn't like the idea of it. I liked knowing we had an ally in town. And I liked having a friend who was good and uncomplicated.

"Not until the renovation is done and my father is buried. But yes, we'll be leaving."

"We've wanted to start a family for so long," May said, "But if these past few days have taught us anything, it's that we can't do it here. We're sorry."

"No," I said, "Please. You two have to do what is best for you. Where will you go?"

"My brother lives in a suburb of Chicago. He said he could find us work and a place to stay. And it's a good place to raise children." Jeff said.

"Yeah man. It sounds great."

And that was it. That was all I could think to say because it did sound great. But I couldn't say I was happy for them because I wasn't. I was a selfish asshole, and I didn't want them to go.

They stayed through dinner. I told them I'd let everyone know that they were leaving, but I think people could tell. Or maybe everyone was just miserable in general. It was probably the latter.

* * *

Thia sat between my open legs, her back pressed against my front. She held on to my arms, which were wrapped around her stomach. Together, we watched the rivulets of rainwater trickle down the glass of our bedroom window. Thia sighed. I felt her ribs expand and contract against my torso. I held her tighter.

"Do you think this is real?" She said, stroking absentmindedly at the hair on my right arm.

"I don't think we're dreaming, if that's what you mean."

"No. I mean . . . us. Do you think this is real?" She laid her head back against my shoulder. I kissed the top of her forehead.

"How would we know?" I said.

"You're not very good at this whole comforting thing, you know." Then she paused. "Sorry. I'm being mean."

"You're not. I just don't know what's wrong." This was three weeks before I lost her. I should have known then. She was already disappearing.

"Nothing's wrong. Not really. I love you." I knew she meant it, but she didn't think it was enough.

"*Nado saranghae, Soyeon-ah.*" Thia had taught me how to say "I love you" in Korean a long time ago, before we were even dating. She had also revealed her Korean name to me after having kept it hidden for so long. I never asked her why she didn't like it. To me, it was the most beautiful sound that ever left my mouth.

Thia laughed. She never really admitted it, but I knew she liked it when I tried to speak Korean. She had a rough relationship with her parents, I knew that, but she loved the sound of the language. It was the language she spoke to her uncle. It was the language of her heritage. She told me once that it was sweet and romantic, like all languages should be. I was more careful with my words around her after that. I wanted everything she heard from me to be sweet and romantic.

"No matter what happens," Thia said, "You never forget this. Okay?"

"You're scaring me a little. Just because we are going to be apart doesn't mean that this is the end." I closed my eyes tight and buried my face in her hair.

"Don't be scared." She said. "It's not the end."

A bolt of lightning illuminated us tangled up as one. I flinched, and she tightened her grip on my arm. Even after all those years, I was still afraid of thunderstorms.

"Don't be scared, Arthur," she whispered. "Don't be scared." *Arthur. Arthur?*

Another bolt of lightning lit her up from behind. For a moment she looked like a monster that had crawled forth from the bayou. Her black hair lay lank and dripping all around her face. Her clothes clung to her form, so much smaller than I remembered. Her hands were splayed open like claws, and her eyes lit up with every move they made. I was paralyzed.

Her name caught in my throat, even though it was the only thing I could think of to say. We had all been waiting for her, not knowing what exactly we were waiting for. And now that she was there, none of us knew what to do. None of us, that was, except Grace. I watched, my eyes threatening to go dark at any moment to save me the confusion of watching as my daughter went and hugged the creature in the doorway, completely unfazed by her soaking form. I watched as they acted like familiar friends. I watched as Grace welcomed her into our home and shut the door behind her.

"You're soaking wet." Grace said, concern clear in her voice. "Come on. Let's get you into something warm and dry."

"Wait just a sec, I think I have to say hello."

I wasn't sure if she meant to me or to everyone else, but the sound of her voice was louder and more jarring than the thunder. My limbs suddenly loosened. I took the opportunity to turn around and walk the other way. I didn't run, and I didn't look at anyone either. I just put one foot in front of the other, deaf to the people calling my name. I heard the sound of footsteps like someone was following me, but I didn't stop. I couldn't deal with it. I couldn't handle seeing her again after all this time, showing up on the doorstep of the place I had thought to be my salvation like the last twenty years had been the painless blink of an eye.

I wasn't quite sure when I exited the Hotel, or where I exited it. I must have walked out of the kitchen doors and stumbled into the rain and mud and thunder. Once I was outside, I just kept walking. I had never even been out that far on the island before. To each side of me, lightning lit up the dilapidated shacks that used to hold enslaved men and women. In the eerie light of the storm, I could almost see the souls clinging to the rotten wood, screaming silently at me as I passed. But I ignored them. I planned to keep walking until I could ignore everything and everyone. If there was one thing I knew in all that mindless movement, it was that I didn't deserve this. I wasn't perfect, but I didn't deserve this.

Whether from exhaustion or mere clumsiness, my legs gave out beneath me. It seemed as good a place as any to stop, especially since I had finally reached the other end of the island, and all that stood before me was swamp. So I let my body stop, my knees slowly sinking into the mud, my body trembling with every crash of thunder, raindrops soaking into my heavy sweatshirt and jeans. I thought maybe if I knelt there long enough, I'd just melt away.

"Arthur?" It was Caleb. I should've known that he'd be the one to follow me. He was my best friend, after all. That's what he said. That's what I believed. But as he knelt down beside me, covering my head with his jacket and holding me close to him, I realized that he knew so little about me. How many of the guests at the Hotel knew what she was to me? Did Grace even know?

I was totally and completely numb. My mind had shut down at the sight of her and it was struggling to reboot. Caleb may have been talking to me, but I couldn't hear him over the racing of my own thoughts. At one point, he brought his hand down from my shoulder to between my shoulder blades. He pressed down there, rubbing firm circles into my muscles.

"What the hell . . . ?" Another voice, maybe Luke's, but it was cut off. I felt Caleb swipe his hand violently backward, slicing the words away. He was protecting me. But the damage had already been done.

Whoever it was that had joined us just stood there watching, until shakily, I stood.

"I can't go back." I said, shrugging away Caleb's jacket.

"Don't be a baby." Caleb said softly, helping me to my feet. I was surprised that I let him, but I couldn't really find it in me to resist. My whole being had gone so loose and ambiguous that I let Caleb and Luke—it was definitely Luke—take me away from the water, away from the rain, and lay me down dry and warm in my own bed.

I didn't sleep. I couldn't sleep. I was exhausted in every cell of my body. I felt that deep sort of sickness—the kind that only comes from doing something foolish, like running outside in the cold rain —starting to creep around my insides. By the next day, I knew I would be feverish. I felt glad for that. It would give me a reason to stay locked inside my room. I wouldn't have to see her if I didn't want to. I could at least control who came in and out of here. I had that much at least.

Luke sat at my bedside wringing his hands. My door opened. Caleb left and Beatrice came in. My two siblings whispered to each other, pretending not to notice that my eyes were still wide open. Maybe they thought if they just wished me to sleep, I would actually fall.

I felt ashamed and embarrassed. Over the past few days, I had suddenly become someone I didn't fully recognize. Someone who allowed his emotions to control everything he did. Some people might have said this was better than how I previously lived life, stifling any emotion that would disrupt the careful apathy I'd managed to maintain. But at that moment, I felt completely overcome with everything I'd kept hidden or banished. I didn't like it. I didn't like how I was acting. All the emotions had become too much for me. I didn't feel human anymore.

"I think you have some explaining to do." Caleb's voice came muffled through the thick wood of my bedroom door.

"Please, let us in." Grace said to him.

"Absolutely not. No offense, but I have no idea who the fuck your friend is. I do know that, whoever she is, Arthur doesn't want to see her."

"I understand your concern—" Grace started.

Caleb's voice lowered to one of those whisper shouts that were sometimes more painful than real shouting. "That's enough, Grace!"

"Caleb." Gabe said, his voice soothing but worried. When had he joined them?

"I know, babe. I'm sorry. But I've got to say this." His voice, softened for his boyfriend, suddenly turned harsh again. "You've done a lot for us, Grace. You really fucking have, but that's enough! We all knew you had your secrets. Hell, we all do. But we just assumed that you knew what you were doing, and that whatever those secrets were, they were for our benefit. So how in the hell do you explain this? He's your family, and I think you knew, you *knew*, that this wasn't right. He's been doing so much for us. How in the hell do you justify this? How?"

There was a long, messy silence. I could've imagined each and every one of their faces: Caleb's tight with pent-up fury; Gabe's tense and uncomfortable, caught in a family quarrel that wasn't his own; Grace's, embarrassed but indignant, not taking kindly to her flaws shoved in her face; and . . . I stopped myself before I could imagine her face. I wouldn't have even known what it would look like after twenty years.

"Caleb, is it?" Her voice punched me in the gut. I groaned, pulling my covers over my face. I was being such a child, but I couldn't stop myself. "You're right. I owe you all an explanation, but before I do that, I think I owe it to Arthur to speak to him first. You may not know this, but Arthur is very important to me. I want him to be okay . . . or at least not mad at Grace."

It was strange. I hadn't even thought of being mad at Grace, but maybe I should have been. The fact that she had kept our bene-factress's identity a secret from me meant that Grace knew. She knew how this would affect me. For a brief second, I thought maybe the two of them were punishing me. It was a pervasive idea. The two of them had come together to create this ridiculous charade all for me. All to make me go mad. Yes, that had to be it. I tried to let that feeling of fury wash over me, but it turned out I didn't have any room left for anger.

"Important to you." Caleb said. He wasn't being sarcastic. It was as if he were simply chewing the words, taking his time to see how they tasted. Maybe Caleb was starting to realize how little he really knew about me. Maybe that hurt him. Maybe that's why he wouldn't let her in. Maybe he didn't want to lose the closest friend he had. Either way, I was grateful. I didn't want to see her. Before, it had been just brief enough that I could pretend it had been a trick of the light. I had spent so long coming to terms with the fact that she was gone. I wasn't sure my tentative reality could stand seeing her face-to-face.

"How about we all deal with this tomorrow?" Gabe said. He took the final step into our fucked-up family. I admired him for his bravery. "It's late and everyone's tired, you probably most of all after your long journey. We should all talk in the morning when everyone is refreshed and . . . calmer. Is that okay?"

"What is your name?" She asked.

"Gabe . . . I'm, um, I'm new."

"Well, Gabe, it's nice to meet you. And yes, maybe the morning would be best." She paused, and then said, "You'll take good care of him, won't you?"

"You can count on it." Caleb answered dryly.

A few moments of silence passed before my door opened again, and someone tugged gently at my covers.

"Can I come in?" Caleb said.

I loosened my grip on the bedsheets and let them fall from my face. A pale pink pill greeted me, lying flat on Caleb's smooth hands. Doll's hands, I had called them once. That had earned me a smack on the shoulder. I took it from Caleb's hand without hesitation and reminded myself to ask Caleb where he got these things and how often he took them. I didn't much like the thought of him being dependent on pills to sleep. Not that it mattered. Nothing mattered to me in that moment. I just wanted to sleep. I let my body fall because there was nothing else I could do.

I stayed in bed long enough so that the halfway-asleep feeling from the pill left my body. It didn't take too long, but once I felt fully in the world, I realized how badly my body ached. As I stood, showered, and dressed, I could feel the feverish creaking of my bones as they rubbed up against each other. I felt hot, burning up as I struggled to work my way into a sweater and jeans. What I really wanted to wear were sweatpants and a tank top, but if I was going to see her, I wanted to at least look presentable.

On my bedside table were two ibuprofen and a glass of water still cold from the night. I took short sips until the glass was empty. Then I opened my door. A hush rushed in like back draft. It seemed like everyone and everything in the Hotel had gone silent out of respect, or pity, for me. It hurt to move forward, my limbs shaking. My eyeballs felt like they might melt within my sockets, but I had to keep going. There was no more avoiding it. I had tried to run, but there would be no more running.

The other guests were about, but like ghosts in the night, they disappeared into the walls as they saw me coming. Soon it was just me, staring at her back as she sat in the library gazing into the fire we always had going. At least there was that piece of consistency still left.

"Thia." My voice came out like a croak, but I didn't clear my throat.

She started and turned quickly. I was glad to see her off her guard a little bit. I doubted if it were something I would have the luck of seeing again anytime soon. At least I knew she wasn't completely made of stone.

"Arthur." Her voice was soft, but disingenuous. "Please sit."

I laughed as I made my way to the seat opposite her. Frowning, she said, "What's so funny?"

"You sound like some kind of prim and proper society woman. Inviting her guest to tea in the sitting room. It's ridiculous." I laughed again, even though the shaking hurt me. I wasn't trying to be mean, but I'd lost any energy to contain myself. Surely she saw how ridiculous it all was. Besides, I'd spent so long accepting the fact that she might be dead. I had no idea of the proper way to talk to a ghost.

She smiled slightly, but it didn't reach her eyes. Overall, she looked pretty much the same. Her hair was maybe a bit less lustrous and the skin around her eyes slightly more lined, but her lips were still full and smooth, and her body was still petite and firm. She had taken good care of herself. I wonder if she thought the same about me. I realized that I really didn't want to look old to her.

"You look sick." She said.

"Yeah, well running around in the cold and wet can do that to you." I said.

"I hope your friend Caleb is all right. He seems like a good man."

"He is. So is that why you're here then? To tell me I've made good choices in my friendships?"

"Don't be cruel, Arthur." It came out more like a plea. That only made me want to be crueler.

"What makes you think you deserve anything more from me?" When she didn't answer, I decided to cut right to the chase. After all, everyone I knew who was eavesdropping outside deserved to know the end of this story. "What the hell are you doing here?"

"I'm the benefactress of this property, and I received word that my investment was in—"

"Thia!" It wasn't a shout, but it was powerful enough to shut her up. "Skip the bullshit. Tell me."

She smiled. "You've grown a lot more confident in the past twenty years, Arthur."

"Good for me."

She frowned, then looked down at her hands. "I'm sorry." She whispered.

"What was that?" It was petty, but I couldn't let her get off that easy. Then I sneezed, and she laughed, and I laughed, and she shook her head.

"I'm being pretty stupid, huh?" She said. "I guess I thought I was prepared for this. She gestured toward me. I guess facing the love of your life, the one you lost, isn't quite as easy as I thought it would be."

"I'm not the love of your life." I said bluntly.

"Why would you say that? Of course you are. You're the only person I've ever loved."

"So you abandon the people you love?"

She flinched. "I suppose I deserved that. And I suppose you deserve an explanation. I won't lie to you Arthur. Do you want the truth?"

"It's the only thing I've ever really asked for."

"Then you'll get it."

And I did. It went back further than just when she had disappeared. Grace was just a child when I went to college. She was seven when I went into my freshman year four years after I was meant to. The first few times she came to visit me in the city, it was with my dad. The next few times, it was with Mari. By my junior year, just after she'd turned ten, she started to come twice a year by herself. Mari would pay for a hotel room for her close to my apartment and I would go stay with her. Thia always knew those random weeks I was with my sister. What she wanted to know was my sister herself.

Apparently, my refusal to allow her to meet Grace whenever she came to visit the city only made Thia more curious, and more determined to meet my half sister-daughter. So she went through my phone, the pass code for which was Thia's birthday. She found out where Grace was staying and worked out a time when I would be in class, and they met. This was senior year and Grace was about to be twelve. Apparently that was old enough for her become friends with an adult. Not surprising, really, given how close she was to her schoolteachers and how mature she was for her age. What was surprising was that she'd become friends with *Thia*.

Thia was up front about who she was to me. Grace was confused, but also not surprised that I hadn't wanted to share her. According to Grace, even though I had always been there for her, she always felt like I kept myself away from her. I kept secrets.

Grace and Thia exchanged numbers and addresses, and then they started to call and write. During that final year of my college life, Grace came to the city more and more often, but not always to see me. There were times when I thought Thia was in class, but she was really meeting Grace for lunch at our usual diner. Thia would tell me she was going shopping for costumes with a theater buddy, and she would instead go shopping with Grace in SoHo. I'd want to see a movie, but Thia said she wasn't interested. Really, she'd already seen it with Grace. Thia never really talked about me with Grace, but Grace told her everything. Apparently starved for a listening ear, Thia soon knew everything about Grace's life. More than I did.

What started out as a kind of older-sister, younger-sister relationship blossomed into a solid and deeply close friendship. By the time Grace was an adult, during the time that I thought Thia was dead, she apparently had no other friends. Her boyfriend had slowly worked to sever all of her friendships until he was her last relationship. Grace hadn't even noticed what he was doing until it was too late. She liked Thia, but Thia knew a large part of their friendship was built on Grace's desperation to have someone outside of her boyfriend. Thia also knew that if Grace couldn't be her own strength, she would have to be Grace's.

I suppose I could have felt betrayed or upset, but really, I was amused. There seemed to be no point to their clandestine meetings other than to just fit into whatever play they were acting out in their heads. Certainly I would have been uncomfortable with the love of my life and my secret daughter becoming such close friends, but I would've dealt. They didn't need to keep it a secret from me, but I suppose secrets beget secrets. It was nothing less than I deserved.

I had assumed that Grace broke up with her fiancé because things simply fell apart in the natural way that relationships do. But things were not all roses and honeysuckle with her engagement. She had never told me that the man she was set to marry was abusive. Not in the physical way, but in the mentally manipulative, emotionally toying way. Kind of in the way Mari was. He liked to control Grace, beat down her confidence, monitor what she ate and who she saw, set a schedule for when and what kind of sex they would have. She had confided all of this to Thia. Eventually, it was Thia, Thia who had been missing from my life by that point for almost a decade, who finally pushed Grace to end things with him and move away.

But where could she move? She was a penniless dancer who was starting to realize that her chosen profession could be just as abusive to her health as her relationship had been. One of her brothers was in a mental institution and her sister was too young to take on her burden. Thia didn't say why Grace didn't come to me, but I could've guessed. I'd never given her any indication that it would even be an option for her. So Grace went back to Mari and Mari's dick of a husband. It was the only place she could think of. For a while, she told Mari that she was still with her boyfriend. Mari, apparently, had loved the guy. Color me unsurprised.

Before any of this, before she helped my daughter escape an abusive man and start life anew, Thia was in London. She was beginning to feel that if we continued the way we were, in love and desperate to see each other but separated by miles and ocean, she couldn't move forward. And she desperately wanted to move forward. She had already taken on the role of Grace's strength. She needed to start being her own as well.

"You always seemed so content to be where you were. I could never feel that way."

Thia didn't have to stay in one place for too long. Her uncle died. It was an unremarkable death, but freakish in its own way.

All his life he had taken care of himself, did everything right, and yet the cancer still got him. Right before he passed, he visited her in London, against his doctor's wishes and barely alive as he was. He wanted her to take over his company. He needed her to because he'd never had any kids. He knew that she could do it. His investors thought he was crazy. His employees thought he was crazy. Thia's parents thought he was crazy. But he knew that she could do it. There was no other option. Thia wanted to say no. She wanted to be selfish, be an actress, eventually find her way back to me. But she said yes.

I stopped listening. Thia inheriting her uncle's entire fortune and his company, thrust into the economic elite of Seoul with only a few months training, somehow it made sense. I could see her showing everyone up, proving them all wrong. It made sense, but I'd heard enough. She still talked, maybe explaining more about what exactly it was she did in Seoul, or why exactly Grace had landed upon this place of all the places in the world to start her future, or why Thia decided to indulge her and fund the whole thing. But none of it seemed to matter anymore. It was as pretty a story as any, filled with drama, intrigue, mystery, and heartbreak. But when you lived lives that already had those things, you searched for simpler stories. I was exhausted just looking at her. The listening ended up being too much of a strain.

Eventually I sensed that she had stopped speaking and was waiting for my reply. So I gave it to her.

"So how do you propose to save your investment from the evils of small-town white people?"

It was meant to sound serious and urgent, but instead came out of my mouth like a British joke, dry, droll, and slow to hit home.

Thia seemed taken aback by my complete lack of interest in her history. It was as if she were offended that I didn't care more. Back when we knew each other, everything she said had been the most interesting thing I'd ever heard. Sometimes I'd listen to her so hard that my head would start to ache. What a far cry from my old self I must have seemed then to her. I wondered what image of me she had kept in her head all those years. I wondered if she were disappointed in what she saw now.

"I have money, lawyers, and a security detail that will protect you. This place will be finished and open for business in no time."

I nodded. "So after the renovation is done, you're going to continue protecting us? Place security guards all around the island? That'll be a nice draw for visitors."

"Arthur . . ." She said, sounding almost desperate.

"Thia, be realistic. What can you really do for us? Your life is in Seoul now apparently. You have responsibilities there. You can't be here all the time."

"But she's here now." Grace walked into the library. I would have thought that she would discourage the eavesdropping that the other guests were no doubt partaking in, but apparently that wasn't the case. "She'll figure it out."

There were a million things I could have said to Grace at that moment, but every important thing, all the burning questions and expressions of anger and hurt, refused to come out. I was overwhelmed, so I just smiled sadly at her. "I'm glad your faith in her is so secure, but I'm afraid money can't solve everything." I stood, my legs tired of sitting.

"Please don't go, Arthur." Thia said. "I know you're angry . . . but . . ."

"I'm not, actually. I think I'm just tired." I shrugged my shoulders. "I don't mean to be making you feel bad. I'm just tired." I thought of ending it there, but I supposed I owed her something more.

"I've spent the last twenty years missing you and wondering what happened to you. I'd pretty much come to the conclusion that you were either dead or so sick of me that you'd made yourself disappear. I mean, you never, ever tried to contact me to explain . . . so what other options did I have? Neither was a particularly comforting thought, and I don't think the truth of it really helps either.

"And I've lied a lot. A lot. I've lied to my family. I've lied to you, so I'm not mad at being lied to. It's just the life I built for myself on the foundation of all my own lies."

"Arthur . . ." Grace said.

I looked at her. Any denial I'd been harboring about whether or not Grace knew about her true parentage was shot to hell. If she could have kept the love of my life secret from me, hiding that small little fact would've been simple, almost laughably easy. I was a fool for thinking I could really hide it. "You already know, don't you? My big secret? You've been dropping hints for a while now."

She nodded shortly, glancing at Thia. "Mari . . . we argued right before I left her place for good. She spat it out at me thinking it would hurt me."

If I had any anger left in me, I would've been furious. Spiteful Mari trying to wound her daughter with something so monumental . . . it would've made me want to hurt her in another life. But I was tired and full of regret. I should've been the one to tell her. "Yeah. I'm sorry Grace."

"You don't have to . . ."

"Yeah I do. I fucked up. I'm sorry."

There were tears in her eyes. I couldn't remember the last time I'd seen her cry. Thia stood up and put her arm around Grace. Looking at the two of them together, they seemed to fit. It was insane, but it was true.

"So," I smiled. "You two are friends, huh?"

Grace nodded. Thia didn't do anything.

"I'm glad." Then I walked forward and hugged them both. Grace buried her wet face in the crook of my neck. Thia gasped, and then grasped the back of my shirt. Other arms surrounded me. Soon the weight of it all sent us crashing to the floor. It wouldn't save us, but at the moment, it was enough.

* * *

After our dogpile of desperation the day before, Thia had disappeared into one of the unoccupied rooms on the second floor and stayed there until well after dinner was over. By that point, I had already locked myself up in Caleb and Gabe's room, playing cards and not talking about everything that had happened. I managed to avoid talking until Caleb refused to keep playing cards with me until I finally enlightened him.

"I'll kick you out of here right now. You know I will." Caleb said, shoving lightly at my shoulders, just enough so that my unbalanced body almost fell off the edge of his bed.

"Babe, come on." Gabe said. "Give the man a break."

"Thank you, Gabe." I said.

"No, not fair. I deserve to know the truth, Arthur Bean."

"You're ridiculous." But I told him anyway. Then I told him to tell anyone who asked him because that was the last damn time I was ever going to talk about what happened.

Even though I had made everything seem like it was okay by embracing Grace and Thia that night, I avoided both of them and everyone else. For two whole days, the only people who could get me out of my self-imposed solitary confinement were Caleb or Beatrice.

"So you loved her?" Beatrice said once after bringing me lunch in bed.

"Yeah."

"Think you love her still?"

I grinned at her, although it felt fake. "So interested in love now that you've got a beau of your own."

Beatrice did not indulge me. "I'm serious, Arthur."

I sighed. "Who knows? Probably. I don't know." I paused, sighing, and continued. "I just don't get why she didn't . . ."

"Maybe she was afraid that if she tried talking to you about it all, you'd somehow convince her not to do it."

249

"I wouldn't do that. I've never tried to stop her from doing what she wanted to do."

"No, but you wouldn't have to try. She probably loves you enough that just hearing your voice would've stopped her."

I rolled my eyes. "Loves?"

"Yeah. Loves."

The next day, construction began again. Jeff said that an inquiry had begun, but then a slew of lawyers came in and tied everything up. They got the go-ahead to keep working as long as minors stayed far away from any power tools. Not that they had anything to worry about. The sound of a nail gun now made Kiki's eyes go wide with fear and his hands reach out to the nearest source of comfort. I doubted the little guy would ever touch a tool again.

Somehow word had gotten out to the construction crew about the origin of our new guest. Jeff knew who had made it possible for them to continue work. The guests knew who paid for their livelihood. Everyone knew who Thia had been to me once. But no one knew what she was to me now. Myself included. That was enough for everyone there to leave the subject alone.

That first day of restarting the renovation, neither Roscoe nor Beatrice's boyfriend showed up. The entire day I'd busied myself with helping out where I could, mostly just so I could avoid Thia and Grace. Not that I really had to work at it. They were locked up in Grace's room discussing all of our futures. I was more than happy to let them be in charge of that. I was done thinking about the past or the future. All I had to worry about was each minute as it passed me by. I had never felt so simultaneously numb and alive at the same time. It was like jumping into a pile of snow in your underwear. Thia and I had done that once on a road trip to Vermont. It was stupid. It hurt. It felt great.

Beatrice had tried calling her boyfriend all day, but he didn't answer. Jeff didn't know where he was either. He was worried as much as she was. Not just about the boyfriend, but also about Roscoe. Last any of us had heard, Roscoe was going to talk to his cousin. No one had heard from him since.

Beatrice was on the verge of tears by dinnertime, wringing her hands so violently until I feared they might pop off her wrists. Finally Mateen grabbed her hands in his, all of us watching as we neglected the food Mrs. K. had set out for us. In recent days, her feasts had become much more mundane. Under stress, all of us became suddenly more normal.

Just as we were all ready to admit that no more eating would be done that night, three thunderous knocks sounded on the front door. It sounded like a battering ram against the gates of a city. Clancy yelped. Sam whispered to her that it was okay. Heads turned first to Grace and then Thia. I was vaguely annoyed with how quickly everyone seemed to fall in line with this idea of Thia as our savior.

I stood, but Sam stopped me. "I'll get it."

"What?" Clancy said. "Why?"

There were three more knocks and then the sound of whooping. Everyone's eyes went wide with fear. Without even thinking, my eyes glanced out the dining room window, searching for a cross on fire in the front yard. I wondered if people still even did that, or if my idea of racism was so antiquated that I didn't even know what to expect.

"I probably look like one of them." He seemed to struggle to get the words out, which wasn't odd for Sam, but the look of shame that accompanied them was less than usual. "Maybe they'll go easy on me."

"No, lad." Thadeus said. "If they'll go easy on anyone it'll be an old man. Now sit down."

I'd never seen Thadeus move so fast before. He seemed to want to avoid any further talk. I was grateful. I wondered if this was going to become a regular thing, the forever question of who will answer the door. What would future guests think of that?

The door opened. Only a few seconds later it closed. Thadeus returned to the dining room with an envelope in his shaking hands.

"Who was it?" Luke asked.

"No one was there. I thought I saw lights near the water, but"—he held out the envelope—"there was only this." There was a large splotch of brownish red against the name scrawled across the front. "It's for Beatrice."

"Give it to me." Grace said, pushing her chair back so forcefully it tipped over.

"But it's mine." Beatrice said. There was no conviction in her voice. She didn't seem to really want whatever was inside.

Grace ignored her and took the envelope from Thadeus's hand gently. I glanced over at Thia in the chair next to Grace's, the chair that had usually been mine. She watched my daughter's moves with laser focus. I realized that somewhere in the past 36 hours, I'd fully established Grace as my daughter in my mind. Any pretense I had built of her sibling status, whatever denial I had carefully constructed, crumbled. The truth now ran rampant in my brain.

Grace opened the envelope and withdrew its contents. She gasped, stepping back into Thadeus, dropping everything. The photographs fluttered to the floor, some lying face down, others face up revealing the horror they documented. Beatrice shrieked, a long, drawn out sound that dissolved into frantic cries. Mateen quickly reached out and held her. Mrs. K. and Clancy both said "oh my god" at the same time, and Sam hid his face behind his hands. All of them had caught a glimpse of the photos on the floor. Luke leaned forward to see what everyone else saw, but Clancy's hand shot out to grab his shoulder. She pulled him back and shook her head, her face deadly white with freckles blaring red like wounds on her cheeks. Thia stood, and so did I. Together we moved forward and picked the pictures up off the ground.

The boy's face was so badly beaten that I wouldn't have been able to identify him if I hadn't already known who he was. One of his arms was bent at an unnatural angle. His bare legs showed burn marks of varying sizes and shapes. Some were from cigarettes or cigars. Others looked like cattle brands. In some of the photographs, he was kneeling with a disembodied hand in his hair forcing him upward. In others, he was twisted on the floor, action shots of him being abused. Involuntarily, my hand turned into a fist. I crumpled the images, tossing them to the floor.

The dining room swam in front of my eyes, and for a second I thought I would be sick in front of everyone. Thia's hand landed heavily on my shoulder. I looked at her. She held up a piece of torn notebook paper. It read, "'If a man has sexual relations with a man as one does with a woman, both of them have done what is detestable. They are to be put to death; their blood will be on their own heads.' Leviticus 20:13."

I snatched it violently from her hands, but she didn't flinch. I felt everyone's eyes follow me as I strode toward the fireplace. Shouting one abrupt, incoherent noise, I threw the note into the fire.

"He's dead, isn't he?" Beatrice sobbed, trembling. "It's all my fault. He's dead! Oh my god . . ."

We tried to convince her that he could still be alive, that he wasn't dead, but our voices were hollow. None of us could wrap our minds around what we had just seen, and no matter how many assurances we gave her that this kind of evil was no one's fault but the perpetrators', I knew that Beatrice would never recover from what had happened.

"So," I said to Thia as I passed her still holding the offensive pictures. "How will you save him?"

Thia looked at me with fury and pain, but she didn't respond. Cruelty begets cruelty. I was not a strong man.

The next day, Beatrice never left her room. Only Clancy went in to see how she was doing, and when she came out, she just shook her head whenever anyone asked anything. All of us wandered around in a state of semiconsciousness. I could tell that the images of that poor boy had burned deep into our minds. Sam flinched every time he closed his eyes for more than a second. For once, Mrs. K. allowed Thadeus to put his arm around her shoulders and keep it there. I hardly knew the boy, but I couldn't shake the images of his suffering from my psyche.

Roscoe still hadn't shown up, and Jeff hadn't been able to find him. I asked after Beatrice's boyfriend too, but Jeff said he hadn't heard anything from the kid either. May had quit her job at the clinic and came with Jeff to the Hotel. She was too afraid to be alone. People had started to terrorize them at night.

"Don't worry," Jeff said through a thin veil of false optimism. "We'll finish what we started."

I wanted to tell him to get out while he still could, but the smallest part of me still held on to the possibility of the Hotel's salvation. Even after everything, I was still a fool.

The day after that, Zorro went missing. I woke to Mateen calling his name, over and over and over, each time growing more frantic. The workers, the few that had withstood the abuses and threats of their neighbors, arrived while we were combing the island in search for the dog. With their help, we soon found him. I just wish it hadn't been Kiki.

His tiny little scream sounded so huge in my ears. By the time I got there, I was already too late to save him from what he'd seen. Mateen had fallen to his knees in front of a large tree infested with Spanish moss. He looked up, his arms extended to the sky, tears streaming down his cheeks and his neck into his shirt. I reluctantly followed his gaze, my eyes already weary of being terrorized.

Zorro hung from his neck, tongue lolling out of one side of his mouth, eyes wide with fear—because how could he know what was happening to him or why? Humans had always been good to him. He only expected kindness from people. It was only once I saw him that I heard the slow creaking of the rope against the wood.

As they brought him down, I prayed for a bullet wound. I prayed for him to have been mercifully killed and hanged only as a sign of their hatred of us. But the poor creature was afforded no such kindness. The awkward angle of his neck and the contortion of his limbs made it clear to all of us. The Spanish bloodhound had been lynched.

Renovations for the day halted. Instead we focused on digging a grave and building a headstone for Zorro. I found Kiki buried in a blanket against Francis's chest as he watched the gravediggers from the porch.

"Is he asleep?" I asked, slightly surprised that the kid could sleep after what he had seen.

Francis nodded. "I can't keep him here, Arthur. Not if things are going to continue this way. He should never have seen that. He should never have seen any of it."

"I understand."

"But this is his home. If there's some way that we can stay . . . I will. You all are his family. He won't want to leave you."

"He's brave."

"He's naive."

The day after that, Mateen joined Beatrice in sequestering himself in his room. A group of twenty strong, armed men and women arrived along with the ever-dwindling construction crew.

"They're here to keep us safe." Thia said.

Everyone eyed the guns warily.

"I don't feel very safe." Clancy said.

That night, Thia caught me in the library after everyone else had gone to their own rooms. I had probably been waiting for her, but it was still hard for me to stay and let her sit down next to me.

"I'm sorry that this is happening." She said after a few heartbeats of silence.

"Yeah me too. I really love this place. Who would've thunk it."

Thia smiled slightly. "You're more like your daughter than you realize. When she found this place . . ." Thia laughed and shook her head. "You should've seen how happy she was about it. And every time someone new came," she shrugged, "Well, I never really got it."

"Yeah, well, call it our island of misfit toys."

We were quiet for a long time. I wasn't sure what I really wanted to say to her. I'd never known Thia to be uncertain, but maybe she felt the same way about me. Of course, she was the first to speak.

"I never contacted you because it was too hard. While I was

still in London, I had planned to write you and tell you that I needed a break. Or call you. I don't know. But I really did just want it to be a break. A long one maybe, but I always thought I was going to come back to you."

"But then?"

"Then things changed and I had to change. It was bad enough a woman without any experience was taking over this massive financial beast. It would've been even worse for me, harder, if you were at my side while it was happening. No one would have accepted you at first, and very few people would've given you the chance anyway. I guess I could say I was trying to save you from what was inevitable for me, but really I was just being selfish."

"I would've understood. If you had told me . . . we could've figured something out."

"Maybe. But I was mourning my uncle. I was figuring out this whole new life . . . and after I settled I'd figured you had moved on without me. I didn't want to drag you back."

I'm surprised that Grace had never told her how lost I'd become. "I never moved on."

Things were easier between Thia and I after that, but they weren't fixed. We didn't have much longer to try and fix ourselves anyway. Two days later the chanting began. At first, I thought I was dreaming. It took me a while to realize that my nightmare had entered the real world.

We all gathered on the porch in our pajamas, wrapped in robes and blankets and each other. The flickering of torches on the other side of the river lit up all the angry faces that held them. They chanted something about pride and unity and other positive words designed to hide their ignorance and venom. To me it just sounded like the chattering of hyenas going for a carcass.

The group of guards that stayed at night all faced the towns-people, staring them down with their guns held visibly in their hands. Shouting and staring, shouting and staring, nothing more. A standstill.

The day after that, the construction crew couldn't get past the angry mob. Some tried and got thrown into the river bloodied for it. We stayed, coward-like, with our armed guard on our island prison. Sure it kept other people out, but it was also keeping us in.

The next day, a boat crossed the river. The guards tensed and held their guns at the ready, but the only person in the boat was Roscoe, tied up and bleeding out his nose. He was barely conscious. A note was pinned to his chest.

"If I could do this to my own son, what do you think I'll do to you?"

* * *

The food grew cold in front of us, as it had the night before, and the night before that. As it had been doing for weeks. I had lost so much weight that I had to punch new holes in my belts with nails just so I could keep my pants up.

"We should leave." Mrs. K. said quietly. Some people nodded, others shook their heads, and others still just stayed still.

"If we leave, they win." Grace said stubbornly.

"They've already won." Luke said. "I mean . . . they've killed someone, for Christ's sake."

Beatrice, who had finally emerged looking thinner and more desperate than I'd ever seen her, glanced at Luke, but didn't say anything. Clancy had told us earlier that day that Beatrice was now holding out hope that her boyfriend was still somehow alive out there. Grace, meanwhile, looked as if she were going to say that Zorro was just a dog, a something, not a someone. Then she caught a look at Mateen's face. For the past two days it had changed from its usual pleasant handsomeness into a mask of gross despair, too disturbing to stare at for long. She shut her mouth.

"I can fix this." Thia said. "I'll get the feds in here. What they are doing is hate crime."

"And after that?" Thadeus said. "How do you propose we start a business in a community that hates us so much? Even if they stop attacking, there are other ways they can hurt us."

"They've proven that." Beatrice said dryly. Outside, the chanting swelled for a moment, and then fell back to its usual even fervor.

"So you all just want to leave? Ruin everything that we've worked so hard for?" Grace was crying. Most of us were flabbergasted by the sight of it. Only Thia and I went to hold her. "Isn't this place worth fighting for?" She asked.

"I think the only thing worth fighting for," Caleb said, "is us."

I stood up. "They're right, Grace. I'm sorry. But we can find another place." Then I began to walk out of the dining room.

"Where are you going?" Grace said.

I stopped but didn't turn around. "I'm going to talk to Roscoe's father." Roscoe himself was in the library, recovering from the beating he'd received from his family.

"Are you crazy? They'll tear you apart." Gabe said.

"Don't be stupid." Clancy said.

"What good will that even do?" Luke asked.

I turned to face them, smiling slightly. I don't know why I felt I should keep things light and airy at a time when darkness closed in on us from every corner. It felt like the only defense I had left. Which stage of grief is denial?

"Last time I checked," I said, "there's a huge mob standing between us and our tickets out of here. We'll need those cars, if they haven't already destroyed them. Maybe if I talk to him—tell him we're going—he'll get them all to back off. I'd rather not go shooting into the crowd with Thia's group of bodyguards."

They all seemed to accept the logic of my argument with relative ease. Eyes shifted to Kiki, who sat at the table looking at me with an unreadable expression. I think everyone was thinking the same thing. If we tried to get out of here with bullets, then probably only the worst would happen. Besides, we all knew that the townspeople wanted the kid. And I think he knew it too. He reached toward Francis and held on to his hand so hard that the pale peach color of his knuckles turned ghastly white.

"If you're going to do this, then I'm going to come with you." Thia said, standing.

I shrugged. "Why not?" It was still too early in our reunion for me to show how grateful I was to have her back at my side.

Thia and I walked quietly across the marshy front lawn, the one Grace had had such grand landscaping dreams for, and started up the airboat together. At the sound of our engine, the crowd fell into a sudden hush. One of the guards, a large man with thick eyebrows and a goatee, climbed into the boat with us, his gun at the ready. I could've laughed at the whole thing if I weren't so terrified. Without even thinking, I reached down and took Thia's hand. She laced our fingers and squeezed.

Once we got to the dock on the other end, the crowd swelled forward with a collective hissing sound like snakes going in for the kill. In response, our guard raised his gun. God it was so ridiculous.

"I'm here to see your leader." Next to me, Thia withheld a snigger. I hadn't been trying to be funny, really. There was just no other way I could think of to say it. But it was pretty funny. Our lives had become a comedy of disastrous proportions. Or maybe it always had been.

"I'm here, boy." Roscoe's father emerged from the crowd, illuminated by the fires of the Party City tiki torches that the mob had used for light. The crowd parted to let him move forward as if he were a prophet and closed in behind him.

"We are willing to leave." I said, not seeing the point of beating around the bush. "But you have to let us go. Have you destroyed our cars?"

"Not yet." He said slowly. He seemed to be mulling over his options. I had offered him pretty much exactly what they wanted, but to take it so willingly would show weakness to his band of ignorant followers. He'd riled them up so much at this point that they were all chomping at the bit for a more violent end to this conflict. Maybe we should've come in with the guns.

"So then we can leave. By Monday at the latest. Then you won't have to worry about us anymore, and we won't have to worry about you."

The man narrowed his eyes. "Why are y'all so willing to leave all of a sudden? You scare that easily?"

"We have lives to protect." I said, simply. "You've made it clear that you don't care about that."

"What about the boy?" A faceless shout from the crowd asked.

"That's a good point." He grinned wolfishly. "That boy ain't in proper care with you folk. I think before we let y'all leave, we're going to need to get him someplace safe."

"The only one making things unsafe for him is you." Thia spoke up. "Francis is Kiki's legal guardian. Not only that, but Kiki is the grandson of a very wealthy, very powerful man. One phone call, and I could bring down his legal wrath upon you faster than anything your god could serve up."

"Oh?" Roscoe's father laughed. "So now you've got a heathen Chink in your ranks?"

Thia snorted. "If you want to be sued out of house and home, be our guest. But Kiki is not going anywhere with you. And I'm Korean, asswipe."

The crowd protested wildly to this, but I could tell Roscoe's father was wavering. He didn't really care about Kiki. I was sure as far as he was concerned Kiki was already tainted goods. What he really wanted was his lily-white town to stay that way.

"You might as well give it up. There's no legal reason to take the boy. And I'm sure we've proven already that we have the money and power"—I gestured back to our guard who had his gun trained on Mr. Bloomington's chest—"to stop you from trying anything like that."

The man's eyes flickered to our guard as if he were seeing him for the first time. He sneered, feigning insult, but I could see the tint of fear in his eyes. He had probably never had a gun pointed at him before. What a privileged son of a bitch.

"Well we can't just let you go for nothing. You've caused a ruckus in this town, and we require payment." A shout of agreement went up from the crowd behind him, tiki torches thrust in the air.

"What do you want?" Thia sounded so fed up with this. I rubbed my thumb against the back of her hand.

Roscoe's father thrust his chin toward the darkness behind us. "That place will do just nicely."

I raised one eyebrow. "You want the Hotel?"

"Sure," Roscoe's father said. "Times been tough around

here"—a murmur of assent from the crowd—"I'm sure a nice big place like that would bring in a lot of revenue." He grinned again, clearly feeling like he'd won. "Give us the deed to that place, and you can be on your merry way."

Clearly we had proven to him that despite our skin or our relationships or our religion, despite all those things that he believed made us so lowly and disgusting, despite all of this, we were more powerful than him. I bet he probably hated that. Going after the hotel, our home, was his only way to assert dominance over us. He needed to feel like he was better than us, and I decided that I didn't give a damn about trying to stop him.

"Fine." I said, gaining shocked looks from both Thia and Roscoe's father. Even the guard spared me a skeptical sideways glance. "On Monday, you clear this place of all your people and we go."

"What about the deed?" He seemed uncertain, as if he were winning this fight too easily. At least he wasn't a complete idiot.

"You come Monday night. Seven. We'll give you the deed and we'll go. But just you."

"I'll need my protection. How will I know you won't do something shifty?"

I smiled. "Fine. You can bring as many men as we've got in that house."

"And how many is that?"

"Four. Because according to you, sodomites aren't men, right? And you couldn't count an old fella as a man either."

"Fine. Fine . . . I'll be here with four men. You've got yourself a deal." He turned to wave away his crowd of followers, maybe regale them with how successful they'd been driving out the filth.

"Wait." I said. Roscoe's father turned around to face me, tired of this conversation and also afraid of what else I might have to say. "The boy whose pictures you sent us. We'll take him with us too. He has no place in this town as much as any of the rest of us."

Roscoe's father smirked. "Oh I'm sorry, but that poor kid died in a car accident. Tragic stuff."

Thia lunged forward, but I caught her. The crowd swelled forward, and our guard cocked his gun, shouting. Roscoe's father and I both raised our hands, palms facing each other.

"Fine." I said through gritted teeth. "Monday."

Roscoe's father nodded. The guard started up the engine to the airboat again and he turned us back toward the hotel, all while keeping his gun up and aimed.

"Thanks man." I said when we finally got back to the dock. He nodded and walked back to his men. I turned to look at the other side of the river. Bobbing flames began to move away from the bank.

"Arthur," Thia said. "They can't have this place."

I looked at her. "They won't."

* * *

P acking was a melancholy affair. Beatrice and Mateen's tears, the sighs of Mrs. K. and Sam, the whispered chatter of Gabe and Caleb and Thadeus—the soundtrack to the end of our lives there. That day I had also called Jeff and told him that he and May should leave as soon as they could. We'd be gone by next week. Jeff apologized more times than he should have. Once was too many. He told me that I'd better keep in touch. I told him that he could count on it.

We ended up keeping the men with the guns right up until the last couple of hours before we left. After all, just because Roscoe's father had agreed to our cease-fire didn't mean that everyone else in town would. Thankfully, no more death or destruction was brought our way in those final depressive days.

Grace and Thia had packed quicker than anyone else and spent the rest of our remaining days in the Hotel searching for where we could go. Our shoddy internet was put to its absolute limit in frantically looking for last-minute housing. Miraculously, and maybe a little backhandedly, they found a place, a quiet little abandoned mansion in the middle of nowhere in New England. It seemed impossible for them to have closed a deal on a place so quickly and remotely, but I'd learned to stop questioning how they did their business. It would be snowing when we got there, I thought. Snow would be nice.

We left the Hotel on Monday in groups of four. Luke, Beatrice, and I went in the first group. Thia and Grace stayed behind to be the last ones to say their goodbyes to the big, beautiful, ridiculous place. Roscoe's father had showed up with his prescribed four men. Truthfully, I had expected him to bring more, but maybe there was some sense of honor buried beneath all of that stupidity and hate.

All of us had made a pact not to say a single word once we hit the other side of the river. Instead we arrived with expressionless faces and silent stares. That seemed to unnerve Roscoe's father the most, although he smirked when he saw his son come across on the boat and begin loading the car with us.

"You can come with us." I'd said to Roscoe the night before we left. "But you have to get rid of that fucking tattoo."

He'd nodded. "Fair enough."

Once all of our things were packed and the last of us were stuffed into the three cars we owned, I handed over the deed to Roscoe's father. He passed it over to the skinny man who had ripped up Francis's papers before. The skinny man examined the document for a moment and then nodded, handing it back to Roscoe's father.

He grinned. "And don't even think of coming back."

My eyes darted toward the Hotel for the last time. Then I walked backward, not willing to turn my back on him, and climbed into the driver's seat of my old sedan. Grace sat next to me. Beatrice, Luke, and Thia were smushed together in the back. Kiki sat on Beatrice's lap.

"Go, Arthur." Grace said.

So, with my car in the lead, we drove away. Roscoe's father and his men watched us go, hooting and hollering as if they'd won something. Distantly, I could hear the sound of the airboat starting up. They were off to examine their prize.

All of us in that car held our breath and waited. As we drove down the dirt road, away from our old life, we waited. We waited for the gas from the kitchen stove to seep into the rest of the Hotel, its toxic fingers caressing the things we'd left behind. We waited for it to embrace the flames from the dining room hearth and the fireplace in the library and the candles lit in Clancy's room and my room and Caleb and Gabe's room. We waited for the ignition. We waited for the boom.

When it came, all of us breathed out, opened our windows, and screamed. My foot hit the gas pedal. The other cars followed me. We went screaming through the main street of town and kept screaming until it was just a dot in the rearview mirror. Kiki screamed louder than anyone. Then he cursed for the first time.

"Fuck you!" He shrieked.

All of us burst out laughing. Kiki blushed and looked around sheepishly.

"You won't tell Francis, will you?"

"Our little secret." Beatrice said.

Then we stopped screaming and looked forward. The road was flat and straight ahead of us. It would take us where we needed to go.

* * *

"Arthur?"

Kiki is standing in the doorway of my bedroom-office. I turn to face him. He's grown so tall in the last year. It always amazes me to see how much his body is changing. He'd been so small when he was a kid. Next year, he'll be going to college. He'd gotten into Harvard, Yale, Columbia, Brown, Stanford, and New York University. But he gave them all up for Howard and a life in D.C. He'll enter college in the fall as a minority for the first time ever. In a way, I think that's what he wants. I shake my head a little and smile.

"What's up, kid?" He's never complained about me calling him kid, even though he's not one anymore. So I've kept it up. Every time I say it, he smiles.

"They're here."

"All right." I stand up, haphazardly gathering the papers on my desk into one pile. Various freelance assignments and newspaper clippings peek out from underneath each other as I move away. My knees and back crack. I curse them internally. Seven years doesn't really seem like that much time, but it was enough for my body to decide it needed to constantly remind me how old I am. I stretch my limbs and walk toward him.

Kiki and I walk together downstairs. A few of our guests see us in the hallway and greet us. We ask them how they are doing and if everything is to their liking. They say yes, and we all smile.

My room is on the top floor. On the second-floor landing, Caleb and Gabe are making out in what they must think is a discreet corner.

"Come on you two, cut it out. There are guests around." I say playfully.

They break apart and look at me, grinning like fools. From the floor below us, their twins, Elijah and Melly, yell at them to hurry up.

"They're here, papa, they're here." Melly shouts, taking her brother's hand and pulling him toward the front door. Some amused guests dodge out of their way. There was never a boring moment with them around.

The four of us make our way down. On the couch in the library, Roscoe is reclining with his girlfriend, Alexa. She is reading to him from an old book, and she has a pleasant voice. A pair of newly-weds from Wichita are listening too. A Christmas tree is lit up in the corner between two bookcases. The twinkle lights blink and shine.

"Roscoe, they're here." Gabe says.

He nods and kisses Alexa on the cheek. She smiles at him and watches as he goes, but she keeps reading for the family.

Mateen is at the front desk as we pass by. Don Juan, his Spanish (German) shepherd, sits on guard next to him, but he wags his tail when he sees us. Mateen rises and smiles.

"Come on, DJ. They're here."

Everyone else is out on the porch waiting for us. Sam and Clancy lean forward over the railing, waving wildly and holding hands. Kiki goes to throw his arm around Francis's shoulders. It's wild to see how they are almost the same height now. Beatrice and Luke are shifting on their feet excitedly. Grace smiles at me from her favorite wicker chair. In her arms is my grandchild, Chester, named after my father. Mateen crouches down next to Grace, placing a kiss first on her forehead and then on his son's. Chester gurgles a little. Then he goes back to sleep. Behind the car that's just pulled up in front of the Hotel, the two apple trees we planted over Mrs. K. and Thadeus's graves sway toward each other in the breeze, their leaves gently brushing against each other.

From out of the back seat burst three children, one right after the other. Melly and Elijah break free from the fathers' holds and rush forward. The five children bounce around happily, screaming and catching each other up with their lives. Jeff and May emerge from the front seat, rolling their eyes and gently scolding their kids. We all walk forward and embrace them, offering to take their bags.

"How's the top-secret project going, Arthur? Grace tells me you've been locked up in your room writing for the past few months." Jeff says.

"I think it's just about done." I say.

"Hey, Arthur." May says, "Look who we found on the side of the road."

I turn and smile, already knowing who it is. Thia stands next to May, a small suitcase in her hand. I walk up to her and catch her in my arms, kissing her on the mouth. The kids all groan and boo. We pull apart laughing.

"How was the flight?"

"Long." She smiles. "But I had one of your books keeping me company."

I roll my eyes. "Oh please, you hate my books."

"Sure I do. But your picture's on the back of them so . . ."

I laugh and shut her up with a kiss. Together we all walk back into the Hotel. Thia and I go up to our room to get settled. We will all have dinner together later in the Hotel's dining room, along with the other guests who are staying with us for Christmas. Maybe tomorrow we'll build a snowman together like we did last year. Maybe this year, it'll actually stand and not just collapse on itself. Or maybe we'll just take a walk to town and get hot chocolate from that little bakery that Mateen loves so much. But right now, I just watch Thia as she unpacks her toiletries in the bathroom.

We only see each other for one month of every year, but for some reason, that's enough. She has her life in Seoul, and it's easier now. People doubt her less. She's more comfortable. And I have my writing, which keeps me locked away for days on end. We are separate and together. It's enough for us.

She catches me staring. "Hey."

I smile. "Hey."

She just smiles and shakes her head, returning to her unpacking, and I walk to the window. Outside, a group of guests have just returned from a long walk. One of them is pointing up at a tree. Maybe there's a bird there. From behind me, Thia wraps her arms around my stomach and squeezes.

"Where are you, Arthur Bean?"

"Just where I want to be." I say, and then I turn and kiss her again.

ACKNOWLEDGMENTS

A writer's journey is not always easy, but the following people guided my passage with their own shining lights. I'd like to thank them for their support, encouragement, and belief in my ability to do this. First and foremost, I owe an incredible debt to my father, John Harrison. Not only did he and my mother allow me to hide out in their home for a year to complete this project, he has, by example, shown me that it is possible to follow your dreams of creativity and still maintain a happy, fulfilling life. He is always the first person to read my manuscripts, and for all of this, I am eternally grateful.

Deena Edwards, who designed the gorgeous cover to this novel, gave the pages of my story the perfect home in which to live. I could not be more blessed to have a talented artist and friend like her in my life. Diante Singley, Lindsay Jean Michelle, and Ellen Hopkins-Fountain all assisted me with launching my crowdfunding campaign, so without them this book truly never would have escaped my computer into the world.

And now for the people whose generous donations allowed me the freedom to present to the world a finished project rather than a first draft; I am not being facetious when I say that *Please Welcome*

Mr. Arthur Bean would never have been published if it weren't for you. Anne Harrison, Leslie Chapman, Ian Harrison, Michael Felsher, Pasquale Buba and Zilla Clinton, Christina Jennings, Nick Mastandrea, Howard Tomb, Lynne Chapman, Ed and Felice Lammi, John Spahn, Richard and Sally Mennen, and Jin Ishimoto . . . I cannot begin to express how grateful I am to each and every one of you. I hope you take some pride in having been a part of this novel's journey, because I am proud and humbled to have people like you as my support.

88458770R00171

Made in the USA
San Bernardino, CA
13 September 2018